Date: 5/22/19

LP MYS JONES
Jones, Stephen Mack,
Lives laid away

LIVES LAID AWAY

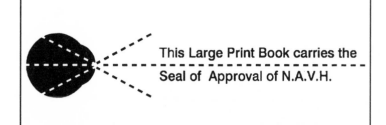

This Large Print Book carries the
Seal of Approval of N.A.V.H.

LIVES LAID AWAY

STEPHEN MACK JONES

THORNDIKE PRESS
A part of Gale, a Cengage Company

Farmington Hills, Mich • San Francisco • New York • Waterville, Maine
Meriden, Conn • Mason, Ohio • Chicago

Copyright © 2019 by Stephen Mack Jones.
An August Snow Novel.
Thorndike Press, a part of Gale, a Cengage Company.

**LIBRARY OF CONGRESS CIP DATA ON FILE.
CATALOGUING IN PUBLICATION FOR THIS BOOK
IS AVAILABLE FROM THE LIBRARY OF CONGRESS**

ISBN-13: 978-1-4328-5994-7 (hardcover)

Published in 2019 by arrangement with Soho Press, Inc.

Printed in the United States of America
1 2 3 4 5 6 7 23 22 21 20 19

For the real heroes.
James and Evelyn L. Jones . . .
. . . my brother JR Jones II . . .
. . . my son, Jacob, who is
becoming the man
I always aspired to be . . .
And to you, the Dreamers . . .

Somewhere there must be storehouses
where all these lives are laid away
like suits of armor or old carriages
or clothes hanging limply on the walls
— RAINIER MARIA RILKE'S
"NO ONE LIVES HIS LIFE"

1

Her secret ingredient was nutmeg.

Not a lot — maybe half a teaspoon or less — but she got the same complex undercurrent effect that she would have with smoked East Indian paprika or authentic Mexican chili powder.

I was in my kitchen, slowly blending half a teaspoon of nutmeg into my homemade salsa — pureed tomatoes from Honeycomb Market, blanched and coarse-chopped tomatoes, chopped jalapenos, minced yellow bell pepper, fresh dill, a quarter lemon, squeezed, garlic, sea salt and coarse ground black pepper. I also added just a bit of chopped cilantro.

While I diced, pureed and blended ingredients, I listened to an old CD of my father's: John Lee Hooker and Santana's classic "The Healer," cranked to top volume on my stereo. Perfect music to accompany a rakishly handsome Blaxican as he made a poor imitation of his mother's salsa. Courtesy of the potent aroma of the salsa and the music, I could feel my hips, my feet moving in the rhythm of a slow rhumba bolero.

And yes, *cabrón.*

I dance a mean rhumba bolero, thanks to my mother's patient lessons and the decades of practice I've had at dozens of Mexican weddings, one Salvadoran/Colombian wedding anniversary and four quinceañeras.

I'd even given salsa and rhumba lessons at Camp Leatherneck and FOB Delhi Beirut in Afghanistan to guys who'd just gotten engaged to sweethearts anxiously waiting stateside. Go ahead. Ask former Marine Corporal Francis "Franco" Montoya (Seattle, Washington) or former Marine Sergeant Dwayne "Wee Man" Nixon (Memphis, Tennessee). Marine killing machines who will freely admit I'm the only guy they've ever loved dancing with.

It had been a week since I'd taken Tatina Stadmueller, my long-distance-kinda-maybe girlfriend, to Metro Airport for her flight home — back to Oslo, Norway. Back to begin her last year of Cultural Anthropology doctoral studies at the University of Oslo. I was still feeling buoyant from her visit. Like Paul blinded by righteousness and beauty.

The air in my house still carried her warm chocolate-and-pepper scent.

One thing I hadn't intended Tatina to see during her time in Detroit was a black Chevy Suburban, windows blacked-out, crawling down Markham Street at ungodly hours of the morning. Tatina had casually noted the SUV twice during her nighttime bathroom visits.

"Who are they?" she asked over breakfast one morning.

"Probably somebody coming home from a late shift somewhere."

Of course, I knew better.

This is Mexicantown. The black Chevy Suburban with blacked out windows was ICE — US Immigration and Customs Enforcement police — trolling in the dark-heart hours, mapping potential "nests" and safe-houses of undocumented immigrants. Their official motto? "Protecting National Security and Upholding Public Safety."

In Mexicantown, we have a different motto for ICE: *Si es marrón, enciérrelo.*

"If it's brown, lock it down."

"Please, Jesus lord," Jimmy Radmon said as he entered through my front door. "Tell me I ain't seein' this."

I was carefully ladling my now-completed salsa into six shiny, sterilized Ball fourteen-ounce storage jars. Celia Cruz had just finished her sexy take on "Oye Como Va." Now I was doing a rhumba bolero to James Brown's *Hot Pants-Pt. 1.*

"You need to learn the rhumba, Jimmy," I said.

"What I need to learn that goofy stuff for?" Jimmy said, walking around me and retrieving an ice-cold bottle of water from my fridge. I kept bottled water in the fridge just for Jimmy and Carlos. They seemed never to be finished making little adjustments, improvements and additions to my house. I didn't really mind, since most of these were invisible to me. One of their last improvements made my house a virtual

Wi-Fi hotspot for the other houses on Markham Street. Not a bad thing since most neighborhoods in Detroit were Internet dead zones.

I found space in the fridge for four of the six jars of salsa and handed two to Jimmy. One for him, one for his loving landlords, my older neighbors Sylvia and Carmela.

"You should sell this stuff," Jimmy said, scrutinizing the jars. "Octavio's Genu-wine D-City Salsa. It's good. Better than store-bought."

"I'll think about it," I said, knowing I wouldn't think about it.

Satisfied with the success of my culinary mission, I grabbed a beer — a Batch Brewing Vienna Lager — and retired to the living room. Jimmy followed along, insisting on boring me with renovation status reports, material and equipment requests and subcontractor bids. We'd just flipped two houses — a detached brick three-bedroom to a young couple who'd moved here from Portland with their three-year-old girl, and a two-bedroom brick duplex to some English charitable foundation guy who insisted on wearing his hair in a man-bun and doing yoga on his front porch.

Then there were the inevitable local newspaper and magazine inquiries.

"This Renna Jacobs from the *Free Press,* man, she keep on calling me," Jimmy said. "Wants to talk to you about bringin' the 'hood back."

"You didn't give her my number, did you?" I said.

"No, on account I know you'd kill me."

"Damn straight," I said. "Probably by making you give up Cheetos and Gatorade and force-feeding you healthy food."

"Seriously," Jimmy insisted. "A little press be nice for the 'hood. *And* for me and Carlos. I mean, we all got to think outside the Markham Street box, Mr. Snow. One house left to reno and flip on the street — then what?"

Jimmy had just asked a question that I'd been avoiding for the past three months. I never intended for house renovations in the southwest Detroit neighborhood of Mexicantown to become my purpose in life. I just wanted my neighborhood — my street — back. Maybe homage to my beloved parents. Maybe reverence for a long-ago way of life that in this moment seemed to hold no more weight than spirits wandering far from their graves.

After being fired from the Detroit Police Department, the trial that followed and my twelve-million-dollar wrongful dismissal award, I'd wanted nothing more than to isolate my shattered self in a safe place. That had been the whole reason I'd renovated my childhood home on Markham Street in the first place, and then, by extension, the neighboring houses toward Mexicantown's business thoroughfare, Vernor Avenue.

Markham Street — and August Octavio Snow — 2.0.

Now, I had a couple good men depending on me for their livelihood.

And I had no answers for them.

"I'll think about it," I said.

Jimmy gave me a sideways look that said he'd heard this from me before. "Yeah, well, either way," Jimmy said, tearing a small portion of paper from his work notebook and handing the shred to me, "here's that reporter's number. A 'neighborhood renaissance,' " Jimmy persisted. "That's what this reporter lady calls what you done did around here. And, I mean, talkin' to her might be a nice chance for you to do some reno on your reputation in this town, you know?"

I feared Jimmy had stepped over a line and into my personal minefield.

But this was Jimmy. A kid who was, by nature, innocent — maybe even naïve — and without a malicious bone in his rail-

15

thin body.

"What reputation might that be, Jimmy?"

" 'Ex-cop who took twelve mil from raggedy-ass Detroit reinvests in raggedy-ass Detroit,' " Jimmy said. "Hometown hero stuff. You could make this work for you, Mr. Snow."

"Like I said, Jimmy —"

"Yeah, I know," Jimmy said. " 'I'll think about it.' "

3

You move to my street, you get a party.

Them's the rules, like 'em or not.

Markham Street had seen three new sets of neighbors move in all within two months: The Bergman-Hallseys, Alan and Michael, a young transplant couple from Portland, Oregon with a three-year-old daughter, Kasey. Mara Windmere, some sort of hotshot tech firm marketing manager who thought she'd give urban living a fun little hipster spin. And Trent T.R. Ogilvy, the man-bun Brit, who moved from Rochester, New York (where he'd moved from Manchester, England). Ogilvy worked for an international charity foundation out of London whose goal was to bring laptop computers and Wi-Fi to Internet deserts. There are certainly enough neighborhoods in Detroit that qualify. Too many people doing job searches through the classifieds in two dying daily newspapers.

"I rather enjoy a drink or five," Trent told me when I dropped by his house to invite him. "I hope that's acceptable."

"More than acceptable," I said. "It's expected."

I made a trip to The Honeycomb Market to put in an order for the summer Markham Street party a month away. You don't live in Mexicantown without making at least a once-a-week sojourn to Honeycomb, a neighborhood institution: pyramids of brightly colored jalapeños, mangos, tomatillos and succulent cactus leaves; shelves crowded with spices, imported packaged Latin American foods; colorful cans and bottles of Mexican and Nicaraguan coffees and soft drinks; fresh handmade tortillas and chorizo, and enough Mi Costeñita candy and Pingüinos sweet cakes to make a child's eyes pop.

I'd been coming to Honeycomb since I was a boy holding my mother's hand. These were the people who converted my father from being a Falstaff beer philistine to a Negra Modelo and Pacifico aficionado who indulged in the occasional cop's guilty pleasure of a smuggled Noche Buena at Christmas.

He was never much of a *michelada* man, however.

"Who inna hell puts hot sauce and lime juice in a damn beer?" I remember him saying.

My mother, head swiveling on her neck, forefinger waving *No! No! No!* in the air, said, *"My* people put hot sauce and lime juice in *everything*! Choo got a problem with that, *cabeza de burro?"*

For this summer's block party, I estimated we were up to at least two hundred chicken and pork tortillas, thirty pounds of rice, twenty pounds of refried and whole black beans, maybe forty pounds of ground chorizo and seasoned ground beef, and God-Only-Knows how many sausages.

At the expansive meat counter at the back of Honeycomb I waited for help.

And waited.

After five minutes, Nana Corazon-Glouster — the meat counter manager — appeared.

"Well, look what the *gato* dragged in!" she said, grinning broadly. "I'd come around and give you a big, wet kiss, but I'm afraid you'd get addicted!"

"Those lips? Those eyes?" I said. "Yeah, it could become a habit!"

"Like hell," Nana laughed. "What can I do you for, Augusto?"

"Well," I said, looking around, "first you

19

can answer me this: Where the hell is everybody? Usually you've got three, four people working the counter."

Nana winced as if she had a bare nerve in a back tooth. Lowering her voice, she said, "People are scared, Augusto. They see them ICE bastards cruisin' day and night and all anybody can think is, 'They're coming for me.' I mean people who've been citizens for ten, twenty — fifty years! None of our employees are undocumented." She lowered her voice and said, "Okay, maybe one or two. But no drugs, no gang tats! They show up on time and work hard. They scrub toilets like they were polishing gold and they say 'Yes, ma'am' and 'No, ma'am,' 'Please' and 'Thank you.' Where's the citizenship path for *these* people?"

She asked if I'd seen any patrols.

I told her about the late-night cruises down Markham Street.

"And they don't scare you?" Nana said.

"Nope."

"Why not?"

" 'Cause I've seen scary up close and personal," I said. "Afghanistan. Pakistan. With me, they got a problem: Deport him to Mexico? Or send him back to Africa?"

My little joke did nothing to allay her concerns.

"You were a cop," Nana whispered. "Can't you do something?"

"I kinda think we've all got our asses hanging out on this one, Nana."

"What about Mrs. Gutierrez?"

My friend Tomás's wife, Elena, was respected throughout the community as a champion of Mexicantown residents and a defender of civil rights in general. Five years ago, a small group of residents and business leaders tried to draft her into running for District 6 city council representative. She politely declined, saying she had a husband and granddaughter to care for — and she was still trying to decide which one needed the most attention.

"She's doing what she can with some Birmingham immigration and naturalization lawyers," I said. "And she's had a couple meetings with the mayor and at Holy Redeemer. But the ICE storm came in fast and hit hard, Nana. People still don't know what — if anything — they can do. I sure as hell don't know."

With every word I spoke, Nana looked as if her soul was slowly being crushed.

"I know this won't help much," I said, "but if they come for you, I'll move heaven and earth to get you back." I made wide puppy-dog eyes and pouted my lips. "And if they come for me, Nana?"

A devilish glint returned to her large brown eyes. With a crisp salute she said, "Sayonara, baby!"

I laughed perhaps a little too loud. "Tha's cold, girl!"

"Oh, you like being spanked. All you macho guys like being spanked. What can I get for ya, Augusto?"

I gave her my list and the drop-dead date. With each item Nana's pretty head gave a decisive nod. "I got your back, big boy."

"Never any doubt, Nana."

I blew her a kiss. She caught it midair and slapped it to her right butt cheek.

Like everybody else in Mexicantown, I usually came into Honeycomb for two or three items and left with seven or eight. I figured I might as well pick up a few staples. Couple extra bags of tortilla chips and a pound of their guacamole never hurt anybody.

As I wandered the narrow aisles, imagine my surprise at running into the rising star of the Detroit Police Department's Major Case Squad, Detective Captain Leo Cowling. He looked like he was dressed for Port Huron to Mackinac Race Week: Navy-blue alligator shoes, cream-colored linen slacks, a crisp white open banded-collar shirt and matching cream-colored linen jacket. Tastefully topping things off was a tan Cuban-style straw fedora with a wide navy-blue silk band. The kind of high-end fedora one could only get from Henry the Hatter.

Improving his overall look was the woman on his arm: tall, glowing bronze skin, athletically built, high-cheek bones, cascading black hair and long, breathtaking legs.

"Well, how's *this* for a Wednesday afternoon surprise!" I said, grabbing Cowling's hand and enthusiastically shaking it. Were it not for his stunning companion, he probably would have yanked his hand from mine and tried to sock me in the jaw with his embarrassingly slow right cross. In this moment, however, he reluctantly went along with the handshake.

"Uh — yeah — s'up, Snow?" Cowling said.

"Nothing!" I said, grinning like the happiest of country bumpkins. "Just a little shoplifting."

"I know you," the woman said, narrowing her eyes at me.

It took me a second, but I finally recognized her.

Suddenly, I didn't find her so attractive.

"Martinez?" I said. "Internal Affairs?"

"Yep," she said. "No hard feelings, right?"

Reluctantly, we shook. From her handshake it was obvious she had the ability to crack walnuts in her fist.

In a slapdash, court-of-public-opinion effort to smear me after I was fired from the Force for looking into the former mayor's criminal malfeasance, an IA case was brought against me: Misuse of department funds (strip clubs, gifts, drugs) and behavior unbefitting an officer of the law; a hooker had been paid to say I'd forced her into giving me free sex and that I'd knocked her around a bit. An unimaginative, classic stitch-up courtesy of the former mayor and his corrupt DPD security team.

IA's case fell apart when discovery failed to produce any strip club expenditures, and the hooker failed to identify me in a lineup as her attacker.

Twice.

It also helped when, after her second misidentification, the hooker stormed out of the viewing room yelling, "Y'all ain't *payin'* my black ass enough for this bullshit! Fuck *all* y'all!"

"No hard feelings," I said to Martinez, still feeling the tweak of a tender bruise on my pride. Fake laughing and slapping Cowling on the shoulder, I said, "Watch out for this guy! I can tell you right now he steals candy from the Fourteenth's vending machine!"

Martinez, not quite knowing what to make of me, excused herself and walked back to the meat counter.

"Making the IA beast with two backs, Cowling?" I said, voicing faux disappointment. "Really?"

"You are such an asshole, Snow," Cowling grumbled.

Leaning into Cowling, I whispered, "Mixed babies are *sooo* beautiful, don't you think?"

Wading through the early June heat and thick humidity back to my Caddy, I felt a bit guilty for having busted Cowling's chops: Very apparent on the left side of his neck near the curve of his shoulder was a long, ugly scar from a bullet that had chewed through his flesh while he fended off some very bad people in a valiant effort to protect his superior, Detective Captain Ray Danbury. Danbury had died. Cowling got the promotion he'd always wanted and never quite deserved. And the two of us were left on opposite sides of a man we had both held in high esteem.

Since Danbury's death, Cowling and I had something of an unspoken understanding between us; for the sake of our dead friend's memory, we would dial back our animosity toward each other.

The Honeycomb Market was what "dialed back" looked like.

Even though the air was thick with humidity and the white noon sun reveled in its skin-shearing, climate-changing dominance, I figured there had to be a few Mexicans out and about. After dropping my purchases off at the house, I ambled back out to the car.

Jimmy and Carlos Rodriguez, Jimmy's equal-share renovation and house-flipping partner, were heading down the street, their skin glistening, tool belts hung like spaghetti-western gunslingers. Since I wasn't in the mood to talk renovation plans, costs, materials or proposals, I moved quickly to my curbed Caddy.

"Yo! Mr. Snow!" Jimmy yelled.

"No time, guys!" I said, waving. "Gotta go!"

I belted myself in behind the steering wheel as I accelerated away from my house, down Markham Street, onto I-75 north toward the city and away from adult responsibility.

4

It's hard to complain about Michigan's suffocating June heat and humidity when you see black kids squealing and laughing alongside German tourist kids in the spouts of water at the Fountain at GM Plaza. Or shirtless black and brown teen boys standing dutifully behind wheelchair-bound grandmothers or grandfathers, everyone smiling up at the descending cloud of cool spray from Isamu Noguchi's Horace E. Dodge and Sons Memorial Fountain.

There are the picture-takers and brick-readers huddled beneath the shadow of Ed Dwight's full-sized Underground Railroad sculpture of a runaway slave family at the last stop on their arduous journey. Even in their frozen bronze stance, the sight of this family looking across the Detroit River to the hope and promise of Canada is moving.

Considering Detroit was built in large part by Native and black slaves, they had every right to stare longingly across the river to the promise of Canada.

Look hard enough at the feet of these sculpted runaway slaves and you'll find a reddish-brown brick engraved with these words: *Still searching. Still hopeful. The Snow Family.*

Once upon a time the three-and-a-half mile Detroit riverfront behind the General Motors Renaissance Center headquarters might have been considered the River Styx: a post-apocalyptic sluice of illegally dumped garbage, washed up sewage and rotting fish seasoned with a dash of mercury and a soupçon of lead. Abandoned buildings along the river served as mausoleums for the bodies of the murdered and the forgotten homeless. It was an open, grey-water grave where dead dreams and lost hopes floated belly up.

Now, with a tenuous revitalization in full bloom, the riverfront had been transformed into a scenic, well-manicured length of greenspace where people strolled, rode rented bikes, casually ate lunch and watched sailboats tack and ride wakes churned up by freighters.

Just up from RiverWalk, near Riopelle Street, there are shiny doors, one red and one blue.

Behind either is a world of hurt.

I was on the second floor of Club Brutus, behind the red door, which bore the Japanese kanji character for "Redemption." Club Brutus is a high-end health and fitness club with panoramic floor-to-ceiling windows looking out on the bright expanse of RiverWalk, the Detroit River and, across the river, the sprawling red brick distillery for Canadian Club where Al Capone and the Purple Gang made their Prohibition-era liquor deals. I was wearing a marine blue *karategi* — the traditional Japanese karate uniform — with black belt.

I was also wearing a bruise just beneath my left eye that would soon become a sickly purple thanks to the club's owner, Apollonius "Brutus" Jefferies.

"Wow," Brutus said as we slowly danced around each other on the mat. "I expected better from a young man."

"Yeah, well, sadly I'm getting exactly what I expected from an old man," I said. "Soft hits, slow kicks and not a takedown in sight. Ain't you supposed to be good at this?"

Brutus laughed as he circled me. "Boy, I'm 'bout to beat you like a rented mule."

Brutus Jefferies was dark-skinned, tall and broad, with a four-inch braid. I wasn't quite sure if he suffered classic male-pattern baldness with his monk's fringe or if he purposely cut his hair this way because he'd seen too many Akira Kurosawa movies.

In the spacious white dojo, there were large red-framed black-and-white photos of Tsutomu Ohshima, Yasuhiro Konishi and Gichin Funakoshi. There were also red-framed photos of black karate masters — Moses Powell and Ronald Duncan, and Fred Hamilton. And there were framed posters for black karate movies like *Black Dynamite* and *Black Belt Jones.*

"Surprised you wanted karate today," Brutus said. Sweeping right kick. Violently disturbed air an inch in front of my nose. "Thought you might want to get in some boxing. Work on that lame right cross. Now yo daddy? Oh, *that* man had him some right cross!"

Boxing was the pain concealed behind the blue door. "Maybe another time," I said. "Right now, I need to work on these skills."

"So, what's going on in Mexicantown these days?" Brutus said. Right round kick, left round kick, punch, punch. "Word is them ICE suckers swoopin' down lookin' to hook some fresh brown meat."

Sweep kick, punch, lapel grab, failed throw, push off. "Just some petty feds with cereal box badges and a weak beef."

"Yo daddy'd be redder than a baboon's swollen butt over this nonsense," Brutus said. Punch, knee thrust, punch, kick. "You don't care they might snatch up some of your neighbors?"

"I care," I said feeling one of my ribs ache from the last kick. "And if it comes to that, then I'll make something pop." Kick. Kick. Leg sweep. No contact. Brutus danced lightly away. "Until then, I got my social security number and marine discharge papers."

"That don't sound like ya daddy," Brutus said. Punch to the chest. Lapel grab. Hip into me. Hit the mat hard. Roll and up again. More ribs throbbing.

"I'm not my daddy."

Brutus grinned. "Oh, I think you more like him than you'd care to think, young blood."

Heel of a hand to my chest. Attack. Wrist grab, twist. Ass-over-head. My full weight crashing to the mat hard. Right heel zooming toward my face stopping an inch from my nose.

Done.

Brutus pulled me up and we bowed to each other.

One of us was out of breath with a few stars dancing in his eyes.

It wasn't Brutus.

"Better," he said.

We walked down a lazily curving staircase to the first floor, where lawyers and doctors, deal makers and politicians were lifting weights, jogging on treadmills or climbing on Stairmasters while watching CNN, Fox News or Bloomberg Television. In one glass partitioned room, people were "spinning" on stationary bikes. In another, people were doing twisty-turny-stretchy things on yoga mats.

I saw the dumpy-and-grumpy judge who presided over my wrongful dismissal trial plopped on a bench wiping sweat from his brow.

He saw me.

From his brief and weary look, I had the feeling he'd presided over a thousand trials since mine, enabling him to forget who I am.

"Holy cow, Brutus," I said. "How many ballers you got up in this crib?"

"All of 'em, now that you here, kid."

In Brutus's glass enclosed office, he stepped on a treadmill fit flush to the floor and behind a black wrought-iron standing desk.

"Really?" I said. "A treadmill at a standing desk?"

"Locomotion is life. Sitting is dying."

A fit blonde woman maybe in her forties and wearing Club Brutus-branded royal-blue spandex entered, smiled at me and handed Brutus a stack of mail.

"Thanks, Geneva," Brutus said, then donned a pair of reading glasses and flipped through the mail. "You want a juice or something, Young Snow? Smoothie?"

"Thanks. No."

"You sure?" Geneva said with a radiant smile. "We make 'em fresh and certified organic."

"I'm kinda wanting an eight-slice Buddy's 'Detroiter' pizza and beer right now."

"Sorry," Geneva laughed as she left. "Can't help you there."

Apollonius "Brutus" Jefferies had been a cop at the same time my dad was on the Force. They had been good friends. They'd even squared off against each other in police boxing leagues. Twenty years into a decorated career, Brutus was shot twice. A failed beer-bunker robbery on Woodward Avenue perpetrated by two liquored up and drugged out teenagers. After a touch-and-go surgery, Brutus had lost a quarter of his stomach, a piece of his right lung and a lot of his weight. He was the living dead.

In an effort to bring himself back from his

dark suspension between life and death, Brutus bought a thirty-by-thirty rattrap of a building along Jefferson Avenue. A few donated heavy bags, speed bags and spit buckets and he was in business — mostly with off-duty cops who felt achingly sorry for Brutus, a bag-of-bones struggling to lift ten-pound dumbbells.

My father may have felt sorry for Brutus. But he never let on. Brutus struggled, fought, pushed and prayed himself back to the land of the living, one ten-pound dumbbell at a time. And now, twenty years later at the age of sixty-five, he was the poster child for healthy living and Club Brutus was where Detroit's elite paid big money to work out.

Brutus had given me the "Friends and Family" membership discount since he had known my father. Of course, part of my amazing bargain was agreeing to teach underprivileged kids beginning karate at an after-school class in the fall. Brutus even threw in a free pair of his personally branded Nike trainer shoes.

Yeah, I have money.

But come on: *Free* Brutus-branded Nikes!

"Sure you don't want nothin' from the salad bar?" Brutus said.

"Sounds good, but I can't," I said, looking out at Detroit's 1 percent making a bid for immortality on ellipticals and stationary bikes. "I'm having lunch with Bobby Falconi."

"Colored kid over at the coroner's office?"

"One and the same," I said. "Though I'm prone to think only old Negroes like you use the term 'colored' anymore." I stood, reached across the desk and shook Brutus's big, powerful hand. "Thanks for the workout, old man."

"Ain't nothin' to it but to do it, young blood," Brutus said, grinning. "Stop dropping your shoulder when you're coming in for a strike. Trust your opponent's aggression to be your source of energy. Stillness is your power, son."

"Any other words of wisdom, sensei?"

"Say 'please' and 'thank you' for small miracles. And always wear a condom."

I showered, shpritzed on a little Clive Christian C for Men cologne (just in case Beyoncé, Christina Aguilera or Wahu were waiting for me outside), and changed into a grey Nautica polo shirt, Buffalo jeans and well-worn tan Cole Haan leather loafers. On my way out, I ran into one of my new neighbors: Trent T.R. Ogilvy.

"If I didn't know any better, I'd think you

were following me," I said.

"Why would I ever wish to do that?"

"Isn't Club Brutus a little out of the price range of a charitable foundation community organizer?"

"It is," Ogilvy said brightly. "Fortunately, Mr. Jefferies — Brutus — was looking for a yoga instructor and I answered the call. You'd be astounded how generous wealthy women can be after a bit of the old Downward Dog."

"Have a good day, Mr. Ogilvy," I said.

"You as well, Mr. Snow," Ogilvy said. "Oh, and should you look in your rearview mirror and happen to see an eight-year-old silver Prius, that's me attempting to follow your Caddy."

I left Club Brutus for lunch with Bobby Falconi.

5

Marie Antoinette took a header off the Ambassador Bridge this past Sunday.

The infamous seventeenth-century French queen, Archduchess of Austria and wife of King Louis XVI, had narrowly missed the bow of the lake freighter *Norquist-Jannak*, its twenty-two-ton break-bulk cargo of iron ore five days out from the Port of Duluth-Superior.

Reaching a terminal velocity of seventy-three miles per hour, Her Majesty the Queen slammed powdered wig-first into the steel-grey channeled waters of the Detroit River. The concussive impact snapped her neck, fractured her right orbital and dislodged the eye from its socket. The *Norquist-Jannak*'s giant propellers churned the queen under for a bit, catching the hem of her ornate gown, unspooling layers of petticoats but sparing her the indignity of being sliced into bloody chunks.

The bridge had been backed up that day. Nothing new; over a quarter of the merchandise traded between the US and Canada crosses over the Ambassador Bridge, which connects Detroit to Windsor, Ontario. The nearly hundred-year-old structure is constantly choked by trucks laden with goods.

Congested as the decaying bridge was, the only eye-witnesses were the usual unreliable ones. No one could recall seeing the seventeenth-century French queen get out of coach, carriage, van, or car, except one witness who swore Madame Déficit had emerged from a blue Toyota Camry and entered the US duty-free shop, presumably to buy cake and champagne. No such car was found and neither the US nor Canada's duty-free shop's closed-circuit security camera had recorded an ornately dressed French queen entering or leaving the premises.

No one from the bridge management company, US Border Patrol, Coast Guard or Homeland Security had anything official or unofficial to say about Ms. Antoinette. Bridge video and lane photo surveillance on both sides — equipment rumored to be the same age as the cameras Charlie Chaplin used to film *City Lights* — had yet to reveal the queen's point of origin or provide a clue as to her motivations.

Word was whoever delivered the queen to her final destination had a stolen Nexus pass, allowing them to quickly enter and exit the US and Canada. Maybe the guard was more engaged in finding a four-letter word for "rodomontade" than checking out his two-hundredth vehicle for the day.

A young black woman who worked in a five-by-five toll booth on the American side apparently busted out laughing when interviewed by a couple of Detroit cops. They'd given her a description of the woman and asked if she remembered such a person.

"I think I'd remember some cray-cray white girl dressed like some dead-ass queen," she'd said.

Until yesterday, it had not been determined whether the queen's demise was in the legal province of the US or Canada. The Windsor and Detroit police departments had cooperated fully with each other, and with Homeland Security, the FBI and the Canadian Security Intelligence Service. Eventually, the Windsor Police Department's considerable lack of resources and eagerness to blame Detroit for all North American crime precipitated the conclusion that the dead queen was in American juris-diction.

"Jesus, Bobby," I finally said. "Coroners have the best stories."

Bobby — Dr. James Robert "Bobby" Falconi of the Wayne County Coroner's Office — and I were enjoying an eight-square Buddy's "Detroiter" pizza — cheese, pepperoni on top, tomato basil sauce, topped with shaved parmesan cheese and magical Sicilian spice blend.

Actually, *I* was the one enjoying the pizza. Bobby, lost in thought after relaying the story of Marie Antoinette, picked at the antipasto salad.

"It's not funny, August," Bobby said. "I did the work-up on the girl. She was eighteen, nineteen tops. Can't tell because nobody can find anything on her: no dental records, nothing in AFIS. Like she never existed!" Bobby flopped back against the padded seat of our booth. "I'm having an acquaintance go over the girl's costume. She's at U of M, my friend. A forensic fiber and fabric specialist."

"Somebody actually majored in that?"

"Works mostly with archeologists." Bobby was still twirling the same piece of salami on his fork that he'd been twirling for the past five minutes. "Auction houses establishing authenticity and provenance. Some police consulting work."

I took a sip of my lemon water. "I take it everybody wants this one closed out fast?" Bobby was quiet for a moment, stirring his iced tea with his straw. Then he looked at me and said, "By 'everybody' I'm guessing you mean your old DPD comrades in arms. Jesus, August — it's not what it was after you were fired. After your trial. They made cuts through the bone and into the marrow. I mean if I hadn't agreed to an eight-percent salary cut, I'd have been God-only-knows where. They could hire a hundred new beat cops and forty detectives tomorrow and *still* be short staffed. It's a mess, August. And the bean counters are scrutinizing each bean as if it were the last. So, yeah — everybody wants this one closed out fast. Some freak chick that got too high and topped herself."

"Everybody," I said, "except you."

Bobby said, "I've seen enough bodies to populate a city. Tag it and bag it, slice and dice. Dictate notes. Go to lunch. That's my day." He paused, drew in a ragged breath of air. "Sometimes — you see a body and you want to know their story. This may sound stupid — but sometimes I can — *feel* — these people — this girl — wanting me to tell their story."

Bobby took a minute to eat some of the salad and a small piece of the pizza. Then he tossed his napkin on the table and stared at it for a long moment. Lifting his eyes to me he said, "She was raped. Systematically. Repeatedly. Vaginally and anally. Three different semen samples in her stomach. Degraded by river water forced in her system on impact." He fell silent, then barked out a laugh.

With tragicomic timing, our waitress stopped at our table and asked if everything was all right. I said we'd take the check and could we have a couple carryout boxes.

Bobby and I were quiet after she left.

Then he said, "Fucking hell, August, I'm still cataloging the drugs that were in her: methamphetamines, MDMA, traces of hallucinogens." He smiled suddenly, a malevolent half-smile. "You were a sniper, right? Afghanistan?"

"Yeah," I said, uncomfortable with the darkening path our conversation was taking.

"Me?" Bobby said. "Army intelligence. Iraq and Afghanistan. I, uh, assisted with some . . . unique interrogation methods on enemy combatants. One of the favorites was the Rollercoaster. Barbiturate injection in one arm — five minutes later, amphetamine injection in the other arm. One minute, you're out cold, the next — *boom!* — shocked awake, heart racing, flop sweat. Four of those and an enemy combatant would confess to the Kennedy assassination. Or his heart would pop like a needle to a balloon."

"Why you telling me this, Bobby?"

"Because I think that's what they — whoever 'they' are — did to this girl," Bobby said. "Put her on the Rollercoaster. Whoever did this, she was their fucking plaything. She wasn't human to them. She was a chew bone to a pack of Rottweilers."

"What the hell was she doing on the Ambassador Bridge?" I said.

"You're the detective," Bobby said. "You tell me."

"Maybe she was being transported," I heard myself say. "Another location. Another party. Risky considering bridge security even at its crappiest. Could be whoever was moving her — if you go with that scenario — had a Nexus card; no stops, straight through. Didn't expect a traffic jam. Maybe she escaped. Or they ditched her. Somebody having suffered that much abuse with that many drugs in their system — maybe she was susceptible to a suggestion of suicide. Get rid of a problem without straight up first-degree."

"She's Hispanic," Bobby said, almost absently.

"What?"

"The girl," he said. "She's Hispanic. That much I know."

He reached into his suit coat pocket and pulled out a sheet of paper folded into quarters. Unfolding it, he positioned it in front of me: the girl on a slab, pristine white sheet covering her from the chest down.

In life she'd probably been very pretty.

Now, she simply looked impossibly pale and eternally sad.

"Eighteen or nineteen," Bobby said again. "Somebody's daughter. Jesus."

I turned the photo face down, not wanting our waitress or other patrons to see it. Not wanting Bobby to look at it and worry about his eighteen-year-old daughter, Miko, some seven hundred miles away in Boston at the Berklee College of Music.

"What do you want me to do, Bobby?" I said.

"I don't know. Maybe show it around your neighborhood. She's Hispanic. Maybe undocumented. Maybe somebody knows her in Mexicantown." His tired, red eyes searching mine, he said, "Maybe somebody's looking for her. Somebody's got to be looking for her, right?"

I refolded the grim photo and reluctantly slipped it in my pants pocket.

"I'll ask around," I said. "No promises."

"I'm too old for promises," Bobby said. "I just need somebody to make a goddamn effort."

Our congenial waitress brought our check and a couple carry-out boxes. Smiling up at her, I said, "For medicinal purposes, I think we could use two Founders Porter beers."

6

Eighty-eight degrees, 40 percent humidity. Air quality index at 163.

If you live off of the I-75 South Highway like me, you're essentially breathing diesel exhaust through a wet wool blanket.

I gave a brief thought to visiting my parents — much cooler in their oak-shaded graves — but nixed the idea. Grief is addictive. As an addict, I had to admit my dependence before I could move on.

Moving on is exactly what I did at the house of my godparents, Tomás and Elena Gutierrez.

I was about to mount the steps to their front door when I heard music and laughter at the back of the house. Los Lonely Boys, "Diamonds."

Tomás and Elena were working in their garden. More accurately, Elena was working in the garden, turning over the black soil, weeding, planning trenched lines where the tomatoes, peppers, onions and chives, kale and spinach, basil and cucumbers would go.

"Hey," I called out to Elena. "How come the fat guy's not helping?"

She laughed. "He's more help *there* than he would be *here,* Octavio!"

"I got a shovel," Tomás grumbled. "Don't make me use it upside your head."

"Nice to see you, too, Shrek."

"You want coffee?"

"Who made it?" I said.

"Me."

"Pass."

"Pendejo."

I finally accepted a cup of his gritty, nearly chewable coffee and we sat on the porch, watching Elena work in the crushing heat. She looked like an Inca princess, onyx-black hair in a thick braid falling over her right shoulder while her bronze skin reflected the rays of a sun jealous of her beauty. It was like watching a myth or a fairytale; a drop of her sweat on the black soil and flowers would bloom in colors only gods and goddesses could see.

My mother, years before her death, had painted Elena, her best friend, in her garden. Maybe it was the heat, but I could swear I smelled the linseed oil of my mother's paints, the seasoned wood of her palette . . .

Between Tomás and Elena under a blue sky, I suffered a brief but all too real sensation of envy. They had something I was yet to experience, even with Tatina; that casual, seemingly inconsequential silent bond that is the essence of a life of love.

"When are you gonna put an awning over this porch?" I said to Tomás after a sip of his road tar coffee.

"Awnings are for pussies," Tomás said. "We're *Mexican*! We don't need no stinkin' awning!"

"You're not afraid of skin cancer?"

"Skin cancer, mi amigo," Tomás snarled, "is afraid of *me.*"

I'd come for a reason, but a lump had formed in my throat. I wasn't quite sure if it was because of what I had come to ask or if it was a congealed bit of Tomás's coffee. I finally found the courage to say, "I need to show Elena a photo."

"So show her the photo," Tomás said dismissively. Then, eyebrows furrowed, he said, "Wait a minute. *What* photo?"

"A girl."

"A girl?"

"Yeah," I said. "A — dead girl."

"Jesus, Octavio! You're kidding me, right? You want Elena — my *wife* — to look at a picture of a *dead* girl? What's Elena got to do with this dead girl?"

"I need to know if Elena recognizes her," I said. I told him about the Hispanic girl in the Wayne County morgue. The dark theatrics of her short, abused life and high-dive death. How a friend of mine couldn't let this young woman become another nameless body lowered into a mud, root and stone potter's field grave.

Elena was the hub of the entire Mexicantown community. Depending on who needed her, she was an altar, a confessional, a bullhorn or a sledgehammer, fighting for the rights of the people in our neighborhood. She knew everyone. "How many baptisms and christenings has she dragged you to, Tomás? How many quinceañeras? Trials and parole hearings? Mom-and-pop restaurant openings? Funerals?" I took a breath. "It's a long shot she knows this girl. But I need to know. Then we — I — can be done with it."

Tomás gave me a long, hard look. "Elena's always been her own woman. Probably seen and stood up to more shit than me — and I've seen and stood up to a lot of shit, Octavio. Still, I'd be lyin' if I didn't tell you I feel like I got an old-fashion, macho husband's duty to protect his woman." He took a moment to glare at me. "And let's be honest: Things *always* start small with you — 'Oh, yes, ma'am — I'll look into that little thing for you!' and 'Oh, yes, sir — I'll fix that tiny problem for you!' — and these 'little' things always end up being mutant fucking atomic alligators chewing everybody's ass off. Tell me I'm wrong."

"Just looking to give my friend some closure."

"Ain't no fucking such thing as 'closure,' " Tomás said bitterly. "Closure is white-folk bullshit. Aw, shit. There it is." He pointed a thick forefinger at my face. "Them puppy dog eyes. You're a *junkie*! You need a *fix.*"

"What the hell are you —"

"A mainline hit of self-righteous hero bullshit."

"Oh, for fuck's sake —"

"See! Right *there*!" Tomás said, jabbing his forefinger at the bridge of my nose. "You *need* to be somebody's hero on account of you think you're the only option for justice in this fucked-up world. Problem is, while you flyin' around with a cape, guys like me tend to get punched in the throat and shot in the ass."

"I'm not asking for anybody's help —"

"That's just it!" Tomás said. *"You never do!"*

"What's going on up there?" Elena said, shielding her eyes from the sun with a gloved hand.

"Octavio wants my permission to show you something upsetting," Tomás answered.

"Perhaps," Elena said, planting her wrists in her waist, "you should inform Octavio that I'm in my fifty-third year of being a grown woman. One who happens to possess an undergraduate degree in Secondary Education and masters in Institutional Management." As is the case with many Hispanic mothers, grandmothers and godmothers, Elena seamlessly transitioned from English to rapid-fire Spanish the more fervent she became. "Also, inform *the child* that I have spent more time tear-gassed and arrested at protests than *el bebé* spent in the Marines."

Tomás glanced at me. With a wry smile, he whispered, "Oh, you done stepped in it now, *cabrón.*"

Elena pointed a finger at the ground in front of her. "Get down here now, Octavio!"

"Yes, ma'am."

I could feel the photo of the dead girl, a dense, solemn weight, in my pocket, as I closed the distance between Elena and myself.

"Anything new on the undocumented

front?" I said in an attempt to avoid my mission.

"Everyone's asking," Elena said, her voice lowered. "Everyone's scared. Old Hispanic men who fought in Korea or Vietnam, *they're* scared! The mayor's not returning my calls. And the Police Chief —"

"Renard?"

"Yes," Elena said. "He says he doesn't have the manpower to enforce any detention orders. But this is the *fédérales* anyway and what Renard does or doesn't do won't amount to much." Elena took off her gardening gloves and fanned herself with them. "I went to Eastern Market the other day. Ventitaglio's Produce. The Latinos who worked there? Gone. Now? Teenage white boys who've never seen produce fresh from the earth trimming lettuce!" Elena gave an exasperated sigh. "I'm doing what I can, Octavio — but this? This is an eclipse no one saw coming."

"What about those immigration attorneys you work with?"

"Ara Tarkasian and Bill Showalter? Ara's serving five days in County for contempt of court because he hid an undocumented Honduran woman who's lived here for eight years. And Bill's fighting disbarment charges from the US attorney general's office for claiming privilege on files of a young Somali man's case. A young man who, by the way, has a three-point-eight academic average at U of M in biochemistry. *These* are the people we're throwing out? I pray to God every day, Octavio. But I can't see His plan. And — I don't know if I'm up for this fight."

"That doesn't sound like you, Elena."

"Well, Octavio," she said with a bit of edge to her voice, "I certainly think I've seen enough to know when a fight is at an end."

"I need to show you a photograph."

"It's bad, yes?" she said.

"It's bad, yes." I sucked in a deep lungful of hot, humid air and said, "A girl. I need to know if you know her. Maybe around Mexicantown."

Elena quickly made the Sign of the Cross. "Okay."

I could see in the micro-changes in the set of her jaw and shoulders that she, not unlike most people, would never be prepared. For a split second I wondered about myself: I had seen a number of bodies in different states, both in Afghanistan and as a cop in Detroit. And with every corpse, I had felt my humanity — my ability to feel empathy or sadness, pity or outrage — recede into shadows. For a moment, watching Elena gird herself, I felt ashamed — embarrassed

— that a portion of my ability to feel sorrow and mourn the unknown dead had receded into the impassive shadows of whatever remained of my soul.

I took the photo out, unfolded it and showed it to Elena.

After a moment, Elena brought her eyes to mine. "I'm going in, Octavio," she said calmly. "This heat. I've been working the garden for two hours. I — need a shower. Then we'll talk."

Elena let her gardening gloves fall to the tilled earth, then walked past me to the house.

"The fuck's going on," Tomás angrily whispered to me in the kitchen. With a paring knife, he sliced oranges, lemons and limes for a glass of sangria. I could hear the water in the pipes from Elena's shower upstairs. "She walks right past me, not a word. The fuck did you say to her?"

"I think she knows the dead girl," I said.

Tomás flashed the glistening paring knife in my face. "You *know* I don't like her being upset, Octavio. You *know* this. But you come and show her a picture of a *dead girl*? Jesus!"

"I was kind of hoping —"

"Let me tell you something, *pendejo*," Tomás said. "You and 'hope' are like gasoline and a fucking blow torch. I can't *wait* for the day when you don't give a shit about hope!"

Against my better judgment, I said, "There's something else going on, Tomás."

"Oh, like this ain't enough?" Tomás dropped the paper-thin slices of lemon and lime in a tall glass. From a pitcher he poured Elena's homemade sangria into the glass, then slowly ran a slice of orange around the lip. "I'm taking this to Elena," Tomás growled. "You wait your sorry ass right here. And don't be using that time to think up any new ways of upsetting my wife, okay, *cabrón*?"

Carrying the glass of sangria as if it were the Blood of Christ, he went upstairs. Five minutes later Elena came downstairs bare-foot and wearing a thick terry cloth robe. Her hair was wrapped in a towel turban.

Elena and I looked at each other for an uneasy moment. Then she drew in a deep breath and said, "What happened to her?"

"Jumped from the Ambassador Bridge."

There was little sense in recounting the grotesque details. The story of the girl's leap into infinity had run three days earlier, saturating TV, radio, newspapers and online news. Reportage included, for whatever reason, a primer on who Marie Antoinette was. But soon the story of the leaping queen was buried beneath an avalanche of other stories as humanity continued its plummet into ever-thickening mud. "Her name was Isadora Rosalita del Torres. Nineteen. Undocumented," Elena finally said "Worked some of the small shops on Vernor. Part of a small group of undocumenteds I was working with. Lived a hard life in Mexico City. Saved enough for a coyote to get her across the border. Nearly suffocated in an eighteen-wheeler parked behind a Walmart outside of San Antonio. She's a — was a smart girl. Good . . . girl."

Elena was trembling.

Seeing Elena this shaken was unnerving for me. Aside from my mother, Elena was one of the strongest, most resilient people I'd ever known. I'd borrowed from her strength when both my mother and father died. I'd been given sanctuary in her un-breakable spirit when I was fired from the DPD and during my whistleblower lawsuit trial. She knew my heart, my mind and spirit. She had helped nurture them since I was a kid.

Now, facing each other, this pillar of iron and the foundation for what bravery I might have shown in my life revealed another aspect of who she was: delicate and vulnerable, subject to the same fears, faults and failings of all the other mortals beneath a common sky.

And that scared me.

"I got Isadora — Izzy — a job in a restaurant in Ann Arbor," Elena continued. "Ara — my attorney friend — he was working her case. Next thing I know — the restaurant's been raided and — she's gone. Scooped up. Hard enough to track somebody with family here. Izzy — she had nobody."

"She had you," I said.

"A lot of good that did her," Elena said, fighting back tears. "Sometimes — they just go. They get scared and they just — go. And there were — are — so many others depending on me."

Tomás came down the living room staircase and made his way to the kitchen. Elena quickly wiped tears from her eyes and cheeks and attempted a smile.

"I'm good," Elena said. "I'm okay."

"You're okay, huh?" Tomás said gruffly. Unsettled by his tone, Elena and I stared at Tomás for an anxious second or two. He was holding a small black leather purse. He reached in and pulled out a Sig Sauer P290 semi-automatic handgun. "This what you callin' 'okay' these days, woman?"

7

Elena, quiet and distant, sat in the living room at the center of their sofa. Her body was rigid save for her slow, rhythmic breathing. She stared blankly at an opposite wall where a small framed painting of a haloed Jesus hung. It had been painted by my mother. Tomás intermittently interrupted her view of Christ, pacing in front of her, the black purse in one hand, the gun in the other. I stood leaning against the archway between the living room and dining room, wondering how this was going to play out.

"You've never — *never!* — carried a gun, Elena. Who's making you do this?"

Elena said nothing. She simply stared at the painting of Jesus. It was hard to tell if she was quietly petitioning Him for answers and strength, or silently admonishing him for not providing either.

I wanted to ask if her recent forays into publicly challenging immigration policies and ICE raids and demanding account-ability of ICE detention facilities had elicited threats. Considering her decades of activism, threats were nothing new for Elena.

But she'd never carried a gun. She hated guns and only tolerated Tomás's knowledge of, affinity for and talent with weaponry because she knew the good and generous heart of her husband. She knew the hard life he'd lived, the challenges he'd met with sheer force of will and keen instinct.

I wanted to ask Elena questions. But this wasn't my home. Perhaps a small part of me enjoyed seeing the emerging tension between them; it was like a reenactment of my parents' arguing. Knowing they were at loggerheads in an effort to better under-stand, respect, love and protect each other.

Of course, a good guest always knows his limits even if his hosts are careening off the rails.

Tomás stopped pacing, standing directly in front of Elena and blocking her view of Our Lord and Savior. "Elena," Tomás said calmly. "Baby, I'm not mad at you. I love you. You know that. But I need to know what's going on. Is someone threatening you? Please. Talk to me."

Without a word, Elena rose from the sofa

and walked to the small study off to the side of the dining room. She returned holding a green file folder, which she offered to Tomás. After putting the purse and the gun down on the coffee table, he took the folder and opened it. His eyes widened as he flipped through the file's contents. I held out my hand.

Tomás glared at me for a moment before handing me the file.

Threats of rape, torture and death.

Your spic ass is going to be white-cocked and tossed over the wall back into Mexican mud where all of you belong . . .

Shut your mouth, you spic cunt, or I'll shut it for you . . .

Nice house, bitch . . .

There were crude drawings of her and an old black-and-white newspaper photo of her with a red-ink swastika drawn over her face. "America *First!*" the sender had hastily written beneath the photo.

"How long?" Tomás said.

Elena slowly drew in a breath. "Six, maybe eight months."

"And you didn't tell me about this because?"

Elena finally met Tomás's eyes. "Because I know you, Tomás. You would have raged against anybody who so much as looked at me sideways —"

"You're goddamn right! I'm your *husband,* woman!"

"I don't like your rage, Tomás," Elena said. "Not because I fear it for myself, but because I fear what it does to you. It eats you up. Consumes you. Takes you away from me. I don't like it when you're away from me."

Tomás sat next to his wife and brought her into him.

I drew in a deep breath, then said to Elena, "You mind if I take the file?"

"Why? What are you going to do with it?"

"Maybe I can have somebody at DPD look into the threats. Shake something loose."

"You still got friends there?" Tomás said.

"Not friends. Markers." I looked back at Elena, now wiping her eyes and looking painfully lost. I gestured for Tomás to follow me to the front door. He did. Elena went back to staring at my mother's painting of Jesus. "Elena know how to shoot?"

"I taught her a long time ago," Tomás said. "Good eye. Rock steady. Licensed. Hates it on 'philosophical' grounds."

"Philosophy and religion get a lot of good people killed," I said. "If she's gonna carry, make sure she's still rock steady with a good eye. If somebody pulls on her, she gotta be ready."

Twenty minutes later, I was sipping vending machine iced-tea and sitting in the pleasantly air-conditioned 14th Precinct office of Detective Captain Leo Cowling.

The precinct was still located in a late-1800s fieldstone mansion on what's known as the Woodward Spine. But unlike the leaky, moldy and mildewed rattrap I'd cut my cop teeth on, it had been impressively renovated.

"Wow," I said, looking around. The office was spacious and modern, looking rather more like a corporate vice president's office than the well-worn workplace of an officer of the Detroit Police Department. "This isn't the 14th Precinct I knew and loathed. Where are the water stains? The cracked walls? Jesus! *Where's Waldo?!*"

"Who the fuck's Waldo?"

"A rat," I said. "About six inches long. White-tipped ears. Got into the old vending machine one night and gnawed at an old egg salad sandwich. Left a trail of diarrhea from here to lockup."

"And this is what you remember from your embarrassingly short career?"

"Pretty much. That and knocking the shit

out of you at a PAL charity boxing tournament."

"Only thing you knocked the shit out of is the truth about that match."

Cowling casually swiveled back and forth in his expensive, ergonomically-designed chair.

"Believe it or not, I got shit to do," Cowling said. "Whatchu want, Tex-Mex?"

I flopped Elena's green file folder onto Cowling's desk. "Death threats issued against a very good friend of mine, a prominent local activist. Elena Gutierrez. I thought you might be able to run 'em by the forensics guys. Maybe pull somebody up on AFIS."

"Why would I want to do that?"

"Because you're all aces?"

After a few tough guy seconds, he spun the file to face him and carefully thumbed through the contents. "This is some fucked up shit," he said.

"It is indeed."

"Who besides you and me has handled this?"

"Elena Gutierrez and her husband, Tomás. You should have Tomás's fingerprints in the system from maybe twenty-five years ago. Mine, too. That leaves Elena and whoever else. Just need to know who the 'whoever else' is."

"I ain't yo giddy-up-'n-go niggah, Snow," Cowling said. "I find something, it's DPD until I say it ain't DPD. You feel me?"

"I feel you," I said. "And doing this might go a long way for you in Mexicantown if you find something actionable. And speaking of 'going a long way,' what's shakin' between you and Lieutenant Martinez? You kids shopping for silverware and china?"

"Get the fuck outta my office."

"Yessir," I said with a crisp salute.

On my way out of the 14th I passed by a large framed photo of a man I once knew: Captain Ray Danbury, looking proud and formidable in his dress blues, his jacket resplendent with decorations and medals. He'd been killed in the line of duty and I couldn't help but feel I'd created the disastrous circumstances that brought about his murder. Danbury wasn't exactly dirty, but he wasn't unerringly clean. For Danbury — like a lot of cops and maybe even me — there were a lot of course corrections along the way, large and small, while making the everyday Herculean effort to stay on a true-north path.

Before leaving, I saluted his photo then made the Sign of the Cross.

8

A couple blocks before turning off Vernor Highway onto Markham Street, I called Tomás.

"She feels guilty," Tomás said. "Like she's backing down. Giving up on the 'hood. Which is bullshit. She ain't never given up on nothin'. Including me — *especially* me! — even when I gave her good reason. You think your cop buddy can pull some prints from that file?"

I spared Tomás the short-yet-intricate history of why Captain Leo Cowling and I would likely never be buddies and said, "He's gonna look into it. I wouldn't hold my breath, though."

Turning onto Markham Street, I saw the last two houses I'd purchased in an effort to complete the picture postcard of my youth. The house nearest Vernor Highway — a red brick duplex built in 1923 — was being professionally cleaned. It had belonged to

Rolf and Germaine Macek and their five kids Ralphie Jr., Ronda, Rebecca, Robbie and Little Pat. The last Germans in an expanding Mexican neighborhood. A family that fed me schnitzel and rouladen and laughed when I turned green at my first taste of sauerbraten.

The brown brick single-family house next to the duplex — once the home of Tina Morales, my fifth-grade crush, and Mamá Victoria — was just about complete. I could almost hear Tina's bright, lilting fifth-grade laugh again.

I was about to wave to my next-door neighbors Sylvia and Carmela when it became apparent Carmela was crying. Seated on a step leading up to their porch, Carmela — small, Mexican-brown and wearing an oversized "Cristo Rey High School Wolves" T-shirt — was being comforted by her friend and roommate, Sylvia. Sylvia — taller, with wild silver hair and untannable Polish white skin. Jimmy Radmon sat a step above Carmela and was gently patting her shoulder.

I parked in my narrow driveway and walked over.

"What's going on?" I said, standing in front of the triptych of neighbors and friends.

Carmela wiped her nose with a tissue and, embarrassed, turned away from me. After a moment, she turned back and tried to smile. The smile was unstable and refused to set.

"F-ing bastards," Sylvia gruffly answered as she glared up at me.

"What f-ing bastards?"

"Goddamn *ICE*!" Sylvia growled. "*That's* what f-ing bastards, Mr. Snow!"

I looked at Jimmy.

"It wasn't good, Mr. Snow," Jimmy said. "They didn't have to be like that."

I knelt in front of Carmela. Put my hands on hers. "What's going on?"

Sylvia rubbed Carmela's back while Carmela purposefully regulated her breathing. Finally, she said, "Sylvia and I were working out front. The flowers along the walkway."

"Chrysanthemums," Sylvia said.

"Oh, we love chrysanthemums!"

"Goodness yes —"

"So colorful —"

"And what happened?" I said, attempting to keep things on track.

"So anyway, this big black car —"

"Chevy Suburban," Jimmy added. "Last year's model. Blacked out windows. Fed plate."

"It parks right *there* —" Carmela jabbed a forefinger at the curb in front of their house. "And — this *man* —"

"He comes up to us, flashes some sort of ID — wouldn't even let me *hold* it!" Sylvia said. "Asks if we know who lives in Carlos's house. Asks about any women or kids in the house."

"And I say we know who lives there," Carmela joined, "but I don't tell him who —"

"Because we know what goddamn *Nazis* look like," Sylvia said.

"So, I don't tell him who lives in the house, but I say they're nice people and they've been here for a while and they're really lovely neighbors. Then — he just — *stares* at me."

I told Jimmy to go in their house and bring out a glass of ice water for Carmela. Sylvia countermanded my order, telling Jimmy there was an opened bottle of rosé and to bring a glass for Carmela and herself. Two minutes later he returned with two goblets of rosé, carefully handing them to the ladies.

"You're such a sweet boy," Carmela said to Jimmy just before she pounded back three full gulps of the chilled wine. "You know how much we love you?"

"Yes, ma'am."

Sylvia filled me in on the rest: The ICE

agent — taking Carmela's brown skin and slight accent as a cue to interrogate — set upon her with what began as a softball probe into her immigration status. It quickly escalated, becoming more intrusive, more demanding and uncomfortably personal.

"Do you know how long it's been since anyone's asked me for proof of citizenship, Mr. Snow?" Carmela said, her voice quivering. "Fifty years! I was *born* here! December thirty-first, 1945, three A.M. at St. Mary's Hospital to Mr. and Mrs. —"

"This *jerk-off* insists Carmela go in the house and produce proof of citizenship," Sylvia said, herself close to tears. Then her voice became a low growl. "I told him to go 'F' himself."

"That's when I got here," Jimmy said.

Sylvia reached across her friend, gripped and jostled Jimmy's hand. "Oh, my *God,* you are our knight in shining armor, Jimmy!"

"So, I axe him I says 'S'up, man?' and he says none of my dang business. And I says, 'It kinda *is* my business on account I live here. Right upstairs.' And he tells me I should back off and I says, 'Hey, man, I ain't crowdin' you. Whatchu frontin' on me for?' "

"And I said everything was all right,"

Carmela said, her voice quavering. "That I'd go get proof of who I was and everybody should just calm down."

"She even offers this a-hole *lemonade*!" Sylvia said. "*Lemonade!* The only thing you offer a Nazi is —"

She pretended to spit and jerked a middle finger in the air.

"Well," Carmela said, "just because some people don't have manners doesn't mean *we* shouldn't be decent." She took in a deep, ragged breath. "So I go in the house. I get my social security card, my driver's license, passport and Target charge card —"

"And I'm sayin' she don't have to show this fool nothin' on account he don't have no warrant or probable cause," Jimmy said. "I mean, they was planting *flowers,* Mr. Snow! So, I go to stand between Carmela, she's holdin' all her ID up and this dude he's already reachin' to take her ID and hits me in the eye."

I took a closer look at Jimmy. There was a bloody scratch and a little swelling around his left eye.

By this time Carmela was nearly inconsolable. Sylvia tried to make her take a sip of her wine, but Carmela just waved it off.

To Sylvia in a low, firm voice I said, "Get her out of this heat. Take her inside."

I stood and gestured for Jimmy to follow me to the sidewalk.

"You get the name of this dumb sonuva-bitch?"

"Hensall," Jimmy said. "No! Hen*shaw*! Tha's it. It was on his uniform. Henshaw. H-E-"

"I know how to spell 'Henshaw,' Jimmy," I said. I nodded toward the duplex down the street that he and Carlos were working on. "You done for the day?"

"Yessir."

"Where's Carlos?"

"Him, the missus and Manny, they out to dinner. I think Dave and Busters, so Manny'd have some fun."

"Okay," I said. "I might be busy for a couple days, so you're the man on the block. *My* block. Got me?"

"Yeah, fo real."

"Call Carlos and tell him he's to go straight to St. Al's downtown," I said. "They should ask for Father Grabowski. Tell him ICE was asking about Catalina and Manny. Father Grabowski will know what to do."

"Yessir."

"I'm gonna look into this," I said. "In the meantime, don't let the girls drink too much. Make sure they eat. Maybe get 'em some sweets from La Gloria."

71

I offered Jimmy a couple twenties, but he waved off the bills. "I got this, Mr. Snow." He said he'd watch *Jeopardy* with them. Maybe listen to some of their old "hippie" albums. "They like that Joni Mitchell, Joan Baez stuff."

"Go for Joni Mitchell," I said. "Joan Baez'll have Sylvia making placards and organizing a goddamn sit-in."

"What if they go for them 'glaucoma brownies'?" Jimmy said.

"*You* serve 'em. One each," I said. "And use gloves when you dole 'em out." Then, after assessing the swollen scratch under Jimmy's eye again, I said, "Do you know how to defend yourself, Jimmy?"

"Yeah, sure," he said, sniffing and thumbing his nose thug-style. "I can handle a ruckus."

"Sure," I said, unconvinced. "I know a guy. Ex-cop. Owns a gym on the riverfront. 'Bout time I introduced you. In the meantime, take care of the girls. You've put your stamp on this street, Jimmy. These are your people now. And you take care of your people, right?"

"One hundred, no doubt."

"Don't forget to call Carlos," I said. "You forget and his wife and son are on a cheap government-paid flight back to where they've got no life." I dug into my pocket and extracted a set of house keys. "Here." I tossed the keys to Jimmy and he caught them.

"1482 Markham," Jimmy said, staring at the keys. "Something wrong with it, Mr. Snow?"

"It's yours," I said. " 'Bout time you had a real stake in the 'hood."

Jimmy gave me a slack-jawed look and started to say something.

"Call Carlos," I said. *"Now."*

Jimmy stuffed the house keys in a pocket of his Carhartt work shorts then quickly pulled his phone from his tool belt.

The last words I heard Jimmy say before I got to my porch were, "You need to listen up fo' real, ma brotha . . ."

I went in my house.

I had calls to make, too.

The kind of calls that required a nicely chilled Negra Modelo beer and a healthy disrespect for federal government surveillance.

9

Upstairs in a dark corner of my bedroom closet there's a shoebox with five "burner" phones in it.

Gifts from a young hacker friend who I — squeezed between a heavy rock and a blood-soaked hard place — sold outto the FBI.

When I was on the job I had occasionally employed a young black hacker nicknamed "Skittles." Normally, Skittles worked out of an artist cooperative on Detroit's crumbling industrial southwest side called Rocking Horse Studios — a reclaimed building occupied by painters, printmakers, graphic artists, musicians and performance artists. I'd always left him the same payment for his hacking assistance: a Costco-sized box of Skittles candy and maybe a few bucks. As much as a young DPD detective could afford.

Then, in a deal struck with a federally authorized devil on a case I had no reason or authority to investigate, Skittles was scooped up by the FBI in exchange for my complete disentanglement from the case. Instead of being fitted for a grey jumpsuit and a job slinging hash in a prison cafeteria, Skittles was given a salary, per diem expense account and all the high-end computers and powerful software he could ever want.

Of course, he was also given a "handler" who reminded him in no uncertain terms that an eight-by-ten federal penitentiary cell was just a phone call away.

And that was all on me.

I hadn't spoken to Skittles in a while.

But between ICE creeping through the neighborhood at night or threatening neighbors during the day, threats to Elena's safety and the Ambassador Bridge death of Isadora Rosalita del Torres, I figured a little on-the-sly dark net IT help might come in handy.

Skittles had given me the phones as a means of clandestine communications. Each was good for one thirty-second off-the-grid call. After the call, I would remove the SIM card, flush it, break the phone in half and leave the pieces in separate garbage bins.

I gave each burner phone a charge, slipped in the SIM cards, pressed zero-one-one-zero-star-pound on each and waited.

While waiting, I had a bowl of broccoli-bacon-and-sunflower-seed salad with dried cherries and poppy seed dressing (an old Grandma Snow recipe). I looked at the morgue photo of Izzy del Torres again and found myself imagining the gruesome deaths of her assailants brought about by my darkly skilled hands. As the Good Book says, "It is mine to avenge; I will repay. In due time their foot will slip; their day of disaster is near and their doom rushes upon them" (Deuteronomy 32:35).

Still waiting for any of the burners to ring, I called Bobby Falconi at the Wayne County Coroner's Office and told him the dead girl's name.

"Thanks, August," he said. "Jenji and I, we're gonna give her a proper funeral. Bury her someplace nice."

I suggested the cemetery where my parents were buried; lots of old-growth oak, maple and pine trees and well-tended by a friend of mine. I could visit Izzy when I visited my folks, maybe leave her a small bag of cashews or an orange like I left for my mother.

"You're one of the good guys, Bobby," I said.

"Somebody has to be or we're all fucked."

After twenty minutes none of the burner

phones had rung. I checked to see if each was holding a charge and had a dial tone. Good on both counts.

Using my cellphone I called a friend at the FBI's Detroit office.

"Hey, O'Donnell," I said brightly. "How's it hangin'."

A quick, exasperated sigh from FBI Special Agent Megan O'Donnell. "What do you want, August?"

"Well, to begin with, how's Frank doing at Quantico?"

Frank was a good friend who had selflessly helped me out of a tight situation awhile back. And though I never would have seen it coming — Frank being a simple soul whose life was an open graphic novel and O'Donnell being uniquely O'Donnell — they had been an item for over a year.

Frank was now in Quantico, Virginia, training to be an FBI agent.

"He's doing better than I thought he would," O'Donnell said with her characteristically brusque truthfulness. "I thought on psyche evals alone he'd wash out. Teacher friend of mine says he's top-doggin' it. Real gung-ho without being a psycho-patriot. Says his physical stamina is off the charts. 'Course I knew that." Then she said again, "What do you want, August?"

77

I told her about Isadora Rosalita del Torres. About the ICE patrols in the neighborhood and how my neighbors were being intimidated. And the threats leveled at Elena.

"You looking for links?" O'Donnell said.

"I'm looking for a reason not to take a baseball bat to the SUV these fed thugs cruise around in," I said. "Anything you can tell me about these patrols and how big a net these yahoos are casting?"

"I have three open cases on my desk right now," O'Donnell sighed. "Each of 'em requires a bald forensic accountant trying his damnedest not to stare at my tits and a couple computer geeks that smell like boiled onions, kale salads and Cheetos. In other words, yeah — I got a few minutes to make an inquiry for you."

"Thanks,O'Donnell."

"And swear to God, August," O'Donnell said. "No goddamn baseball bats, okay?"

"No promises."

We disconnected.

After another hour and the onset of evening neither of the burner phones had rung. I had the very distinct feeling that Skittles had moved on from any association with me. Or the choke hold the FBI had on him left little to no digitally covert wiggle room.

At about seven thirty that muggy evening, the sky turned deep blue with hazy orange streaks running through the horizon. The day's high of eighty-five hadn't budged. Even so, I sat on my porch steps, sipping orange and mint iced tea, feeling my skin dampen in thick humidity, looking at the revitalized houses decorating my personal memory lane and wondering in which direction I should move on anything: Izzy del Torres's death. ICE and the ethnic cleansing of Mexicantown. Or Elena.

For whatever reason, I gave more thought to Izzy del Torres. A young woman I'd met only through a coroner's photo. A person who, until Elena identified her, had died nameless and degraded. I wracked my brain, searching for a Catholic prayer that spoke specifically to her. All I came up with was *"Since indeed God considers it just to repay with affliction those who afflict you . . ."* from 2 Thessalonians.

Then again, I may have just been meditating on what special and bloody gifts I held in my hands that might help Isadora del Torres be remembered by those who had sinned against her.

Carlos pulled his white Dodge Ram 2500 truck into his narrow driveway across the street and parked.

Neither Catalina nor his son, Manny, were with him.

I quickly surveyed the street for any signs of the feds' black Chevy Suburban then gestured for Carlos to come over.

"What the hell's going on, Mr. Snow?"

Carlos — looking weary and confused — sat next to me on the step.

"ICE agents were inquiring about Catalina," I said. "And Manny."

"Jesus," Carlos said. Attempting to hold onto a thread of hope, he said, "Señora Elena's been looking into citizenship paths for —"

"Right now, my friend," I said, "there *are* no paths. Only landmines."

"Is she — are they safe? My boy? With Father Grabowski?" Carlos said. I might as well have just punched him in the gut. At least that would have left him with a bit of air in his lungs.

"Father Grabowski has been running his undocumented underground for ten years," I said. "He's exactly the guy you want your wife and son with right now. Feds get the heebie-jeebies when it comes to squarin' off with religious organizations. You can thank Thomas Paine, Waco and Ruby Ridge for that. The good father knows when, how and where to move people."

"He's so — old," Carlos said.

"Don't mistake advanced age with diminished capacity," I said. "Catalina and Manny are in good hands. You'll get through this. We'll all get through this. And all we need is a little faith."

"Faith is what got us here to America," Carlos said. "And your faith in me — my wife and son — has helped sustain us."

"Go home," I said. "Try to get some rest. If these guys show up and start grilling you, tell 'em Cat and Manny are at Disney-world and maybe they should hitch a ride on the fuck-you-train to Orlando."

I watched Carlos, sunken into himself, walk across the street and into his house.

Inside my house, the burner phones remained silent.

I called Jimmy and asked how things were going with Carmela and Sylvia. He'd gotten them carry-out from Forbidden City Restaurant near the Wayne State University campus. Neither of them had a "glaucoma" brownie, but they'd emptied a liter bottle of rosé while listening to an old "hippie" vinyl recording of The Who's *Quadrophenia.*

"The whole thing?" I said, vaguely familiar with the so-called rock opera.

"The whole. Dang. Thing," Jimmy said.

Convinced at midnight there was little else

I could do, I figured I'd turn in and start fresh in the morning.

"Fresh" on what, I wasn't quite sure.

Halfway up the stairs I heard a timid knock on my door.

Fairly sure it wasn't Tatina, Rosario Dawson, Eva Longoria, Viola Davis or Shakira come to help me into my jammies and tuck me in for nighty-noodles, I quickly found my Glock, flipped the safety off, racked one in the chamber and peeked out of the living room window at the timid knocker.

I opened the door.

"Feel like a donut?" Father Grabowski said.

10

"Isn't it way past your bedtime, old man?"

I was in the front passenger's seat of Father Grabowski's rusting 2003 Ford Windstar van, holding on for dear life as he raced north on I-75. We were heading for the Lodge South exchange leading into the city.

"The devil doesn't sleep, so why should I?" he said. The interior of the van smelled like Catholic mass incense and old man. "Besides. I got a spastic colon. Wakes me up at all hours."

"I take it we're not really going for donuts," I said. "In which case I will be sorely disappointed."

"Actually," Father Grabowski said, nodding enthusiastically, "we are."

"Are Catalina and Manny okay?"

Father Grabowski sighed. "For now. They're both pretty upset and scared. Who could blame them? But they understand."

"Where'd you stow 'em?"

Grabowski shot me a glance. I assume a big yellow-toothed grin had formed somewhere beneath his thick entanglement of white beard.

"If I told you," he said. "I'd have to give you Last Rites, then kill you."

LaBelle's Soul Hole Donut Shop is on Michigan Avenue in an area that was among the first to show signs of revitalized life in Detroit. Near where the old and venerated Tiger Stadium once stood on Michigan Avenue and Trumbull and along this stretch of pot-holed four-lane road, you'll find such nationally recognized restaurants as Slows Bar Bq and Mercury Burger & Bar. Even the looming perpetual shame of the decaying former train station which had been closed for decades can't take the shine off these diamonds. (Ford Motor Company recently bought the decrepit station, giving some Detroiters cautious hope of sustainable city rebirth.)

Presidents, prime ministers, princes and princesses from around the world had photos taken with the five-foot-nothing, round-bodied Lady B, grinning broadly while holding "Put Yo Mouth on It!®" T-shirts or wearing Soul Hole logo baseball caps. You could also buy coffee mugs,

aprons and refrigerator magnets to com-
memorate your trip to the Soul Hole.

Father Grabowski parked on 14th Street
near the Michigan Avenue intersection and
we walked to the front door, which was
locked. The inside of the donut shop was
dark, save for the softly lit length of pastry
display case. Far in the back was a faint
rectangle of light outlining the door to the
kitchen.

Father Grabowski pulled a phone from
his brown frock and dialed a number. He
listened for a moment before saying, "Yeah.
Me."

"Do I wanna know where you keep your
phone in that thing?" I said after he disconnected.

The kitchen door at the back opened and
light spilled into the store front. A couple of
harsh overhead lights flickered on, revealing
a round, chocolate-brown woman wearing
crisp chef's whites and a hip-slung holster
filled with a Smith and Wesson Model 629
.44 that was about as long as she was tall.
Walking toward us, waving and grinning,
the proprietor of the Soul Hole, Ernestine
"Lady B" LaBelle, unlocked the door and
before I could say anything, clutched my
face with two strong hands and brought me
in for a kiss.

"Well, if it ain't the Snow boy," she said, releasing me from the cheek-hold and opening the door wide. As soon as Father Grabowski and I were in, she closed and locked the door. "You're late, Father," she said, waddling ahead of us toward the back kitchen. "Parley don't start till everybody be here."

" 'Parley'?" I said.

"Yeah, well I had to get young blood here," Father Grabowski replied to Lady B..

"Ain't nobody gonna be none too happy you brought Young Snow in," she said. "Supposed to be just the core group in parley. This could add a whole new dimension of ugly."

"What the hell's going on here?" I said, only to be ignored once again.

"I don't care," Grabowski said. "He lives there. They don't."

"Suit yourself." Lady B flicked off the overhead store lights. Before opening the door to the kitchen, she stopped and looked up at me. "Don't mean nothin' 'bout you, baby," she said. "Just don't like no surprises. Like the song say, Jack of Diamonds is a hard card to play. And tonight, baby, you the Jack of Diamonds." She opened the kitchen door and made a grand gesture toward three people seated at a round table.

Very little these days surprises me or throws me off guard.

This achieved both.

"Before you shit yourself or shoot some-body, sit down, shut up and listen," FBI Special Agent Megan O'Donnell said.

"You want some coffee, baby?" Lady B said, gently touching my arm.

"How 'bout three-fingers of that Two James Bourbon you keep in your locker," I said, my mind spinning as I stared at O'Donnell. Sitting next to O'Donnell was a middle-aged man with a chiseled jaw and white crew cut. He was wearing an Immigration and Customs Enforcement uniform.

But the biggest surprise sat on the ICE guy's right.

"Elena?" I heard myself say.

"Hi, Octavio," she said. "I didn't want you involved. But with Izzy and now Carlos's wife and son . . ."

I sat next to Elena and she took my hand in hers and squeezed.

"You mustn't tell Tomás about this. He thinks I'm with my girlfriends."

"Frankly, I wouldn't know what the hell to tell him," I said.

Lady B splashed bourbon into two coffee mugs. I took one and Father Grabowski took the other. She offered bourbon to the ICE agent and O'Donnell. Both waved it off, but O'Donnell said, "You have any honey crullers left, Lady B? And coffee?"

"Sure, baby," Lady B said. To the ICE agent she said, "How 'bout you, sugah?"

The agent simply shook his head and stared at me.

"August," Father Grabowski said, raising his mug of bourbon.

"Father," I said gently knocking my mug to his. Looking at O'Donnell and the ICE agent, I said, "To what do I owe the pleasure of meeting with the Village People Tribute Band at goddamn midnight?"

11

I downed my last bit of coffee mug bourbon and indicated to Lady B I could use more. She obliged. Father Grabowski gently laid a hand on my forearm — the forearm that was helping bourbon reach my mouth — and quietly said, "Easy, August."

"Padre, we left the land of 'easy' five minutes ago. We're in the Knockma Woods at the Gates of Guinee right now." I cut a look to the Immigrations and Customs Enforcement agent with the white crew cut. "Especially with ICE Agent Crew Cut over there."

"His name is Captain Mason Foley," O'Donnell said. "He's deep cover DEA."

"How many federal agents does it take to change a light bulb?" I said. "Forty-three thousand, but one of them's got to believe in light first."

Foley cut me a look that might have eviscerated a lesser man.

"Listen, August," O'Donnell said, "it might be helpful if you tucked your ego back into your skivvies for five minutes."

I tucked and O'Donnell talked.

"Most federal agencies have their 'white whales,'" she began, "Stories, myths and legends behind an investigation that become bigger, stranger and more convoluted than the actual investigation. Most white whales are just bullshit; a secret dossier here, a high-level Deep Throat there. Filler that gives an investigation a more colorful, dramatic narrative."

O'Donnell took a moment to assess each of us at the table. Her eyes stopped at me.

"ICE operations in Michigan, Ohio and Illinois currently have their own white whale and it is this," she continued. "Six months ago, a total of one hundred eighty-three detentions and arrests were made across the three states. One hundred sixty-seven of those people were actually documented, deported or released."

"And the sixteen?" I said.

"ICE records of detentions and arrests have always been loosey-goosey," Foley said. "Strong on the enforcement side, weak on the administrative side. From an administrative viewpoint, the truth is whatever ICE says it is."

"In other words," O'Donnell said, "we don't know what happened to fifteen of those people."

"And the sixteenth?"

"Raúl Lopez," O'Donnell said. "Picked up in a Chicago sweep five months ago. Three months ago, in March, a body was discovered in the Sonoran Desert with two kilos of cocaine. Body fit Lopez's description but we didn't have any DNA or dental records on him, so . . ."

"Maybe he just got in with the wrong crowd back in Mexico," I said.

"He wasn't deported," Foley said. "He was detained, but got lost in the shuffle either by design or screw up. I'd like very much to know which so the problem can be addressed."

"Speculation is that there is a small, highly effective rogue operation within certain ICE units responsible for human trafficking," O'Donnell said. "Sex trafficking, work enslavement, even selling some disappeared detainees back to coyotes as drug mules."

Lady B returned with a large plate pyramided with all manner of colorful donuts and small cakes. She sat the plate in the middle of the table, then went back to standing by the kitchen door.

"So," I said. "Everybody sitting around

91

this table is involved in a rogue operation investigating the rumor of a rogue operation." No one said anything. "Why read me in?"

Elena said, "I think Izzy might have been caught up in whatever this is."

"Izzy?" Foley said.

"The young woman who jumped from the bridge last week," O'Donnell said. Then she cut her piercing blue eyes at me. "And we're not quite rogue, August. But we're out on the raggedy edge while a small, authorized group of FBI and DEA directors wear the armor of distance and deniability."

"Is Phillips part of that group?" I said. Phillips, director of the FBI's Detroit Field Office, was O'Donnell's boss.

O'Donnell stared hard at me for a moment before saying, "No."

"Puts you in a helluva squeeze, doesn't it?" I said.

O'Donnell said nothing.

"You've rebuilt a nice bit of community, August," Father Grabowski said. "People love and respect what you've done and continue to do in Mexicantown."

"Let me guess," I said. "You want me to back off ICE when they come scurrying around looking to stitch-up little girls and grandmas."

"You're a grenade, August," O'Donnell said. "A very observant, very dangerous grenade. And if you go off like I've seen, you could set this whole operation back months. These guys would just metastasize somewhere else and we'd be left picking your shrapnel out of our asses."

"You're asking me to turn a blind eye to one disastrous wrong so you have a chance at *maybe* correcting a fed family fuck up?" I said. "Is that about right?"

"Listen," Foley said. "I've been DEA for close to twenty years. These ICE guys? They're like me. Former military. Mustered out with honorable discharges and just want to make a difference. They're not bad guys. They're just doing their jobs the best they know how according to the law. Keeping America safe isn't some buzzword bullshit to these guys; it's an everyday, boots-on-the-ground duty that they embrace. You think I wanna be here potentially ratting out people I work with? If it were up to me I'd tell all of you to go to hell — no offense, Father and Lady B."

"None taken," Father Grabowski said.

Lady B simply stood silent.

"I serve at the pleasure of my director," Foley continued. "I'll do what it takes to root out the few bad apples. No more, no less."

"Is a guy named Henshaw under your command?" I said.

"Yeah," Foley said. "Sergeant Corey Henshaw. Good man. A little gung-ho, but a good man to have on your six. What about him?"

"He's an asshole," I said. "When you're in Mexicantown, keep a short leash on him. You don't and I can guarantee you it'll take a Henry Ford Hospital trauma team to pry my foot from his ass. He harassed a neighbor of mine — nice lady who's been a citizen longer than he's been wearing long pants — and fucked up a friend's eye."

Then I looked at Lady B and said, "So what's your take on all this menudo?"

With arms folded across her ample chest, Lady B laughed. "I'm just Switzerland where the world comes to parley, baby. I will say this much, Young Snow: If'n yo daddy was sittin' there he wouldn't hesitate, equivocate or fluctuate. He'd be sayin' 'Who,' 'What,' 'When,' 'Where,' 'Why,' and 'I know how.' "

And there it was again; me, hung on that golden hook of my father's immutable reputation. Not necessarily a bad thing since my father was the best of the best. Not necessarily a good thing since I had my own goddamn name and life.

After an hour and a half of strident back-and-forth, the parley ended with no agreements or consensus: Foley held his cards close to the vest, defending his "mission" for the DEA while maintaining his cover as a dutiful ICE cop. Elena protested the tactics and legality of both and challenged him to give everyone an idea of what his end-game looked like. Father Grabowski raged against the moral, ethical and spiritual impact those missions were having on real people, real families. And O'Donnell tried in vain to play peacemaker and overall mission specialist.

I sat back and drank bourbon.

At the end of the meeting I pointed to Elena and said to O'Donnell, "You watch this lady's back and I'll back whatever play this little cabal agrees on for as long as I can from the bleachers."

"Oh, I'm sorry, August," O'Donnell said with the hint of a smile. "Did I say I wanted you in the bleachers on this one?" Whenever O'Donnell smiles I feel a shiver spider-walk up my spine.

"So, Lady Macbeth," I said. "Wha'd you have in mind?"

O'Donnell told me in private exactly how

95

I could be helpful.

"You're kidding, right?" I said.

"I actually thought you'd enjoy my little assignment for you."

"Does Frank know how evil and manipulative you can be?"

"Yes. And yet somehow it doesn't bother him."

After O'Donnell and I talked, I took Father Grabowski aside and said, "Do O'Donnell or Foley know about your little underground railroad?"

"No," he said. "I mean, they do, but the network me and a couple other priests, reverends and rabbis have built over the past fifteen years is good. I've even got a border patrol contact. I can move or hide twenty people a year and they wouldn't miss a meal or a day of school."

"Yeah, well, don't get cocky, old man."

"So, *you're* the only one allowed to get cocky?" He said he'd drive me home but I told him I'd catch a ride with Elena.

After all.

Elena and I had a few things to work out, the least of which was the uncomfortable necessity of keeping her involvement in the White Whale Club a secret from her husband, my godfather and best friend.

The silence was thick between Elena and

me as we headed southeast on Michigan Ave.

Finally, she said, "You *can* not tell Tomás, Octavio. Promise me that."

"That's a hard promise to make, Elena. You still carrying?"

Reluctantly, she said, "Yes."

"And if somebody pulls on you, you ready to do the same, only faster?"

"I — don't know."

"Jesus, Elena," I said. "Tomás should know —"

"*No,* Octavio!" she said. "It would kill him knowing I was still out here doing what I have to do. Especially with the threats. Tomás and I don't have secrets between us, Octavio. But telling him this? He would tear the world apart to protect me — and I can't have that. Not right now. Not when people may be in danger of more than being detained or deported."

I didn't say anything for a minute or so, trying to find an acceptable balance between not telling Tomás about his wife's involvement in a dangerous venture, or telling him and having the venture blow up entirely. Certainly, Elena had been on the front lines of civil rights protests long enough to have had several targets on her back, politically and personally. But this was different. No one had ever threatened her safety before. And she'd never found herself tangled in a web of three government agencies — DEA, ICE and FBI — working one ill-defined case at cross purposes.

After two minutes, I came to the conclusion there was no acceptable balance.

There was only a hard choice.

"You're my godmother," I finally said. "I love you like I still love my mother. I won't tell Tomás, but secrets find ways of creeping into the light. And when this one finds light, you need to be ready." I took a breath and said, "If this is gonna work at all, you need to do one thing for me and not doing it is not an option."

"What's that?"

"That gun in your purse?" I said. "Practice shooting. Tomás says you're good. You need to get better. The threats to you are real and the only people who've got your back are me, Tomás and maybe O'Donnell."

"I — I don't want to hurt anyone —"

"And I don't want you dead," I said curtly. "I've already buried my mother. I'm not ready to bury you."

It was too early for her to go home; her girls' nights usually lasted until at least two in the morning. Tomás would not go to bed until she was safely at home. There was no need for her to coordinate a lie with her friends: They knew Elena sometimes met into the late evening hours with attorneys, politicians, residents and business owners. All her friends needed to know was when she was going out so as not to call the house.

And frankly, the likelihood of Tomás asking what the girls had talked about was slim to none.

We landed at American Coney Island and sat at a table near a window.

"All you need is a yellow felt hat and a green coat," I said after a while. She resembled the forlorn woman in Edward Hopper's painting *Automat, 1927.*

Elena gave a quick smile. Then she went back to staring into her cup of coffee.

I ate two Coney dogs, extra chili, cheese and onions.

And large fries.

Finishing my second Coney dog, I continued to wrestle with the question of how best to keep a secret from Tomás. The only conclusion I came to was there were no good options.

While Elena quietly, discreetly prayed the rosary stowed in her purse next to her gun, I listened to the tumult of waiters and cooks laughing, talking and arguing in their native Greek. And I wondered about the dynamic secrets played in even the most loving relationship. Were there secrets my parents held from each other, innocuous or volatile? And though I could swear I'd been sweepingly honest about my life with Tatina, deep down I held a small, black lock box of secrets from her: The ten-year-old boy I'd not seen who took my bullet to his head as it traveled through a Taliban militia leader. Father and son. Killed in an embrace.

And other bloody intimacies.

My little black box was the exact dimensions of the distance I kept between myself and anyone I cared about.

12

That night and the next two nights I slept downstairs — not much of an inconvenience since I love my forest green leather sofa almost as much as I love Tatina and chili-lime seasoned steak fajitas.

Early Sunday afternoon, my phone rang.

It was Tomás.

"They've got her," he said breathlessly. "The bastards have got Elena."

"Who's got her?"

"ICE," Tomás growled. "I'm picking you up in two minutes. Get strapped."

From my house, it took us less than three minutes to get to Café Consuela's.

Tomás brought his truck to a screeching halt behind a black Chevy Suburban SUV with fed plates. There were at least twenty people huddled around the porch steps, craning their necks and holding up cell phones to capture video.

Tomás and I pushed our way through the

small crowd of mostly young white men and women and shouldered our way up the café's steps.

A young, chinless ICE agent held up his hand up in an effort to stop Tomás and me. "Hey, whoa, guys! I can't let you —"

Tomás brought a quick right cross to the agent's jaw. An ugly crunching sound before the agent crumpled to the ground, blood pouring from his mouth. We pushed our way in.

"Unless you have probable cause, I'd say you pathetic wankers are about three seconds away from a bloody fucking lawsuit!" Mr. Man-Bun himself — Trent T.R. Ogilvy. He was in the face of Mason Foley, the undercover DEA/ICE agent from O'Donnell's White Whale Club.

"Sir, our probable cause is the belief that undocumented aliens are working on the premises," Foley said.

At a glance, there were four terrified women — Elena and the women of Café Consuela's — and Trent Ogilvy. They were facing off with the usual overkill of feds; seven ICE agents in a space that could barely hold twelve customers. Each agent was trying his damndest to look imposing in "POLICE ICE" tactical vests. One fat ICE bastard hard-eyeing me had a splotch of guacamole on his vest. I was ready to make him eat his guacamole vest.

Foley gave me a quick glance, then said, "We're just making inquiries —"

"You gagging arseholes haven't even paid for the lunch you gobbled down!" Ogilvy shouted. "I'd call that theft, ya miserable —"

One ICE agent tried to put Ogilvy in an arm lock. It didn't work out well for the agent; Ogilvy flawlessly spun to meet the agent's efforts, grabbing the agent's wrist in the process, twirling the agent as if in a ballroom dance and pushing him away. Unwisely, the agent pulled his weapon.

"Really?" Ogilvy laughed. "Jesus! Guns just solve *every*thing in America, don't they?"

In the space of an eye's blink, Ogilvy swept the agent's gun from his hands and put the agent squarely in the sight of his own gun. It was a move only highly-trained hand-to-hand-combat experts could achieve without getting themselves — or somebody else — shot.

Tomás spotted Elena sitting in the single booth of the restaurant. She'd been crying, and was rubbing her upper arm.

Tomás pushed his way through to her.

"Did they touch you?" he barked.

"Tomás," Elena said. "It's okay, mi amor. Everything is —"

He turned and shouted, "Which one of you piece of shit motherfuckers put his hands on my wife!"

"Sir, I'm gonna have to —"

That was as far as a fourth agent got before Tomás landed a solid right to the agent's chin.

Elena screamed.

The Café Consuela women — Martiza, Louisa, Nina and Dani — screamed.

Two agents descended on Tomás, managing to pin him against the wall.

Another agent pointed his weapon at me.

The name "Henshaw" was on his black-and-grey shirt.

"Go ahead," Henshaw spat. "Do something, fucker."

After contemplating taking his gun away from him and beating him senseless with it, I smiled and said, "Since when do you guys need justification to shoot?"

Then I turned, placed my hands behind my back and waited for either a bullet or handcuffs.

Tomás and I were stripped of our weapons, handcuffed and, along with a handcuffed Ogilvy, were thrown into the back of the black Chevy Tahoe SUV. Tomás was swearing bloody revenge on whoever had touched his wife. As the agents dragged us down the steps, I told Elena to call my lawyer, David G. Baker, and let him know the situation.

Apparently in an effort to stop the agents from entering the kitchen of Café Consuela's, Elena and Trent Ogilvy had blocked the door. One of Foley's agents got a little enthusiastic, grabbing Elena by her upper arm and yanking her away from the kitchen.

Ogilvy reciprocated with a punch to the agent's kidney.

"Looks like you heroes bought yourselves *muchos problemas* today," Henshaw said, climbing into the SUV behind the steering wheel and grinning back at us.

"Listen," I said. "If you're planning on driving us out to Lovers' Leap and making us blow that tiny pink pecker of yours, fine. But I need me some ChapStick — *somethin'.*"

Ogilvy nearly doubled over laughing.

It's a well-documented fact throughout history that some morons of the male persuasion can be lit up quickly when their sexuality is called into question.

Henshaw was one of those morons.

Pulling his weapon, turning and pointing the black barrel at me he said, "Oh, you're

just a little smart-assed faggot, aren't you?"
He pushed the barrel of his weapon closer
to my nose. "You wanna suck on something?
Huh? Do ya?"

"Henshaw!"

Standing at the open passenger's side door
was Foley.

"Stand down," he said.

"Yes, sir!" Henshaw said, suddenly adher-
ing to the strictest of military obedience.
He quickly holstered his sidearm and turned
to face the front of the vehicle.

Foley stared at the three of us for a very
long time, "You broke one of my agents'
jaws," Foley said to Tomás.

"And one of you *pendejo* motherfuckers
put his hands on my wife," Tomás said. He
was breathing like a bull teased by the
matador's cape and tormented by the horse-
man's picador. "I don't care who you think
you are or what kind of badge you pulled
out of a cereal box. You lay hands on my
wife, I lay hands on you."

Foley nodded that he understood this type
of urban quid pro quo.

The Café Consuela women, led by Elena,
pushed their way out of the café and down
the steps. A couple of agents tried as best as
they could to restrain them.

"Tomás!"

"I'm okay, baby!" Tomás shouted in Spanish. "Just go home! I'll call you! It's okay!"

"You gentlemen realize I'm obligated to take you into custody," Foley said. He cut his ice-blue eyes to Tomás. "You because of the aforementioned breaking of a federal agent's jaw. You —" he turned to me, "— because I'd like to know what compels a once good cop to become some sort of neighborhood vigilante."

"You were a policeman?" Ogilvy said to me.

"Once upon a time," I said.

"And now?"

"I flip houses."

"Oh."

"And you?" Foley continued as he stared at Ogilvy. "You took one of my officers' weapons and turned it on him before surrendering it. And frankly, I just don't like limeys."

Before we drove off, I noticed Tomás had his head oddly cocked. He was staring at Henshaw in the rearview mirror with one eye squinting and the other eye wide open.

"The hell are you doing?" I whispered.

Without breaking concentration Tomás whispered, *"Los ojos!"*

The "Evil Eye."

13

We were taken to the 14th Precinct, but we weren't booked.

Rather, ICE agent Foley had a few words with the DPD desk sergeant, pointed to us, then left.

The desk sergeant — a short, stout, balding white guy with the name Kosinski — escorted Tomás, Ogilvy and me from the recently renovated lobby to the dungeons below.

"Are we being charged?" I said as we descended to the cages.

"Nope," Sergeant Kosinski said. "Just cooling you off, as per the vanilla ICE guy. Would you *like* me to charge you? Kind of a badge of honor for the three stooges?"

"You're not really intimidated by us, are you?" I said.

"What is today? Sunday?" Kosinski said. "Naw, see, around here we alternate days to be intimidated by tough guys like you. Me?

I'm Mondays, Wednesdays and Saturdays. Sorry."

While the city had invested a sizable amount of money revitalizing some of the older precincts like the 14th in an effort to make them more "camera ready" for the press, the subterranean holding cells hadn't seen a red cent; they were still medieval and smelled of several decades' worth of sweat, urine, clogged toilets, blood and vomit. Somewhere was the sound of water dripping and an ancient ventilation system threatening to die a gruesome death.

The three of us, locked in one of three cages, settled in.

Tomás and I had experienced such incarceration before.

I wasn't sure about Ogilvy. He appeared to take our situation in stride, sitting on the bench in lotus meditation position.

"You okay, big guy?" I said to Tomás.

"Somebody's gonna pay, Octavio," Tomás said. "Somebody's *got* to pay."

After a while, Tomás stared at Ogilvy and said, "What's with the hair?"

I may have blushed with momentary embarrassment, but I had to admit the question had crossed my mind.

"Well, I suppose I'm a bit of an Akira Kurosawa fan," Ogilvy said with bright enthusiasm and still holding his lotus position on the bench.

"Akira Who?"

"Japanese filmmaker," I said. "You've seen *The Magnificent Seven?*"

"Who the hell hasn't?" Tomás said. "He made that?"

"No," I said. "He made the movie *The Magnificent Seven* was based on — *The Seven Samurai.*"

"My choice of hairstyle," Ogilvy said, "is based on the hairstyle of the noble Japanese samurai military class from around AD 790. Beneath the hair, they adhered to a strict code of ethics, behavior and loyalty. The Bushido."

"The guys with the swords and flip-flops?"

"Exactly!" Ogilvy said. "It's emblematic of my aspirational belief system: Honor. Integrity. Humility. Generosity. A reminder of who I should aspire to be on any given day."

"Still looks goofy," Tomás mumbled.

"Be careful insulting our cellmate," I said. "He's more dangerous than he looks. Check out the tattoo on his left forearm."

Even in the dim, flickering light of the holding cells, it was easy to see Ogilvy's discreet bluish tattoo of what looked like a winged sword with an unfurling banner beneath that read "Who Dares Wins."

"You're the first in five years to take full and apparently informed note of it," Ogilvy said. "Other than a Portland barista who asked who the tattoo artist was."

"I suppose you told him Her Majesty Queen Elizabeth II?"

"Something like that," Ogilvy said, grinning.

"So, you're a badass, huh?" Tomás said to Ogilvy.

"*Former* badass," Ogilvy said. "British SAS. These days I prefer helping people become *organized* badasses to meet their personal life goals and community needs." Ogilvy laughed, then said, "Might I assume you're something of a badass yourself, mister —"

"Gutierrez," Tomás said. "Tomás. Some folk call me El Sepulturero."

"Oh, for fuck's sakes! *Nobody* calls you 'The Gravedigger,' " I said.

"Yeah, well —"

"Never seen someone shatter a jaw with one punch," Ogilvy said. "Impressive."

"You handled yourself pretty well back there, too," Tomás said. "Thanks for, you know, tryin' to help the ladies out."

"I'm English on my da's side and Scottish on my mum's side," Ogilvy said. "Gallantry and raising hell's in the blood, mate."

"Hey," the man in the next cell groaned. "You — you fuckers shut up."

He was dressed in an expensive suit and was lying on his cell bench. Occasionally he moaned and burped while nursing his right eye with the broad end of his tie.

"You okay?" I said to him. "You want me to call someone for you?"

The man struggled into a sitting position and tried to focus me with his one good eye. He adjusted his one-eyed focus and grumbled, "Fuck you, nigger," then laid back on the bench. Ogilvy, outraged by the epithet, started reply to the man until I touched his arm, smiled and said, "I've been inoculated. Leave it."

After an hour of playing "What Movie Is This Line From?" we had our first visitor for the day: Detective Captain Leo Cowling.

Cowling was dressed in his summer finest: A powder blue linen suit, navy blue monogrammed shirt and tan silk tie. The shoes were tan buckskin loafers. Capping the look was a cream-colored Panama straw hat and a shiny gold shield hooked to his alligator belt.

He was also wearing a grin that stretched nearly ear to ear.

"Lord, *Lord*! It *must* be Christmas 'cause it ain't my birthday!" he said, stepping up to the bars of our cage.

"Howdy, Leo," I said. "Long time, don't care."

"Oh, this is just *too* good," Cowling said. Reaching into a coat pocket, he retrieved his iPhone. He held it out for a selfie with the three of us in the background.

"Wait a minute," I said.

I put my arm around Tomás's shoulders and he put his arm around mine. Ogilvy, not knowing exactly what was going on, quickly got into the spirit of things and laid his head on Tomás's shoulder.

"Friend?" Ogilvy asked of me concerning Cowling.

"Not exactly," I said.

"Foe?"

"Not exactly."

We grinned and simultaneously flipped Cowling the bird.

Cowling took several pictures.

"By the time my lawyer's done with you," the well-dressed man in the adjoining cell snarled at Cowling, "there won't be enough of your coon ass to hang from a goddamn tree."

"Oh, you absolutely *must* tell us who this gent is," Ogilvy said to Cowling.

"And you are?"

"Benedict Cumberbatch," Ogilvy said. "An associate of these ruffians."

"No accounting for taste," Cowling said. Then he nodded to the man in the next cell. "Nice little Muslim girl with a pretty floral print hijab, just sitting on a Campus Martius bench, reading a book, waiting for the bus. Wayne State student. Anyway, Mr. Charm School here had one too many at lunch. Sees Muslim girl. Starts yelling some really awful things at her."

Tomás, deciding to have a bit of perverse fun, stood close to the bars we shared with the man's cell, and began whispering to him in Spanish.

"This is *America,* you dirty *spic!*" the man yelled at Tomás. "Talk fucking *English!*"

"Did the girl hit him?" I asked in reference to Charm School's puffy black eye.

"He might have tripped and fell on my fist," Cowling said.

"Tell this wetback shit stain to shut up or swear to God, I'll shut him up!"

"Oh, now you just hush," Cowling said dismissively to the man.

"God*dammit!*" the man shouted. Suddenly he charged at the bars between us. Both hands and arms came through to our side — just before his head slammed into one of the iron bars.

The man, unconscious, fell back, landing hard on the concrete floor.

"Oh, my God," Tomás said. "That was — *beautiful.*"

"You are a genius at provocation, compadre," I said, slapping Tomás on his shoulder. Then to Cowling, I said, "Any prints from that file I gave you?"

"Nothing usable," Cowling said. "Frankly, I wish there was. Don't much care for grown-ass folk who got the time and inclination to draw nasty, psycho shit like that."

An hour later, FBI Special Agent Megan O'Donnell showed up, greeting us by saying, "Whichever one of you knuckleheads just pissed himself does *not* ride with me."

The three of us pointed to the unconscious man in the next cell.

The guard unlocked our cell.

"Whoa, hold on, bucko," O'Donnell said, placing her hand firmly on Ogilvy's chest. "Who the hell are you?"

"He got tangled up with us at Café Consuela's," I said.

"Just enjoying a bit of lunch is all," Ogilvy said. "Suddenly things go tits up!"

"I'll vouch for him," I said.

"Like that means something?" O'Donnell said.

Tomás and I signed papers and retrieved our weapons, and O'Donnell drove us back to Mexicantown.

She dropped Tomás off first.

Elena ran out of their house and leapt into his arms. They kissed. Suddenly, Elena pulled out of the kiss and slapped Tomás hard across the face. Arms flailing, the two argued in Spanish until they were inside the house.

Then we dropped Ogilvy off just down the street from my house.

"Strange times, eh?" Ogilvy said, climbing out of the back seat.

"Strange times," I agreed. "I've got a sixteen-year-old Islay whisky at the house. We should talk sometime."

Once Ogilvy closed the door, O'Donnell said, "You got scotch at your house?"

She sat at my kitchen island staring at the tumbler of Lagavulin I'd poured her.

"Café Consuela's was on a pre-approved ICE watch list," she said. "Foley had nothing to do with planning the raid. And Elena just happened to be there, talking with Dani about her sister's son — undocumented, hiding and scared."

"Swear to God, O'Donnell," I said. "Another raid like that and fuck you and your little junior detective's group — I'll put

Foley and Henshaw down —"

"Another girl turned up dead, August," O'Donnell said.

"Jesus."

"Hispanic. Eighteen, nineteen. Dressed like Dorothy from *The Wizard of Oz* right down to the ruby slippers. Washed up near Zug Island. She'd been — branded." O'Donnell quickly knocked back her glass of scotch. "Swastikas."

14

To my knowledge, no one has packed fried chicken, potato salad and beer for a nice summer picnic on Zug Island since 1876.

In fact, I doubt anyone has enjoyed a lazy sun-and-sand day on Zug Island since furniture and real estate entrepreneur Samuel Zug first drained 334 acres of swampland to create his exclusive River Rouge family get-away. By 1886, the affluent Zug family — exhausted from battling the ravages of flooding — sold the island in the biggest American real estate deal of the decade for $300,000.

The island hasn't fared any better in over 100 years. It's become its own circle in a Hell even Dante could not have imagined: Gaping, red-mouthed blast furnaces and grim mountainous fields of coal, coke and iron ore. Tall chimneys belched out thick, dark clouds while generations of men took the black, sooty air deep into their lungs.

Generations of rain water runoff helped turn the surrounding river water into a murky, poisonous soup.

Even now communities near Zug Island complain of a consistent, low thumping sound emanating from the island . . .

. . . like maybe the devil's heartbeat.

The remains of the second Hispanic girl, branded seven times with a swastika, had been steeped in the acrid chemical stew of the River Rouge near Zug Island, which had exacerbated her decay and left little if anything to point to her killer or killers.

"You making a link between the girl's murder and this white whale thing?"

"Circumstantially, yes," O'Donnell said. "She was fantasy dressed and there were traces of barbiturates and amphetamines in her system. At least what was left of her. Problem is, if the news media sinks its fangs into this thing then we've got a serial killer panic on our hands. And that could muddy the already-dirty waters." She polished off her second scotch. She didn't request more and I didn't offer. "I need you to get to those people I asked you to talk to, August. I do it and nobody talks. They just size me up for a thong and four-inch Lucite heels. *You* do it — a disgraced cop — and maybe they'll feel an affinity with you and open up."

"I think it's only good manners not to call me a 'disgraced cop' while drinking *my* sixteen-year-old malt. Just for future reference."

"Sorry," O'Donnell said, uncharacteristically. "Just find out what they know. And I need to know before anymore shit hits the fan."

Shortly after O'Donnell left at the onset of evening, I got a call from Tomás.

"You home?" he said.

"Yeah. What's —"

He disconnected.

Five minutes later Tomás was pounding on my door.

"You knew," he said.

"Knew what?"

"About Elena! About her and this ICE guy, Foley! And the priest and all that secret bullshit at LaBelle's! And nobody told me *nothing*!"

"Listen —" I said in a calm voice.

That's as far as I got before Tomás put my lights out.

When I came to on my living room floor, it was night.

Standing over me, a thick fist clamped

around a bottle of Negra Modelo beer, was Tomás.

" 'Bout goddamn time," he said. "I didn't hit you that hard, Tinkerbell."

"How long?" I said.

"Long enough for me to catch the last inning of the Tigers and Cubs."

I struggled myself off the floor, shook my head to clear the cobwebs and leaned against the back of my sofa. There was a little blood from my nose and, though I could feel my nose throbbing, it wasn't broken.

"Who won?"

"Cubs," Tomás said. "Eight to three. Ain't our year. You wanna beer?"

"And a shot," I said. Now I knew what it felt like to be on the receiving end of Tomás's jagged and callous knuckles. "Tequila. You *hit* me, goddammit! In *my* house!"

"Yeah, well, you deserved it, you little punk-ass."

Even though I knew it would do little to appease Tomás, I explained why I kept Elena's involvement with the White Whale Club a secret. And I suggested Elena had every right to a private life, even within her marriage, and to decide her own adult fate. A suggestion that was met with dismissive grunts and the occasional punctuation of a disbelieving "bullshit."

I knocked back my shot of tequila, and then we took our beers and sat outside on my porch steps.

It was a warm night. Maybe low eighties with thick humidity.

Neither of us said anything for several minutes.

We just looked at the houses along Markham Street, listened to dogs barking in the distance and the continuous whoosh of night traffic on I-75 and the nearby Ambassador Bridge. Above the neighborhood was a waxing crescent moon in a mostly black and starless sky, the stars having been washed out by I-75's nocturnal glow.

Tomás finally pointed to Carlos's house across the street and said, "Elena told me about his wife and kid being forced into hiding. How's he doing?"

"Not good," I said. "He spent a long time up here without them. He finally gets 'em here and now this. He's trying to keep busy and Jimmy looks out for him. But — he's not doing good."

Tomás nodded, took a long pull on his beer. "My pops? One hard-workin' sonuvabitch. Jesus, that man could work! The family? Started out harvesting apples, moved on to asparagus and beets, lettuce and peppers, melons. Hated watermelons!" He took a moment, and another swig of beer. Craning his neck, he looked up at the night sky. "My younger sister, Angie — she worked harder than me. My mamá and Angie. Like machines. Sometimes, my pops, he'd beat the livin' shit outta me." Tomás laughed, full and long. "He'd say, 'This is your *family,* you little bastard! You work *hard* for family!' Then when he was done whippin' my ass he'd say, 'You think that hurt? Wait till *gringos* get a hold of your lazy brown ass!' " Again, Tomás laughed, but this time in the pale light coming from inside my house I could see his eyes flooding with tears. "Sundays would come. Him and Mamá sitting at a rickety table in some migrant motel or farmer's roach-infested migrant housing. Mamá counting the money, writing shit on a scrap of paper. Then I hear my pops whisper, 'Can we do it?' After a couple minutes, Mamá would touch his arm, smile and say, 'Si.' Then he'd turn to me and Angie and say, 'I think we should get some ice cream. You guys think we should get some ice cream?' Same man who beat the shit outta me, he's got his arm — *brazo grande y fuerte!* — around my shoulders. And we're eating ice cream."

"These days," I said, "he'd probably be arrested for child abuse."

"Fucking white people," Tomás said with a slight laugh and shake of his head. "They ruin everything, don't they?" Then he took a deep breath and said, "He taught me how to be a man. How to be strong for family. Protect the family. Showed me how important the right woman is. A woman that sees bigger dreams — bigger possibilities — in her man. A woman that knows how to patch you up, lift you up and get you back in the fight. I got that in Elena. *More* than that in Elena. She's the only reason I kinda believe in God, Octavio, 'cause somebody like Elena don't come from random. Angels ain't accidents."

"Sorry I didn't tell you."

"Sorry don't cut it, *pendejo,*" Tomás said. "On account there's only four things keeping me rooted to this shit-heap earth: Elena, my daughter, grandbaby June — and you."

Tomás looked up at the night sky for a moment, then knocked back the rest of his beer.

"Whatever you need done to make my wife safe and get things back to a regular amount of shit, I'm there, Octavio," Tomás said. "But you gotta be straight with me. No secrets, lies, or bullshit."

"Tomorrow I'm heading out to Royal Oak. You wanna ride shot gun?"

"What's in Royal Oak?"

"Duke Ducane."

Tomás gave me a look. Once upon a time that name had unleashed the hounds of Hell, at least in Detroit.

"He's not still inside? Or dead?"

"Nope," I said. "Been out two years."

"And why would we be going to see that son of Satan's whore?"

"Because he used to run girls in Detroit," I said. "Newfoundland to Toronto through Detroit and on to Kentucky and Tennessee. Russians, Chinese, Nigerians. They were a quarter of his business. Had pipelines and safe houses not even the FBI could track or trace. He knows the players in the sex trade. At least he used to."

"What's that evil fucker doing in Royal Oak?"

"He's in the music business."

"Jesus," Tomás said. "From bad to worse."

15

Royal Oak was once a funky little upper-middle-class hippy enclave fourteen miles northwest of Detroit where aging white liberals could get their "freak" on. The smell of pot and clove cigarettes hung in the air wherever you went: from hip little coffee bars with beat-up sofas and bad paintings of nude women to hole-in-the-wall specialty bike shops to the expansive farmer's market where, I suspect, the words "organic" and "gluten-free" were first overused. You could buy vintage clothing in one shop then pop next door to be fitted for a latex bondage outfit. Long before being accused of "cultural appropriation," white kids with lip-piercings and blond dreadlocks skateboarded up and down Main Street, past this little overpriced art gallery or that coveted greasy-burger joint. Film aficionados, stinking of Gauloises or Gitanes unfiltered cigarettes, worshipped at the flickering alter of the Main Art Theater where every week was a celebration of François Truffaut, Roberto Rossellini or Ingmar Bergman.

And there were rattrap, collapsing storefront music clubs where rock bands furiously performed in front of stoned teenagers resplendent in primary-colored hair, tats, piercings, mercilessly ripped jeans and unlaced Doc Martens boots.

Royal Oak is to Michigan what Austin is to Texas: a small citadel of music-loving, free-wheeling, progressive white social liberalism plopped in the middle of a Sargasso Sea of gun-toting, cross-burning, right-wing militias and reactionary neo-con politics, with all the black and brown folk on the outside, staring in with fear and loathing at both.

Royal Oak is what happens when wealthy white people gentrify an area populated by middle-class white people.

For all of my gripes, I had a few squishy spots in my heart for Royal Oak.

When I was ten, my folks took me to see a director's cut remastered rerelease of *Alien* at the Main Art Theater when the Main Art finally realized pop culture paid the bills. My mother had seen the original with girlfriends. She'd told my father *Alien* was "like a Mexican children's story only in space!" Unimaginable monsters and insatiable evil pitted against the virtuous in lands where virtue and righteousness rarely won. My father wondered about my mother's sanity for a while after that.

There was now defunct Dave's Comics and the long-gone R&J Café. Mercifully, the Red Coat Tavern was still serving one of the best burgers around with butter-sautéed onions.

My lawyer — David G. Baker — lived here.

"Remind me again why he just did a nickel in Jackson for extortion instead of life for murder, drugs, racketeering, human trafficking and prostitution?" Tomás said as we inched our way north through heavy afternoon Woodward Avenue traffic toward Royal Oak.

"Expensive legal team," I said. "Not to mention half the judges and politicos in the state were in his pocket. If he went down for everything, they went down for more. And the legal system in Michigan crumbles into Lake Erie. I've always had the uncomfortable feeling I won my lawsuit against the old mayor because Duke Ducane decided to cut bait with him."

"Even so," Tomás said, "you was the one who perp walked him. A lot of cops tried —

including your old man — but you got the collar, young blood."

I remained unconvinced of my own heroism when it came to arresting Marcus "Duke" Ducane.

Before leaving on our quest north to Royal Oak, we made the obligatory stop at the large gun locker in Tomás's basement.

"Jesus," I said, staring at the gun locker. "What the hell's this?"

Gone from the locker was the poster of a maniacal looking Generalissimo Emiliano Zapata Salazar, replaced by a poster of popular Mexican-American comedians George Lopez, Gabriel Iglesias, Paul Rodriguez and Cristela Alonzo. The bare light bulb and pull chain in front of the locker was now outfitted with an imitation stained glass shade that read "¡El hogar es donde está el corazón!" — "Home is where the heart is!"

"Elena did that," Tomás said. "Zapata kept freaking her out when she came down to do laundry. Something about the eyes following her."

"Dear God," I said unnerved by the changes. "It looks like you keep frijoles and puppies in there now."

It took a lot for me to convince Tomás that maybe one — just one — semi-auto rifle might be good enough for our visit to Duke's Royal Oak recording studio, Sound-Nation. Reluctantly, he settled on the impressive-looking IWI Tavor XB95.

"But I'm taking two clips," Tomás said. "If I gotta kill that fucker, I wanna make damned good and sure he's dead."

Instead of a second assault-style rifle, Tomás settled on a Beretta 92 Series 9mm with a shoulder rig, a Ruger .357 Mag snugged in a back-belt holster and a Ka-Bar Snody "Snake Charmer" knife in his left cargo pants pocket.

"Feel like I'm fucking naked," Tomás grumbled as he closed the locker. "Coupla goddamn peashooters and a Mexican tooth-pick."

I well understood Tomás's reluctance to see Duke Ducane without heavy artillery.

There are dark legends in the Detroit crime world. The Purple Gang, a notori-ously vicious prohibition era gang com-prised mostly of Eastern European Jews. Vito "Billy Jack" Giacalone and his brother Anthony "Tony Jack" Giacalone, Italian Mafia bosses who were suspected in the disappearance and murder of International Brotherhood of Teamsters president Jimmy Hoffa. And notorious black drug kingpin Frank Usher, who so impressed his Italian mob partners with his business acumen and unrepentant violence that he was given the moniker "Frank Nitti" after Al Capone's vicious enforcer.

Then there was Marcus "Duke" Ducane: Drug dealer, extortionist, gun runner, numbers runner and human trafficker.

By the time I came to the force, Duke Ducane had already outlasted two mayors, a DPD commissioner, three Ducane task forces, one joint DPD-FBI investigation, and a mistrial.

Like Tomás said, I was the one who perp walked Duke Ducane into the 14th Precinct.

And I was the one he winked at as he walked away from eight charges that could have landed him in a super-max prison for life, drawing only five years for extortion. That's when I came to the uneasy realization that Duke let me arrest him. He dangled just enough bait in legal waters to get him out of a business that had become a decentralized, depersonalized and anonymous global machine. Autonomous nation-states with byzantine agreements, shadow contracts and mountains of snakes each with multiple heads, each with killing venom.

I was Duke Ducane's last, best shot at

131

retirement without a double-tap to the back of his head. Maybe that's why he hadn't seemed to hold much of a grudge against me.

After my wrongful dismissal trial I got a letter from Ducane.

"Sorry for your troubles, Detective Snow," the letter began. "You may not believe this, but I am truly sorry for your trial and tribulations. Wherever your path, know this: I am changed because of you. Perhaps not transcendently — I am not Saul. Just remember Deuteronomy 31:6, 'Be strong and courageous. Do not be afraid or terrified because of them, for the Lord your God goes with you.' "

Even the devil quotes scripture.

I pulled into the small parking lot behind a two-story red brick building just off of Main Street a couple miles north of I-696 and parked.

Duke Ducane's SoundNation Recording Studio.

Tomás and I did a quick safeties-off weapons check.

Satisfied we could fend off any number of small island nation armies and quickly be coronated we went inside.

16

The sign next to the simple polished maple wood door for SoundNation Recording, Inc. could very well have discreetly announced the entrance to a CPA's office.

Inside, it quickly became apparent this wasn't a CPA's office: The walls had a Jackson Pollock-on-a-bourbon-and-cocaine-bender splatter vibe to them. Hung from the ceiling was a white frosted glass chandelier in the shape of a giant bottle of Jack Daniels.

There were two curved loveseats on opposite sides of the hallway, both done in white-and-black leopard print, adding to the nausea-inducing effect.

Sitting some thirty feet away at a frosted glass desk outlined with white LED lights was an attractive young woman with impossibly white skin, Emo plum-purple hair, black eye shadow, matching lipstick and a silver nostril ring.

"Hi!" the young woman said enthusiastically. "Welcome to SoundNation!"

"I'm August Snow," I said, returning her enthusiasm. "This is my travel companion and personal chef, Tomás Gutierrez. And you are?"

"White Girl!"

"Uh — okay," I said. "You wouldn't mind if I called you by your Christian name, right?"

"Not a Christian," she said. "Buddhist. And it's Dahlia Alanis Delaney."

I told her that I'd very much like to see Duke. She made a brief call on a white phone that looked like it had been designed for the Queen of England. After a second or two she said, "Yessir," then hung up.

"Mr. Ducane will be with you in just a minute, Mr. Snow," Dahlia Delaney, aka White Girl, said. "If I could just get your weapons?"

Tomás and I gave each other looks.

"How'd you —"

Dahlia pointed to her computer screen: A frozen image of Tomás and me was on the screen rendered in X-ray black and white. It clearly showed all of our weaponry.

"Seriously?" I said.

Dahlia opened a desk drawer and retrieved a Smith and Wesson 686 Plus and pointed it casually at me. "Seriously."

"What about Duke or the Compton twins?"

"The *Compton* twins?" Tomás said in disbelief. "Oh, this just gets better and fucking better."

"Mr. Ducane, yes," she said, still holding the shiny business end of the gun rock steady on me. "The twins, no. Everybody — guests and clients — surrenders to me. Best practices and industry guidelines for the twenty-first century."

Reluctantly I surrendered my Glock to her. She stowed it away in a lockbox and gave me a ticket: No. 26.

Then she looked at Tomás.

"No way," Tomás said. "No fuckin' way."

Her desk phone rang and she answered it while holding her gun on me and smiling. She listened for maybe five seconds, nodded, lowered her gun and said, "Of course," then hung up. "You may retain your weapons," she said to Tomás.

"Thanks, doll-face," I said.

"What the hell was that?"

"Bogart. Maybe you're too young —"

"That was the worst Bogart I've ever heard," she said, her nose turned up.

"She's right," Tomás said. "You never could —"

"Okay, I get the point!"

White Girl gave us instructions to get to Duke's office and we started our long walk down the nauseating hallway.

Along the way we passed four recording studios: In the first, a young black woman was singing her heart out while an engineer adjusted levels on a massive control board. Seated behind the engineer was a young black man, eyes closed, head slowly bobbing to a rhythm neither Tomás nor I could hear.

In the next studio, a tall white guy was reading from a script on a music stand. Two corporate-type women held an animated discussion with their engineer. The sign on the studio door said SOUNDNATION WELCOMES THE WESTERN MICHIGAN FORD DEALERS ASSOCIATION.

In the third was a young black man wearing jewel-bedazzled sunglasses, a colorful silk shirt, blue velvet bell-bottom pants cinched with a wide white patent leather belt and white jeweled cowboy boots. His bushy afro and sideburns completed his Elvis Presley look. He was talking to an engineer and pointing to sheet music laid out on the sound board.

The fourth studio was dark.

A small young woman wearing business

professional clothing and carrying a nice leather briefcase passed by us. She smiled and winked at me before heading toward reception.

I stopped and looked at the woman as she walked away.

" 'S the matter?" Tomás said.

"Nothing," I said. "Could swear I've seen her before."

"Guys like us think we know every *chica guapa,*" Tomás said. "Let's get this shit-show started."

We made a right turn and heard the Compton twins, Duke's muscle and, in a weird and dangerous way, his ever-loyal surrogate sons. I hadn't heard either of them in five years since they went away at the same time as their boss. A chill snaked its way up my spine and I found myself reaching for a weapon I'd relinquished at the reception desk.

I hoped the twins didn't hold a grudge against me for slapping the cuffs on them five years ago. If they did, this could be a very short and painful visit.

"Oh, man," one of the twins said in a mountain troll baritone. "Bitch be dead."

Tomás and I peeked around the corner into the conference room; the twins, their massive backs to us, faced an impressively large wall mounted flat screen TV. On the highly polished maple conference table between them were the remains of what I suspected was every item offered on a Taco Bell menu. On the TV, the body of a young woman lay at the bottom of a moss-covered cliff. The woman, dressed in '40s clothing, clutched a black sequined handbag.

"Hey, guys!" I said.

The twins spun in their chairs, stood, and instantly took offensive guard positions.

"Pause that shit," one of the twins said to the other. I think it was Fergie, but the egg had split so precisely I was never quite sure which twin was which. Fergie's brother Fin grabbed the remote control from the conference table and hit the pause button. The TV screen froze just as an old woman, wearing white lace gloves and a lace doily for a hat, appeared and stared mournfully at the body of the young woman.

"Miss Marple?" I said. "Seriously?"

"The fuck you doin' here?" Fin (I think) said with no small amount of irritation. "Why ain't White Girl call us? And who's this Speedy Gonzales-lookin' mothafucka?"

"So many questions," I said. "So little interest. I guess your receptionist was so overwhelmed by my charm and good looks she forgot to call you guys. And this gentleman is my friend, confidant and spiritual advisor. By the way — he hates being referred to as a 'Speedy Gonzales-lookin' mothafucka.'"

Simultaneously — and with no short amount of spine-tingling creepiness — the twins nodded to me and said, "What y'all niggahs doin' up in here?"

"Got an appointment with your zoo-keeper," I said.

"So, we can't hurt you?"

"Not today, boys," Tomás said opening his shirt a bit to reveal his gun in the shoulder rig.

"We owe you a hurt, Snow," one of the twins said. "Y'all know that, right?"

"Guess it's just gonna have to wait, Chuckles," I said.

I grinned, saluted the twin sociopaths, and Tomás and I continued on our way.

I was about to knock on a set of tall maple wood double doors when they whispered opened.

"*As-salamu alaykum,*" Duke said from behind his large antique rosewood desk.

"Back atcha, toots," I said, entering the relative darkness of his office. I knew Tomás had one hand around the knife in his cargo pants pocket and the other ready to make a quick withdrawal from his shoulder holster.

"Prison conversion to Islam?"

"Just hedging my spiritual bets is all," Duke said. "Could have said *'Shavua Tov,' 'Namaskaram,' 'Allah Abho,' 'Jai Jinendra,' 'Hamazor Hama Ashobed'* or 'Peace be with you.' If I recall, that last one's more your style, right?"

Duke's office was narrow and long. He sat behind an antique desk dressed in an expensive lime-green polo shirt and white Kangol driving cap. Behind him was a monogrammed golf bag and set of clubs leaning against illuminated glass shelves bearing, among other things, a few books, small Chinese jade carvings, framed photos and, for whatever reason, a woman's silver necklace with heart-shaped pendant, a diamond at the center.

"For that special someone?" I said, pointing to the necklace.

"Not anymore," Duke said dryly.

The most interesting thing the shelves held was a collection of Highland single malt scotch bottles.

One caked with dust.

"So," I began, eyeing the two tufted leather Chesterfield chairs in front of the desk. I claimed one. "Sure looks like working in the prison cafeteria paid off."

"Always plan your future, young Snow,"

140

he said, reaching behind him and extracting three crystal tumblers from the shelves. "The Royal Bank of Canada, Bank of Nova Scotia, Bank of Montreal and Scotiabank Negril helped me plan mine before my trial and subsequent incarceration. Whiskey?"

"Sure," I said. "How 'bout the dusty bottle?"

Duke offered a whiskey to Tomás, who graciously grunted his refusal.

Duke slid a tumbler of malt whiskey to me and simultaneously we took appreciative sips. "This whiskey's over seventy years old, son, so don't go gulpin' the shit down like we cousins at the Elks Club on a Saturday night," he told me. "So. Word on the street is you looking for wisdom on sex trafficking in our fair city. Thinkin' about a new career since that cop thing didn't work out?"

I gave Duke the lowdown, then slid my empty glass back to him. He was kind enough to pour me another two fingers. "I grew to hate that business venture. Never was a sentimental fellow, but after seeing too much desperation and fear in too many women I got out of that business. The hard truth is some of them bitches *wanted* me to move 'em through the Land of the Free and Home of the Brave. Better than bein' raped by some new Hong Kong millionaire or

Saudi prince. Or beat to shit as Moscow or Turkish drug mules." Duke took another sip of his scotch. "But here we are, right? Glorious new century. Glorious new possibilities."

"Your magnanimity is truly inspiring, Duke," I said, nauseated by his cavalier assessment. "Real Nobel Prize stuff."

"Get to the fucking point," Tomás growled at Ducane.

The two men traded hard stares before Duke smiled and said, "The point is you got some off-book ICE units scoopin' and skimmin' Hispanic and Middle Eastern girls, moving 'em through a new private network. Heard they even pinched some white Irish girl, overstayed her visa. I mean, they can't move 'em theyselfs on account it's too risky, right? And the pros I know — *used* to know — don't want no partnership with the feds — dirty or otherwise — 'cause feds got a way of sittin' on they hands and chokin' on they thumbs. So, who they dealin' with?" Duke took a moment to hold Tomás and me in suspense. "Skinheads, neo-Nazis, white supremacist biker gangs. And I mean if theys one thing Michigan got in more abundance than apples, cherries, walleye and deer, it's white hate groups. Most of 'em just inbred, squirrel-eatin' mothafuckas couldn't find they ass with one hand nailed to it and the other holding instructions. And since the bigger ones be strapped for drug and gun cash, what better way to collect coin than to move girls? Move 'em through strip joints. Through high-end members-only sex clubs. Hook up with a couple big, badass biker clubs out of California and Texas." Duke retrieved a notepad and Mont Blanc pen and began writing. "I was you? Thems the folks I'd talk to." He tore the piece of paper from the notepad and handed it to me.

"You're being especially helpful," I said. "Why?"

" 'Not through the blood of goats and calves, but through His own blood, He entered the holy place once for all, having obtained eternal redemption.' Hebrews 9:12. Not everybody walks the same path to redemption, Snow. This is my path. And my path has been carved out by my own blood. My history. This business? *My* business? A hundred legit. That's a path that's reduced my involuntary mortality odds by at least eighty percent. I like them odds." Then he smiled. It was a smile I'm sure approximated that of the snake in the Garden of Eden. "Besides. I get my donuts and haircuts same place you do. And the wise pay homage to donuts and haircuts. You see what I'm sayin'?"

I did.

"You just like yo daddy," Duke finally said. "Honorable man. A little slow on the up-take, but still it's my belief that we, as honorable men, can disagree without poppin' caps up each other's ass."

"And what about the Compton twins?" I said.

"I will, of course, inform the boys that you are no longer persona non grata and should be treated with the utmost respect," Duke said. He laughed and added, "Of course, I may have to repeat this several times before it sticks, so . . ."

I finished my scotch, stood and offered my hand to Duke. Surprised, Duke stared at my hand for a second before standing and shaking it.

"Be careful out there," Duke said. "I may have need of your friendship at some future date and I'd hate to see you get popped before then."

I looked at Duke in his lime-green polo shirt, white Kangol hat and white belted hot-pink shorts.

"Are they shooting a remake of *Caddyshack*?" I said. " 'Cause I mean you? Nailed it!"

"Get the fuck outta here," Duke laughed.

"See ya 'round, boys," I said to the Compton twins as we passed the conference room. They had resumed watching *Miss Marple*. "Try not to miss me too much, n'k?"

"Assho," Fergie said.

"Assho," Fin agreed.

"Enjoy your visit?" Dahlia, aka White Girl, said as I traded her my ticket for my gun.

"Feel like I need a shower with sacramental wine," I said.

17

"This could get real ugly, real fast."

Tomás and I were waiting for our lunch at Tom's Oyster Bar in Royal Oak. Tomás had wanted to sit at a table outside in the eighty-six-degree heat and 40 percent humidity. For Tomás, heat like this made cold beer taste better — though I'd noticed he had no problem enjoying the stuff during a midwinter Michigan blizzard.

"Ugly and fast I can handle," I said. "Right now, all I've got is boogeyman stories and a half-ass lead from an ex-con."

"But you trust your FBI lady friend, right?"

"O'Donnell?" I said. "Yes. I do. But she's not always right or quick to follow her instincts. The government employee syndrome."

Our waitress — a young woman with a bright smile, buoyant spirit and a cryptic upper arm tattoo that read "Camus Was

Right" — brought our drinks. Tomás had a New Holland Dragon's Milk stout (proof that not all was bible-thumping Dutch Reform conservatism in Grand Rapids). Having already indulged in Duke's Highland malt, I opted for a club soda, lots of ice, with a slice of lime. Maybe next time a Valentine Vodka martini, chilled, up, two olives.

Tomás devoured his Baja Fish Tacos while I savored every bite of my shrimp po' boy. I still had half a sandwich to go when Tomás, finishing his last taco, said, "Shoulda done the world a favor and put Ducane down like a rabid dog."

" 'Keep your friends close and your enemies closer,' " I said, quoting either Sun Tzu or Machiavelli. "As long as he's doing his recording studio thing, he's no threat to us."

"And the Compton twins? You think he can keep those King Kong mothafuckas on a short leash?"

"The Compton twins don't eat, sleep or shit unless Duke tells them to. Plus, if Duke wanted me dead, it would have happened long before now." Then I said, "You still with me tonight?"

"Si."

"Good," I said. "Pick me up at around

eight thirty."

"I'll bring a hundred bucks with me," Tomás said. "In singles."

He laughed.

Me, not so much.

Nicky Karnopolis may run one of Detroit's most popular strip clubs on 8 Mile Road west of the Southfield Freeway, but dear God — he's dumber than a bag of tube socks.

Nicky's father — Christophanos "CK" Karnopolis — once owned three clubs: The Barbiton in Greektown, Aphrodite's Pillow in Grand Circus and Leto's on West 8 Mile. The clubs were mostly clean and the strippers toed a very strict don't-get-drunk-or-do-drugs line enforced by CK's steroid-juiced security thugs.

Karnopolis made no bones about not liking black people — "Why I got to let niggers in my clubs? Niggers, they *animals*! Don't fucking tip!" He barely survived a couple racial discrimination lawsuits brought about by a few black patrons and one stripper.

Having reached the ripe old age of seventy-eight, the cigar-chomping, ouzo-swilling CK decided strip clubs were a young man's game. He sold two of the clubs and left the third largest — Leto's — to his idiot son Nicky.

"He screw up?" CK once uncharacteristically confided in me. I think half a bottle of ouzo was floating his brain. "Fuck him. Always make more boys. Still got Greek Fire in the sack, you know what I say?"

If Nicky knew anything about kidnappings, prostitution or human trafficking, he probably forgot it five minutes after his last line of coke or his fifth glass of marginally drinkable champagne.

Still, he was on Duke Ducane's list and FBI Special Agent Megan O'Donnell's mind.

For Nicky, the club was easy money. It was how he got laid. It afforded him a six-bedroom house on a suburban lake and a private pier for what had been a twenty-six-foot pontoon party boat (recently repossessed).

Tomás and I were in Nicky's cluttered back office.

"Guys," Nicky said, flashing a million-megawatt grin. "Seriously? Trafficking girls? Do I *look* that needy or stupid?"

I chose not to answer.

"Nobody in here from local or state cops? Maybe ICE?" Tomás said.

"Whoa, whoa — *whoa!*" Nicky said, his

hands dramatically pumping the brakes. "State cops? Fucking *ICE*? Guys, this is a *respectable* adult entertainment venue! Local po-po, yeah. Sure. But they usually just get a bellyful of my beer and a face full of complimentary tit, right? We ain't had *no* trouble from *no*body."

"Mind if we just hang for a while?" I said.

"As long as you want, Detective," Nicky said with his uniquely irritating and nervous screech of a laugh. I didn't correct him on the "detective" thing. "I'll even spot you drinks! Lap dances? I got these twins — Bosnia, Belgrade, some fuckin' Middle East country — make your dick a diamond cutter, swear to God!"

Walking back into the soupy darkness of the club, Tomás said, "Is it me or is that guy tweaked like nobody's business?"

"Like nobody's business," I said.

The club's DJ — a white dude with blond dreadlocks and an oversized Brooklyn Dodgers sweatshirt — was blasting some rap song about "phat stacks and mad pussy" while two women helicoptered around stage-to-ceiling poles.

One of the women, with red-clay skin, large dark eyes and jet-black hair, barely looked legal. She spotted me, smiled and winked.

For whatever reason I got an uncomfortable chill.

Like I knew her from somewhere.

If there's one thing about strip clubs that's always churned my stomach, it's the smell: Humid funk. A sickly stew of sweat, farts, mold, dicey food, flat beer and premature ejaculation. The bathrooms are like walking into a tire fire.

Aside from the smell and the sexually reductive denigration of women, I've always been bothered by the lack of poetic imagination in stripper stage names: Jade Green, Tiffany Diamond, Honey Potts.

A caramel-colored woman exhibited a bit more initiative in adopting her stage name "Marqesh de Sade." She walked with imposing sexual confidence on impossibly high Lucite heels up to our small table and said, "Looks like you sad-faced boys could use some stim-a-lation."

Before I could dismissively thank Marqesh for her interest in alleviating the sadness in our faces, she'd mounted my lap and pulled my head into glistening breasts intent on breaching the banks of her black imitation-leather bra. She smelled like moderately expensive perfume and a night's worth of hard grinding.

Tomás laughed. "My friend *is* a sad-faced

boy, Marqesh. Think you can turn that frown upside down?"

"Oh, I can do better than that, lover," she said. Then leaning in to my ear, she said, "Outside, fire door, five minutes. Got some ICE shit for ya."

After a few minutes of grinding on me to concussion-inducing music, Marqesh winked at me, stood and walked back into the overheated crowd.

"Was that as much fun for you as it was for me?" Tomás laughed.

Five minutes later, Tomás and I stood by the club's fire emergency door.

The door clanked open and Marqesh came out wearing a purple polyester "Sailor Moon" kimono and fuzzy pink bunny slippers.

"Y'all got a cigarette?" she said.

"Smoking kills," I said.

"I strip for idiots who wanna animal-fuck me by that dumpster," she said, pointing to what appeared to be a twenty-four-hour, all-you-can-eat rat buffet. "A cigarette ain't gonna kill me any quicker than this job."

"Regular or menthol?" Tomás said.

"Menthol."

Tomás reached into a cargo pants pocket and pulled out a pack of Salem Menthol 100s. He handed the box to Marqesh and she knocked one out. Tomás lit her cigarette and said, "Keep the box. Tryin' to quit."

She nodded her thanks and dropped the box of cigarettes into a pocket of her kimono.

"I know you," she finally said, narrowing her eyes at me. "Cop who busted the mayor."

"Sorry, I don't —"

"No," she said quickly. "You wouldn't remember me. You came to his contractor buddy's house in Indian Village. Bastard was trying to bribe you. I was at the top of the stairs polishing some jagoff's knob from the State's Attorney General's office. You told the mayor's buddy to go fuck himself. Then you punched him in his stupid face." Marqesh took a deep drag off the cigarette and blew two columns of smoke from her nostrils. "I'm nobody's hooker, but — easy money's easy money. Sex has always been a negotiation. Ask any wife."

Marqesh took a last, deep drag off her cigarette, dropped the butt and crushed it with a furry bunny slipper.

"Heard you and Nicky," she said. "Fucking idiot. Yeah, there was a couple of them ICE dudes in last week. Four of 'em. No — three. Fourth guy looked like a biker dude: scraggly-ass beard, leather vest. Couldn't

153

see no club name. Drank like goddamn fish. One of 'em pays a C-note for lap dance from one of the white girls. Russian girl. Fucked up on meth and vodka." Marqesh lit another cigarette and took a deep drag. "When was the last time you heard of some government grunt whippin' out a C-note for anything? So anyway, this guy's trashed, right? Wasted. Starts yellin' shit like 'I should check your papers, honey' and 'you know how much we could get for that sweet commie ass?' That's when his buddies stuff a couple twenties into the Russian chick's G-string, snatch him up and they're in the wind."

"Can you describe any of these guys?"

"White," she said. "I guess. Shit, you know what the lighting's like in there. Coulda been Chinese circus midgets. But I know they was ICE. When they come in a couple of 'em flashed their creds at DaShawn like that would get 'em free lap dances. Assholes."

"DaShawn?"

"Bouncer. Gone now. Nice guy just tryin' to make ends meet."

Tomás and I thanked Marqesh.

I started to fish out a couple bills from my pocket. "Keep it," she said. "Just promise me you'll skull fuck these guys. I do what I do 'cause I *choose* to do it. Some girls don't got the chance to choose. You find these guys, awright?"

"We'll see what we can do," I said.

As Tomás and I walked to my car, I said, "Regular or menthol?"

"You want somebody to talk in a strip club?" Tomás said. "Chances are they want a smoke. Makes for a moment of camaraderie. They didn't teach you that at the academy?"

"Must have been out sick that day."

18

"So," O'Donnell said. "You boys have fun tonight?"

It was late Monday evening and I was stripped down. The shower was running when O'Donnell called.

"Some of us had more fun than others," I said.

"Anything for me?"

"Love and respect," I said. "Other than that, I got jack shit."

I gave O'Donnell a download on our visit with Duke Ducane. And I told her about our evening at the strip club where a very stupid, very nervous Karnopolis gave us nothing and how a brave stripper named Marqesh de Sade gave us our first solid lead.

"Marqesh de Sade?" O'Donnell said. "Best stripper name I've heard in years."

"In the meantime, since you're FBI, seems we've got neo-Nutsies and bikers somehow mixed up in this thing now. If I were you,

I'd start collecting intelligence on bike-mounted Michigan hate groups, Lower Peninsula and local varietals."

"We're monitoring eight such groups in our Wire Room right now," she said. "Plus, we've got a guy inside the BMCs — Blutsbrüder Motorcycle Club — in Howell. Loose affiliation with the west coast BMCs. Nasty bastards, but mostly weapons and drug distribution. No human trafficking that we know of."

"Eight groups and one guy on the inside?" I said.

"You have any idea how many of these whack-job groups there are in Michigan?" O'Donnell said.

"The Southern Poverty Law Center puts it somewhere north of a buttload," I said, standing in the thickening bathroom shower steam.

"You get me a group name and location and I'll get a warrant for a wiretap. What's that sound?"

"That's me waiting to shower off an evening at a strip club."

"Jesus, Snow," O'Donnell said. "I had no idea you were such a choir boy."

After my shower, I slipped on a well-worn pair of Wayne State University faded gold sweatpants and a black hoodie, climbed into bed and prepared to read a couple poems by Antonio Machado. Something that would help guide my dreams to water wheels and cathedrals.

Of course, there are nights when I sleep on top of the sheets. Just in case Izzy comes for a visit to remind me that that corpse once held her soul, or the dark alleyways of my mind revert back to Kabul and Kandahar, Ghazni and Gardez. Nights when I wait for "the call." The order to pull the trigger and watch the body fall.

After forty minutes of reading, I was no closer to sleep.

I was ready to make the trek downstairs in desperate hope that a couple ibuprofens and maybe twenty minutes of SportsCenter would be enough to lull me into a dreamless sleep.

I'd just pulled myself into a sitting position on the side of the bed when I heard it.

A noise at the back of the house. Maybe just the air conditioning traversing the ductwork.

Then again, maybe this was "the call."

I slipped on a pair of Adidas cross trainers, pulled my Glock from the side table, checked the clip and made my way downstairs.

At the back of the house, the shadows of

two men trying to crowbar the security pad of my shed.

Another man approached the shed, low and quick. He seemed pissed at the two men and gestured toward the house.

I made my way in the dark to the front of the house.

A bearded man crouched by my door, the low metallic sound of a picklock scratching at the keyhole. I let him scratch and took a position near the sofa below the window.

Doorknob turning.

The door slowly opening.

The jet-black barrel of a 9mm semi-automatic peeking through the door.

Then the bearded man stepped through.

I stood and brought the barrel of my gun to his throat. He fell, gasping, clutching his throat. His gun slid across the floor. A second skinny man wearing a white T-shirt and black leather vest rushed through the door, baseball bat raised. Before he could take a swing at me, a large silhouetted third man appeared behind the skinny guy and clamped a shadowed hand over his mouth.

A muffled scream from the skinny man. The bat dropped, clanging on the floor.

The skinny guy limped quickly out of my house, leaving the bigger silhouetted man standing with a blood-soaked hunting knife

159

gripped in his right hand.

Tomás.

"Two more in back," I whispered.

I grabbed the first man's 9mm and gave him another good crack on the head before Tomás and I made our way around to the back of my house.

"Come on, asshole!" someone called from inside the truck to the limping man.

The limping man scrambled into the truck bed and the truck rumbled away.

An unconscious man wearing a black Blutsbrüder Motorcycle Club "cut" was sprawled in my narrow driveway near the shed. Someone was standing over him. I leveled my Glock at the standing man.

"Hey," Tomás laughed. "It's Man-Bun!"

"Usually out for a walk at this hour," Trent T.R. Ogilvy said. "Clears my mind. Nourishes the soul." He pointed to the unconscious man at his feet. "This especially helped clear my head."

I said, "Another guy in the house."

"Rendered neutral?" Ogilvy said.

"Rendered neutral."

Ogilvy knelt and began rummaging through the unconscious man's pockets. Tomás and I ran to the front of my house just in time to see the man I'd laid out in the living room hobbling his way down

Markham Street toward what looked like a tricked-out Harley-Davidson.

"No," I said catching Tomás's forearm. "Let him go."

"Gerald Brecker," Ogilvy said, holding a small flashlight over the unconscious man's driver's license. "332 Palm Grove Drive, Spring Lake Township." Ogilvy brought the beam of the flashlight up to me and said, "I take it you're not acquainted with Gerald Brecker of Spring Lake Township?"

"Never heard of him."

"And, of course, there's this."

Ogilvy brought his flashlight to Gerald Brecker's left forearm: A tattoo of an angry bearded man wielding a large hammer inscribed with Scandinavian rune symbols. Beneath the bearded man tattoo were script-style letters: "BMC" followed by the German words *"Heimat. Bruderschaft."*

Homeland. Brotherhood.

"I don't think you gentlemen want to be around for part two of this. Just in case the cops get involved," I said. Then, turning to Tomás I said, "And just what the hell are you doing around here?"

"Haven't slept good since the threats against Elena," Tomás said. "Some nights I read. Some nights I cruise the neighborhood. Tonight's your lucky night."

"Jesus," I said. "You *read*?"

"Excuse me, gentlemen. There's a 'part two' to this?" Ogilvy said. "I take it part two doesn't involve the police?"

"No," I said. "It does not involve the police. And it doesn't involve you either, Trent."

"Well," Ogilvy said, standing and stowing his flashlight away. "I have to differ on that particular point, as I'm the one who put in considerable effort in taking this gentleman down."

Tomás held up his bloody knife. "It's midnight on a Monday and I'm a cholo holding a bloody knife over a neo-Nazi. What else I got to do?"

"What about Elena?"

"At baby girl's house for a couple days," Tomás said, meaning his daughter. "Nothing ever happens in Ferndale, 'cept maybe a stoner steals a pair of Crocs."

"Okay," I said to both men. "But this ain't gonna be pretty."

Neither man said anything.

I punched in the code to open my shed.

Ogilvy and Tomás dragged the unconscious Gerald Brecker into the shed.

"I assume you have zip ties?" Ogilvy said as I closed and locked the door.

19

Carlos and Jimmy had built the shed at the back of my house with painstaking detail. One of those details included a double layer of stone wool soundproofing; they'd known there would be times when they worked late into the night and maybe needed to cut a length of pipe or piece of wood. More recently they'd taken to restoring the Olds/ Hurst 442 they'd gifted me in their off hours.

The soundproofing would come in handy this early Tuesday morning as we sweated Gerald Brecker.

We tied the neo-Nazi biker to a metal chair ten feet in front of the Olds 442 and set up three very bright work lights on stands around him.

He was conscious now, and not liking it one bit.

"What — what're you gonna do?" Brecker said, swallowing hard and squinting against

163

the work lights. "You can't do this! It ain't right, goddammit!"

"Trying to put a beatdown on me in the wee hours of the morning 'ain't right,' Mr. Brecker," I said. "I'm sure the only part that 'ain't right' to you is the fact that you got caught."

"My brothers'll be back for me," he growled. "Locked and fucking loaded, asshole."

"One of your biker brothers is miles away nursing his right shoulder and probably a perforated kidney," I said. I pointed to Tomás and said, "Courtesy of this man —"

"Hey," Tomás said, waving to Brecker. "How's it goin', jizzface?"

"Another one of your playmates I'm pretty sure has a broken jaw, busted nose and dislocated right arm." I pointed to Trent Ogilvy and said, "Thanks to this gentleman."

"Cheers, mate," Ogilvy said with a nod to Becker.

"And I knocked your other buddy so hard in the throat he'll be sucking breakfast through a straw for a month," I said. "So, I don't think your scary neo-Nutsy buddies are coming back for you anytime soon."

"These are the weapons we took from your friends," Ogilvy said, pointing to the weapons he'd arranged in a semicircle in front of Brecker: two 9mm semi-automatic pistols, a piece-of-shit revolver, three long-blade knives, a set of brass knuckles, a retractable metal baton and an aluminum baseball bat. "Who uses brass knuckles anymore?" Ogilvy wondered out loud.

"*And* an aluminum baseball bat?" I said to Brecker.

"Fuck you, mud boy," Brecker growled.

"You're more than welcome to make a play for any one of these weapons," I said to Brecker, "if you manage to struggle free from your bindings. But I can assure you — by the time you reach any one of them, you'll be in pieces. And those pieces will then be fed to a mutant strain of walleye in the Detroit River with teeth as big as my real estate agent's dentures."

"What do you want?" Brecker said.

"Who sent you," I said, casually checking the clip and chamber of my Glock. "Why. How much. And who holds the purse strings. Or are you just garden variety, stupid-as-fuck white supremacists, come to steal from lower-to-middle-class blacks and Mexican-Americans?"

Brecker nervously assessed each of us individually — me, Ogilvy and Tomás — then cut his eyes to the semicircle of weapons laid out in front of him. He struggled against his bindings before mumbling, "You're breakin' the goddamn law."

"Oh, so *now* you wanna talk the law?" I laughed.

"This is bullshit," Tomás grumbled before walking to one of five toolboxes kept in my shed. Retrieving a pair of snip crimpers, he walked back to Brecker. Kneeling, he removed Brecker's right boot and sock.

"Hey!" Brecker said. "Hey, what the fuck, man!"

"Yeah, Tomás," I said. "What the fuck?"

"You're gonna talk. Right goddamn now," Tomás said to Brecker as he fit Brecker's little toe between the snip crimper's blades.

"Who, what, why and how much," I said. "Or swear to God, Tomás will cut —"

Bone snapping.

Blood spirting.

Screams.

"Jesus, Tomás!" I said. "What the *fuck*!"

"I thought you said 'Cut it!' "

Brecker, his eyes rolling back into his head, thrashed about in the chair. Ogilvy moved quickly and stuffed a rag in Brecker's mouth to stifle his screams.

"I didn't say 'cut it'! I was just *threatening* the guy! Fucking hell!"

"Well," Tomás said, "you need to *enunci-*

ate, goddammit!"

"Frankly," Ogilvy said as he gagged Brecker, "I thought you gave the order, too."

"Oh my God! Seriously, guys? Really?"

Brecker passed out.

It was ten minutes before he came around. I brought a fifth of tequila, a bottle of hydrogen peroxide and Tylenol from the house. Ogilvy cleaned and dressed where Brecker's little toe had been.

"You — you cut my fucking toe off," Brecker cried. Then, trying to bring the pills I held in front of him into focus, he said, "What's that?"

"Pain killer."

He gladly took the pill, washing them down with the shot of tequila I poured into his mouth.

"Let's try this again, *pendejo,*" Tomás said.

Contrary to extensive studies conducted by the CIA, State Department, DOJ and the Pentagon, it seems torture *does* on occasion yield honest and vital information. In this case, Brecker opened up like a well-watered rose in full sunlight . . .

. . . or like a man who'd just had his little toe clipped off.

He belonged to the local neo-Nazi chapter of the BMCs, headquartered in a biker bar called Taffy's on the Lake, on the less affluent outskirts of Spring Lake, nineteen miles northwest of Detroit. The group — twenty or thirty, mostly men — dealt marijuana, PCP, MDMA, crystal meth and pharmaceutical grade oxy knock-offs from Canada mostly to teenagers and lake rats. At least that's all Brecker — a grunt in the organization, I assumed — knew of. Occasionally they got a batch order for oxy, pot and Viagra knock-offs from an ambulance-chasing attorney with a big lake house and a long-rumored but never proven appetite for underage girls.

And occasionally they got an order from "some Greek guy who owns a strip club."

"What's the lawyer's name?" I said.

"Olsen," Brecker said, surrendering to the tequila and painkillers. "Barney Olsen."

I poured another shot of tequila in him.

" 'You want justice?' " Tomás said. " 'You want *Barney*!' That guy? The fat fuck on the billboards and buses?"

"Yeah," Brecker said. "Him. You cut off my goddamn toe, you piece of shit spic!"

"You got nine more," Tomás said.

"Fuck you!"

Tomás walked to the toolboxes and retrieved a sizable pair of metal shears.

"Oh, God!" Brecker pleaded. "Jesus! No! No, please! I'm sorry, man!"

After a moment, Tomás put the shears back in the toolbox.

Brecker said the BMCs got a cash infusion of a couple grand from Olsen just to rough me up and warn me away from looking into "his business."

"And what's 'his business'?" I said.

"I don't know," Brecker said close to tears. "And I don't fucking care. It was good money and the club needed it."

"Olsen probably pulls down a couple mil a year chasing ambulances," I said to Brecker. "And you and your buddies come after me for beer money? Fucking hell. I always knew racists were stupid, but I had no idea they were *this* retarded."

"We don't use that word anymore, August," Ogilvy said invoking the royal "we."

"Twenty grand ain't no beer money," Brecker said. "You're gonna have BMCs straight up your jungle monkey ass when I tell 'em what you did to me! We'll see who gets cut up then!"

I knelt in front of him. "I'm guessing you won't be going back. I'm guessing your buddies are gonna tell Olsen that I've been taken care of. But, hey — the 'nigger' might need another tune-up. I'm guessing they'll squeeze him for more. You? They see you gimping through the door and they'll wonder how much you squealed. And bikers don't like squealers. Maybe you'll end up with another club. Maybe some hydrocephalic half-wits shooting squirrels for stew and running pathetic army drills." I pushed the barrel of my Glock to the center of his forehead. "Either way, you're done."

Brecker squeezed his eyes shut and began weeping.

Then he pissed himself.

Once the shed had been hosed down and Brecker's toe had been flushed in my downstairs toilet, I thanked Ogilvy for the assist and told him to go home. Then Tomás and I drove Brecker to the outskirts of Spring Lake and rolled him out of the bed of Tomás's truck near a dried-out marsh.

I stood over him, and said, "If I even think you farted in my general direction, I'll find you and kill you. Understand me, Gerald Brecker?"

Then I got back in Tomás's truck and we drove off.

We were silent for a moment before Tomás said, "Swear to God, Octavio — I thought you said to cut his toe off."

"Can we just get some breakfast and not talk about it?"

"Yeah. Sure. Breakfast," Tomás said. "But no sausage links —"

■ ■ ■ ■

Tomás and I did some serious carbo-loading at a Denny's on our way back to Mexican-town.

There was a chance — slim at best — Gerald Brecker would hobble his way to the cops. My guess was he already had an extensive petty crime rap sheet including an affiliation with drug-and-gun biker lake rats. More trouble than maybe a little toe was worth.

"You think Markham Street would alibi us if he did go to the cops?" Tomás said.

"I think Markham Street would swear on a stack of King James bibles we were saving a box of kittens from drowning in the Detroit River."

Tomás gave me a sly smile.

"For a Catholic kid, you sure take a lot of liberties, Octavio."

" 'If we confess our sins, He is faithful and just to forgive us our sins and to cleanse us from all unrighteousness.' "

"Yeah. Like I said . . ."

It was eight on Tuesday morning by the time Tomás finally dropped me off at my house.

I was about to call FBI Special Agent

171

Megan O'Donnell to let her know that her mythical white whale had given us a very real dorsal fin slap on the ass when I got an uneasy feeling. Like a trail of someone's residual electricity dissipating in the air.

I pulled my Glock and tripped the safety off.

There.

Eleven o'clock.

Elevation, eight feet.

Descending the staircase, fresh out of my shower and wearing only a white towel, was a petite young woman with reddish-brown skin and wet, coal-black hair. She was athletically built and pretty in a stoic, uninterested way. Like a magazine model who found everything save for her own existence excruciatingly boring.

The pole-dancing stripper who'd winked at me in Leto's strip club.

The saleswoman leaving Duke Ducane's SoundNation recording studio.

"If I put my hands up, the towel drops," the young woman said plainly. "I don't much give a shit. But you. What's your take on that?"

"Who the hell are you?" I said.

"I'm the IT Department."

20

Unconcerned by the business end of my 9mm, the young woman resumed her staircase descent and walked to my kitchen. Without a care, she proceeded to open my refrigerator and give the contents careful consideration.

"So," I said. "The gun's not impressing you?"

She pulled her head out of my refrigerator, gave me a hard look and said, "Yours ain't so big and scary. Is that *real* salsa? Like, homemade? No gluten or GMO shit? You got any chips?"

I put away my less-than-scary gun.

"You know, it's really not nice to fool us old folk," I said, reaching into her large desert camo Army surplus backpack on my sofa. I held up the wig and bikini she'd worn at Leto's Gentleman's Club.

"Yeah," she said. "But it is *so* much fun.

Don't you got any Mountain Dew or Gatorade?"

"Put some clothes on and I'll fix something."

She started to grab her backpack.

I stopped her. "No. The backpack stays here."

Inside of her backpack were two laptop computers, an assortment of flash drives held together on a big loop-style keychain, well-worn Vasque hiking boots, a couple pairs of khaki shorts, two graphic T-shirts — one for an '80s rock band called Redbone, the other for an EDM band called A Tribe Called Red — underwear, toiletries and a Marttiini Lapp hunting knife in a leather sheath.

And there were more disguise elements: false teeth, three different colors of contact lenses, another wig, various glasses, spirit gum and prosthetic noses.

Her name was Lucy Elise Pensoneau, originally from the Bay Mills Indian Community in Michigan's Upper Peninsula. Most recently from electromagnetically tricking one-armed-bandits to pay out in Las Vegas as a few tokens and modified keycards from the Bellagio, Ceasars Palace and ARIA suggested.

After ten minutes, she came downstairs

wearing oversized, multi-pocketed forest-green cargo shorts and a T-shirt that read, "There are two types of people in this world: Those who can extrapolate from incomplete data."

She also had a Sig Sauer P220 10mm pistol pointed at me.

"Seriously?" I said, exhausted from a crappy late night and shitty early morning. "You know how many times people have pulled guns on me in my own fucking house? *Do you?* Now put that peashooter away before I dip it in salsa and make you eat it!"

"Sorry," she said, lowering the weapon. "Habit."

"Jesus." I grabbed the gun from her. "What kind of situations make that a god-damn 'habit?' " I ejected the bullet in the chamber, took the clip out and laid the now impotent piece of metal on my coffee table. "Now go sit down," I said, pointing to the stools at my kitchen island. "And tell me who the hell Lucy Elise Pensoneau is —"

"Actually I prefer Lucy Three Rivers."

I cut her a look. "Just tell me who you are and why I shouldn't toss you out on your ass."

"Oh, my God," she said. "You always this emotional?"

175

"Talk!"

While she talked, I calmed myself by making vegetarian tacos with chopped and grilled Vidalia onions, flash-grilled jalapenos, black beans, tomatillos and *queso fresco.* I opened a jar of the salsa and dropped a spoon in it.

In my mother's old stovetop percolator coffeepot I made four cups of Michigan cherry-infused coffee and sat down at the kitchen island with a cup.

"I saw some beer in there," Lucy said, nodding to my refrigerator.

"Yeah," I said. I opened the refrigerator, retrieved a can of naturally flavored cherry seltzer water and handed it to her.

"Hey, I'm old enough for beer."

"Maybe in the Netherlands or the Philippines," I said. "Not around here."

"You saw my driver's license," she said. "I'm twenty-two."

"It's good," I said after a bite of taco and a quick swig of coffee. "Just shy of undetectable. How old are you really?"

"Skittles said you were a piece of work."

"He said that?"

"Yeah." She grabbed another taco and gobbled it down. "Said you fired up some burners he gave you a while ago. Said you might need some help. I'm the help. Don't

I look twenty-two? I mean the guy at the strip club thought I did."

"The guy at the strip club had a nose full of coke and a belly full of champagne," I said. "Not exactly the stuff of sound judgment." After a sip of coffee, I said, "Why the reindeer games?"

"That's me helping you," she said. "Got it on the down low you was heading to that recording studio. I spoofed your phone there and laptop when I got here."

"And the strip club?"

"Just wanted to see if you were some kinda perv," she said, her left cheek rounded with a large bite of taco. "The guy you talked to in the back office —"

"Nicky Karnopolis."

"Yeah," she said. "Him. He was pretty shaken up after you and the big guy left, so I knew you wasn't there for the tit show. Called some doofus named Barney Olsen. Speaking of tits, that chick who gave you the lap dance and motorboat jug job? You get off on that or what?"

"Aren't you a little young to have such a bad attitude?"

"Live a year on my rez," she said. "Then ask me again. And be the only girl — only *red* girl — in Michigan Tech computer science classes for two years. So anyway, wherever you went, I got there first. Figured you might want some intel beyond old school shoe-leather shit. I blue-jacked the strip club guy's phone. And that black guy — Duke Whatever."

"Jesus."

"I don't trust people as easily as Skittles," she said, snatching the last taco and slathering it with my salsa. "I had to make sure you was legit."

"And?"

"You're okay I guess," she said. "You feel guilty about what you did to him?"

"Yes."

"He said you would," Lucy said with her mouth full. "But I wouldn't be here if he hated your guts. Skittles? He's cut different."

"So I noticed."

"By the way," Lucy said. "Your phone? Somebody else spoofed it. Somebody else is monitoring your calls."

"Who?"

"Don't know," she said, finishing the taco and licking a couple fingers. "Weird configuration. Not feds. Not local PD. Just — weird. I can find out if you give me an hour. Which room is mine?"

"The one next door," I said. "I don't need my neighbors wondering why a nineteen-year-old girl is bunking at my house."

"Wow. Skittles said you were an old-school altar boy."

I called Jimmy Radmon, who was at my door within five minutes. As was usual, his knock was just a courtesy; he opened the door and bounded in.

Seeing Lucy sitting at my kitchen island was apparently a bit too much for Jimmy; his eyes became as big as saucers and his jaw slackened. If I was his age, I probably would have reacted the same way: she was as a budding beauty.

"Jimmy," I said. "This is Lucy . . ." I hesitated, unsure of which name I was supposed to use.

"Three Rivers," she said.

"Lucy Three Rivers," I repeated. "She's going to be staying with us for a while. She's taking your place at Carmela and Sylvia's. That's Lucy's stuff." I pointed to the backpack on my sofa. Then to Lucy I said, "Carmela and Sylvia are very special people to me, so behave or you're out on your ear, IT department or not. Don't go pulling a gun or knife on anybody, okay? And whatever you do, don't eat their brownies."

Lucy said to Jimmy, "You seein' anybody? You're kinda cute."

Jimmy's jaw just about hit and bounced

off the floor.

"I — uh — I got me a girlfriend," Jimmy stammered. "But — you know — thanks."

"In an hour, I wanna know who's crawlin' around in my phone," I said to Lucy. "Besides you."

Lucy saluted, took a big pull of her cherry-flavored seltzer water, burped, then said, "Are you really a tough guy? Skittles said you were a tough guy. Real Rock-'Em-Sock-'Em Robots kinda shit. You ever, like, beat somebody senseless?"

I cut my eyes to Jimmy and said, "Get her settled at Carmela and Sylvia's. Now."

21

I was wearing a black summer-weight Tom Ford suit with light grey silk pocket square, white shirt, black tie and a pair of black Santoni double-buckle shoes. Perfect for the grim business of kneeling by the coffin of a young woman I had not known and, into folded hands, whispering, *Ave Maria, gratia plena, Dominus tecum* . . .

I emerged from my house at the same time Lucy Three Rivers bounded out of Carmela and Sylvia's.

"Dude!" she said.

As I made my way across the street to Carlos's garage to retrieve my rental Caddy, Lucy walked backwards in front of me.

"I got something for you, tough guy —"

"Not right now, Lucy," I said, unsuccessfully trying to sidestep her.

"Yeah, but this shit's really new-metrics weird." She skipped backwards so she could continue to face me. "That second spoof of your phone? It's so *old* tech it's *new*! It's like a pterodactyl with a jet pack!"

Jimmy Radmon, appearing out of nowhere, stepped between me and Lucy. Facing Lucy, he said, "When Mr. Snow say 'Not right now,' he mean 'Not right now,' Miss Fire."

Lucy stopped skipping and planted her fists firmly in her waist.

"It's *Three Rivers,*" she said. "And if you weren't so cute, I'd probably deck ya."

Jimmy turned to me. "You okay, Mr. Snow?"

"No," I said. "Not really. Thanks, Jimmy."

As I continued walking to Carlos's garage I heard Lucy behind me say, "Wow. What's his serious problem?"

"He don't like good people gettin' hurt," Jimmy said. "And he really don't like seein' 'em buried."

Since its founding in 1880 on the corner of Junction Street and what's now Vernor Highway, Most Holy Redeemer Catholic Church has gone through three building phases: the modest clapboard parish built on hard dirt and thick mud, the spired red brick European Gothic-style cathedral built sixteen years later, and its substantial 1927 remodeling which stands today.

As the façade of the church changed, so

did the face of its patrons; from white European immigrants thanking God they hadn't drowned or gotten dysentery on their journey to the promise of America to Mexican and South Americans thanking God for pretty much the same reasons.

To step inside Holy Redeemer is to step inside the Basilica of St. Paul's in Rome. Breathtaking frescos, a high and expansive altar, side altars and devotional shrines. Kneeling in a pew on a prayer rail you might half expect to raise your head and see a contemplative pope at the altar smiling at you.

This mid-June Tuesday morning, there were no smiles.

No benevolent pope smiling at the faithful.

Lying in a shiny grey coffin with chrome rails at the head of the altar was a nineteen-year-old girl who'd been drugged and brutally raped.

Bobby Falconi and his wife, Jen, stood by the main door of the church greeting people as they entered for the service. They were footing the bill to give Isadora Rosalita del Torres the modicum of dignity in death that she'd failed to find in life.

"Thanks for coming, August," Bobby said as we shook hands. "What you've done? I owe you, brotha."

"You owe me nothing," I said. "You doing this for her is more than a lot, Bobby."

I gave Bobby's Japanese-American wife of twenty-three years, Jen, a kiss on her cheek.

Much to my surprise, at least sixty people were already in attendance.

Sixty people who most likely didn't know the girl in the coffin, but who came to pay their respects and offer their prayers. Many of these people were friends and associates of Elena Gutierrez: Nadine Rosado, the District 6 City Council representative; community activists, Mexicantown business owners. There were the ladies from Café Consuela's and, of course, a phalanx of *abuelas,* their elderly heads covered by black lace mantillas. They may not have known the girl in the casket, but they knew she was young, Mexican and dead. Enough to mourn and say the rosary.

Much to my surprise, Carmela and Sylvia were seated in a pew.

"We're so sorry about your friend, Mr. Snow," Sylvia whispered, taking my hand in hers and squeezing.

After giving an emotionally drained Elena a hug and kiss on her cheek, I took a place next to Tomás.

"You clean up nice," I whispered.

"This tie," Tomás whispered back. "It's like being choked by a baby."

Ten minutes before the service began, several other of my Markham Street neighbors entered the church, including Jimmy, Carlos and Trent T.R. Ogilvy. I'd never seen Jimmy or Carlos in suits and the sight both managed to stun me and fill me with a strange sense of pride.

And Lucy Three Rivers was with them dressed in torn black jeans, black Converse All Stars and a black Bellagio casino t-shirt. The closest she could come, I assumed, to respectful funeral wear. I recognized the look on her face as she passed by me. It was the "shit just got real" look. The look of youth suddenly realizing the young could die.

The arrangements Bobby and Jen had made at Holy Redeemer included the church's choir — twenty members, young and old, resplendent in white robes — seated near the altar.

And may flights of angels sing thee to thy rest.

Father Irwin Prescott may not have been of Mexican descent, but you would never have known from his command of Spanish and the emotionally effusive way he delivered the funeral mass and his homily.

Concluding the service was the choir, forming a semicircle around Isadora's casket and singing some 1980s song — "Yah-Mo Be There" — in Spanish.

Not a dry eye in the house.

Except for mine.

And Tomás's.

Tears would have obscured our view of the blood and bone vengeance we intended to take in Izzy's name.

After the mass, Bobby stopped me at the door and said, "You coming to the luncheon?"

"No," I said. "I gotta see a man about a thing."

Bobby knew better than to ask. He'd known better since my days on the Force.

"Hey!" Tomás said, catching up with me in the parking lot. "You goin' to the lunch thing over at Armando's?"

All I could do was look at him.

Compression of intent.

Concentration of purpose.

Focus of rage.

Target acquisition.

He turned to Elena and said, "I'll see you at home, baby."

"Why? Where are you going?"

Tomás briefly glanced at me. Then to

186

Elena he said, "I gotta see a guy about a thing."

She quickly made the Sign of the Cross over her chest and said, *"Mia madre."*

"Go," he said, handing her the keys to his truck. "I'll see you later. Promise."

Then we got in my Caddy and left Holy Redeemer.

We made one stop.

Tomás's house.

His gun locker.

"What should I take this time?" he said.

"Take it all."

"Oh, shit."

And from Tomás's house in Mexicantown we took the fight to the northern Detroit suburb of Southfield.

I wanted justice.

I wanted Barney.

22

Travel the highways and byways of Metro Detroit and you're bound to see the always startling moon face of Barney Olsen, Esq. plastered on billboards and buses. Next to the multimillionaire ambulance-chaser's massive, grinning face is the quote that has been his advertising tag line for the past twenty-five years: "You want justice? You want *Barney*!"

Olsen has been occasionally plagued by rumors of raucous parties at his multimillion-dollar modern split-level, eight-bedroom Spring Lake house. Nothing new, considering most people with homes hugging the shore of the lake are well-off and enjoy drunk boating, drunk fireworks and drunk barbeques in the summer and especially on the long Fourth of July week-end. (Nothing says "I Love America!" like losing fingers to fireworks and beer-bloated rich people fucking on powerboats.)

The stories of Olsen's parties included the added bacchanalian debauchery of under-age girls engaging in sex and drugs. Rock 'n roll was optional.

Now that I'd shaken a branch of the trafficking tree, Olsen had called out some mentally deficient neo-Nutsy bikers to do me bodily injury.

And that just wouldn't stand.

I brought my Caddy to a screeching halt in the parking lot of Olsen's five-story office building along the Mariana Trench of the Lodge Freeway in Southfield, prepared to do to him what he apparently had intended to do to me.

"Listen, Octavio," Tomás said. "Don't go in there guns blazing."

"Said the man who broke a federal agent's jaw."

Olsen employed a number of other attorneys each taking a percentage of slip-and-falls, car and motorcycle accidents, medical malpractice lawsuits, etc. But Olsen chose to occupy the expansive fifth floor all by his fat-ass lonesome.

Tomás and I each carried Coach 20-gauge shotguns. And those were just the weapons you could see. With irreproachable authority Tomás flashed his wallet at the security guard.

"Need backup, officers?" the security guard said as he made sure his shirt was properly tucked in.

"No," I said. "Just fifth floor access."

"Yessir," the guard said, swiping his card in the elevator's reader and pushing the button for Olsen's private floor. He saluted us and the doors closed.

"Amazing how far a driver's license and Macy's charge card can get you at thirty paces," I said to Tomás.

"Ain't it though?"

On the fifth floor we walked past a fully equipped gym, large conference room, law library and, oddly enough, a sushi bar where the Japanese chef stood leaning against a wall, looking bored and reading from his iPad.

Finally, we arrived at a tall, curving oak desk where a slender brunette sat.

"Where is he?" I growled. "Where's Olsen?"

The woman stood, visibly shaken by our hard-charging march toward the doors leading to Olsen's office. I yanked on the glass double doors behind her. They rattled and remained locked.

"Do you have —"

"No, I don't have a goddamn appointment," I said. "But I'm sure he'd just love to see me. Now open the damn door!"

Tomás made his way around the receptionist's desk and found the button release for the doors.

"Sir!" the receptionist said, following Tomás and me into the executive offices. "Sir, Mr. Olsen is —"

"Mr. Olsen is what?" I said standing in the wide doorway of a large empty office bearing the nameplate "Barnard J. Olsen, Esq."

"That's what I'm trying to tell you, sir," the receptionist said breathlessly. "He's not here. Mr. Olsen hasn't been in the office for a couple days now. Nobody's heard from him. Partners. Associates. Clients. Nobody. He's missed two court dates and three depositions. He's not answering his phone. We're all kind of — you know — worried." Nervously, she glanced at our shotguns. "Are you — clients?"

Tomás and I left.

From the Southfield offices of Barney Olsen, Tomás and I headed even farther north to his Spring Lake home. It wasn't hard to find; it had been featured a few years earlier in *Hour* and *Detroit Design* magazines and looked very much like the fever-dream fantasy child of a feudal shogun and Frank Lloyd Wright.

191

It sat on five acres of prime lakeside property with its own private pier and surrounded by a not-so-subtle iron gate. Next to the gated entrance which bore the large scroll initials "BO" rendered in iron was an old-style red enamel British call box.

"If you gotta call to get in," Tomás said as we drove up to the gate, "then you ain't gettin' in."

"I don't think that's gonna be a problem," I said, pointing to the entrance gate. It was already partially open.

Tomás got out of the car and opened the gate all the way.

When he got back in the car, he gave me a look and said, "Safeties off?"

"Safeties off."

It's never a good sign when a house appears to be empty and the main door is open; Tomás went in high and I went in low.

Nothing. No one.

Tomás indicated he would take the upper level of the house while I took the first and lower level.

The house appeared to be completely empty and thoroughly scrubbed down: Empty refrigerator, kitchen cabinets, pantry and closets. No furniture. The two first floor bathrooms stank of bleach. There was a media room with bare wires dangling out of holes and the steel wall brace where a TV had once hung.

The expansive open-concept dining room and living room still held their breathtaking view of the lake, but aside from that, they too were empty.

The lower level was the same.

Big and empty.

As I was about to mount the steps leading back upstairs, I noticed something out of the corner of my eye. A small white square peeking out of a corner of the crème-colored carpeting. I knelt by the white square; a piece of lace stuck under a wall. I tugged at the lace and it came free from the wall. Three inches of it. Stained at one end with what might have been blood.

It didn't take long to find the release for the false wall.

I pushed it open and was nearly over-whelmed by the burning stench of ammonia.

Barney's private party room. The room was a large, windowless rectangle. It looked as if a quick renovation of the room had begun and just as quickly abandoned; spackle had patched over some holes in the wall while other holes were left open and gaping. Drag marks of furniture or equipment on the carpeted floor. At the far end of the room was a bar with empty liquor shelves, a few toppled over barstools. Hung from the ceiling over the long bar were three chains, one equipped with a pair of furry white handcuffs. In corners of the ceiling there were more holes where multi-colored wires dangled lifeless.

A door off to the left near the bar: Five smaller rooms, three with mattresses saturated with bleach. The fifth room was soundproofed. Empty racks where electronics once resided, a small desk and four wall-mounted closed-circuit monitors, their screens smashed.

I would get the lace to Bobby Falconi at his Wayne County Coroner's Office for trace analysis, but I had a sickening feeling Izzy had known these rooms.

"Octavio!"

I raced to the second floor and found Tomás in what might have been a bedroom facing the lake.

"What do you smell?" Tomás said.

"Bleach," I said. "And paint."

Taking out his pocket knife, Tomás crouched by the wall and sank the tip of his knife blade into a soft spot. He brought the tip of the blade up for me to see.

"Spackle." I pointed to where Tomás had dug the still drying spackle out. "A bullet hole? What the hell's going on here?"

Tomás stood. "I think I know where Barnard J. Olsen, Esquire is."

"Where?"

He pointed out to the expanse of the shimmering lake.

23

On the way from Olsen's house to the biker bar, Taffy's on the Lake, I made two quick calls.

The first was to my lawyer, David G. Baker.

"Jee*EEE*sus, August!" G shouted. "Remember *last* time? Remember I had to use a goddamn crate of crowbars to free you from the gnarly talons of the FBI? How many times do I have to tell you — I'm a *contracts* lawyer, August, not a criminal lawyer! You know, your father —"

"I don't have time for a virtual spanking from my dad, G," I said. "I need to know you've got my back on this."

There was a considerable pause. Then G said, "Depends on who pulls first, how and if that's verifiable — which, mind you, it almost never is. A badge would help, but of course you don't have a badge anymore. I'll ask Janet Layne. Criminal attorney I partnered up with last year. Run a couple scenarios by her."

"Weren't you sleeping with this Janet Layne last year?" I said. "Compact? Great smile? Killer legs?"

"You're about to walk into a neo-Nazi biker kill box and you wanna know who I'm sleeping with?" he said. "Listen. Tatina needs to move here. Or you need to move there. Either way, my love life couldn't *possibly* be more interesting than you being tried for murder. Or worse, me sitting shiva for you."

My next call went pretty much the same way.

I told Megan O'Donnell about my recent experience with Gerald Brecker and his neo-Nazi biker crew. I told her about our visit to Barney Olsen's Southfield office and how she might want to get an FBI forensics team to Olsen's Spring Lake home. And I told her I was on my way for a beer-and-a-couple-shots at a little biker bar called Taffy's on the Lake.

"You're being stupid," O'Donnell said.

"You wanna know what's stupid, O'Donnell?" I said. "Five people sitting in the back of a goddamn donut shop talking about 'white whales.' In the meantime, brown girls from my neighborhood are disappearing or showing up dead."

"Hey, asshole, don't you *dare* play that goddamn brown card with me!"

"If it's the only card dealt," I said, "then it's gonna get played."

I disconnected.

After a moment, Tomás said, "If I ask a question, you gonna punch me in the mouth?"

"Not like I don't owe you a punch in the mouth."

"If you're jacked and ready to unload," Tomás said, "why you callin' these tiptoeing hush puppies and givin' 'em a head's up?"

"I'm tired of sitting on the sidelines, watching things go to shit," I said. "Tired of people who *should* do something just sitting back, drinking coffee and claiming plausible deniability when things go fubar. If I'm in the shit, then *everybody's* in the shit." I could feel Tomás staring at me. I cut my eyes to him and said, "What?"

"You're very tense for a young man," Tomás said.

It was late afternoon when Tomás and I rolled up to Taffy's on the Lake, a rattrap ranch-style building well on the outskirts of Spring Lake's tonier waterfront residential developments. The parking lot contained a nicely restored sapphire-blue 1959 Ford

F-100 with whitewall tires, a beat-up puke-brown 2004 Buick Rendezvous and five black Harley-Davidson bikes gangsta-leaning on their kickstands.

"How you wanna play this, jefe?" Tomás said after checking the 15-round clip of his Baretta Brigadier Inox.

"See how we're dressed?" I said.

Tomás gave me a curious look before assessing how we were both dressed. "Like real James Bond classy kinda shit."

"That's how we open," I said. "With class."

"And if that don't work?"

"Then we put our foot up in it."

Tomás parked and we walked into the urinal cake and vomitorium that is Taffy's (Nowhere Near to Being) on the Lake.

The lighting was low and even though the air was cool, it was thick and musty and stank of stale cigarettes and pot. There were eight tables and three booths, most still littered with empty beer bottles, shot glasses and the red plastic baskets fries and buffalo wings come in. There was a Wurlitzer Bubbler jukebox with a Confederate flag hung over it and a large poster of a prominent scraggly-haired Detroit rocker wrapped in the American flag and flipping the bird.

I could feel the soles of my very expensive

shoes sticking to whatever biological matter had congealed on the floor.

Behind the bar was a broad-chested man with a full grey beard and wearing a T-shirt that said "FU." Over his T-shirt he wore his "cut" — black leather vest with various patches on it. I'm fairly certain none of the patches was earned for helping little old ladies across the street.

Two other guys — both wearing their cuts — were seated at the bar, smoking and drinking.

All eyes were on Tomás and me.

"We're closed," the bartender growled.

"Actually, that's a good thing," I said. "See, we'd like to have a nice, uninterrupted conversation with the manager of this fine establishment."

"He said we're fuckin' closed," the customer to the right said. "Or don't you and your buddy speakee dee English?"

The three men laughed.

I slowly reached into my back pants pocket and, with two fingers, extracted my wallet. From my wallet I pulled three hundred dollars. "Tell you what," I said. "Three hundred for three minutes of the manager's time. How's that —"

"Your money's no good here, Buckwheat!" the barkeep said, slamming his meaty fist on the bar. "Now get your asses outta here!"

"Whoa, whoa, whoa, Hatcher," a heavy baritone voice said from the shadows. "Money's always welcomed everywhere — including here. *Especially* here."

A mountain of a man emerged from the shadows. He was zipping up the fly of his jeans.

"You boys five-oh?"

"Oh, heavens, no," I said. "My name is Mr. Snow and this is my associate, J. Paul Yeti. We're just a couple of interested parties making inquiries."

"Interested in what?" the big man said.

"For starters, the relationship between the BMCs and a lawyer named Barney Olsen," I said. "And if we get around to it, why a couple club members tried to give me a beatdown last night in Mexicantown."

The big man stared hard at us for a moment. There was a slight whistle from his nose as he breathed.

The bartender slowly reached beneath the bar.

The guy on the left at the bar had slipped his hand beneath his vest.

"Tell you what," the big man finally said. "Why don't you leave the money on the table along with your email address and we'll get back to you."

He turned and started to walk away.

"Gee, I'm afraid I can't do that," I said. "See, I need answers in a timely manner since a girl — *two* girls, in fact — have been murdered and I think your club and Barney Olsen have something to do with their murders."

The big man stopped. He turned back to us.

"I thought you said you wasn't no cops?" the big man said, crossing his massive arms across the wide geography of his chest. "If you ain't cops just who the fuck are you?"

I took a couple steps closer to him, smiled and said, "I'm the vengeance of the righteous, motherfucker — and if you don't give me answers in the next sixty seconds, I will rip your asshole out through your left eye socket."

The whistling from the big man's nose suddenly got louder and faster.

After a moment, he looked at the bartender and said, "Take 'em."

The bartender suddenly pulled a sawed-off shotgun from beneath the bar at the same time the patron on the left pulled a .38 revolver.

Tomás, having five minutes earlier decided which of the three men at the bar he would put rounds in first, fired twice at the bartender. The bullets ripped into the bartender's right shoulder and trigger hand. His shotgun fired and a portion of the ceiling exploded.

I fired my Glock at the patron with the .38 revolver, catching him in the knee and hip.

He tumbled off the barstool in agony.

The big man fired a long-barrel revolver at Tomás but missed.

From a crouched firing position I made a seven-foot leap at the big man and brought the grip of my gun once into his nose and once into his mouth in quick succession. His nose and teeth crunched, blood slopping out of both.

He wasn't done.

"Motherfucker," he slurred before catching me in a rib-crushing bear hug and running me into a wall. Hitting the wall squeezed out the last bit of air from my lungs.

Tomás would have helped had he not been busy with the second man at the bar, who was now in possession of a machine pistol set on full auto; bullets ripped up the wall and door of the bar. Tomás dove to the side of the jukebox, waiting for his shot.

I was about three seconds from passing out.

Still holding my Glock, I squeezed three — four — rounds down toward the floor.

The big man dropped me and stumbled away. I gulped in as much air as I could.

My bullets found a path down his left thigh and into his knee.

I fired at the guy with the machine pistol.

No choice but put him down.

One in the right temple.

Done.

The big man had crawled to a wall and sat himself against it.

"You're dead," he half grunted, half laughed. "You are so fucking dead. You're gonna see all of us soon. Real soon, motherfucker."

"Shut up," Tomás said before bringing the butt of his gun across the big man's jaw.

We stood in the doorway of the big guy's office.

"Jesus."

On a black metal desk was a kilo of cocaine. Apparently, we had interrupted sorting the coke into small baggies. On a chair in a corner were two large bags of pills. And there were the four stacks of hundred-dollar bills.

I spotted a small black safe and decided it was coming with us.

My phone rang.

"I got a Spring Lake police unit on its way to some biker shithole out there," O'Donnell said. "Is that you?"

"That'd be me," I said.

"God*dammit!*"

Just as Tomás and I were about to bug out, the beat-up sofa in the office moved. We pulled our weapons on it. Cautiously, I jostled the sofa away from the wall; a young woman — sixteen or seventeen — naked, huddled and scared out of her mind. On her upper right arm was a recent brand of a swastika. Her fully dilated pupils told me she was higher than the International Space Station.

She stared like a wounded animal up at me waiting for the killing shot or mercy. She was trying to say something. I knelt slowly, assuring her everything was alright.

"Get her something to cover up," I said to Tomás.

She tried to speak again.

I got closer.

This time I heard her: "Nigger."

I took the big man's riding jacket from Tomás, draped the jacket around her shoulders and stood.

"We gotta go, jefe," Tomás said.

Leaving Taffy's would have been so much easier had the tires of my rental Caddy not been slashed. It also looked as if someone had tried to crowbar the trunk open.

"Shit," Tomás said. "Now what're we gonna do?"

Tomás had always wanted a classic Ford truck in sapphire blue with whitewall tires.

And frankly, I think I look pretty good in the saddle of a Harley Softail Fat Boy . . .

24

"You know how many useless UHF antennas and first-gen satellite TV dishes are sitting on top of houses and apartment buildings and office buildings in Detroit?"

I was sitting on my sofa staring at the small black safe from Taffy's on the Lake on my coffee table.

I've done a lot of things in my life.

Cracking a safe is not one of them.

Lucy sat on the granite work surface of my kitchen island eating from a bag of tortilla chips. An open jar of my salsa was next to her.

"Sit on a chair," I said still staring at the safe. "Don't sit on my island. I prepare food there."

"Well, I don't know *exactly* how many UHF antennas and TV dishes there are on buildings in Detroit," she continued unabated. "But I'm guessing a shitload. Just sitting there being nests for pigeons and hawks and falcons."

I sighed and flopped back on the sofa. "Is there a point, Lucy? Or is this just you free associating?"

"Oh, there's a point, big guy," she said, hopping down from the kitchen counter. She took a seat next to me. "Okay, so I couldn't figure out who spoofed your phone besides me. I mean, I can usually trace a piggyback in my sleep. I wouldn't be much of a digital-diva if I couldn't do that, right? But this one? Pure freakin' genius!" She paused. Then she said, "You want me to open that for you? I mean 'cause it ain't gonna open itself."

"You can crack this?" I said.

"Oh, my God!" she laughed. "A *five-year-old* could crack that! Move."

I slid down the sofa a bit and Lucy took my position.

"It's an old Nationwide Class B combination safe," she said, staring at the metal box on my coffee table. "Thicker metal makes hearing the tumblers a little harder."

"You've really had a misspent youth, haven't you?" I said.

Lucy slid off the sofa and, on her knees in front of the safe, gently placed an ear against the door of the safe.

No sooner had she done this, Jimmy

knocked on the door. As usual, he entered without waiting for an invitation. Seeing me on the sofa and Lucy with her ear against the metal door of an office safe, Jimmy said, "Uh — bad time?"

"Hi, Jimmy!" Lucy said without taking her ear from the safe door.

Jimmy was carrying a deep purple Club Brutus gym bag and wearing a white *gi* — the uniform used in the practice of jujitsu — tied at the waist was a yellow belt.

"Holy shit," I said. "You've already earned your yellow belt?"

Jimmy stood a little taller. He smoothed his *gi* with a hand. "Yessir. Mr. Brutus says I'm a fast learner."

"And Brutus doesn't just hand out compliments," I said.

Lucy pulled away from the safe and turned to look at Jimmy.

"Wow," she said. "Ain't you a sexy beast?"

Had Jimmy's skin tone been a bit lighter, his blushing would have been very apparent.

"I, uh — I's just wondering if everything was all right," Jimmy said. "Mr. Ogilvy said you had some trouble the other night? Something about the shed?"

"Just a couple rats, Jimmy," I said. "We shooed 'em away."

"Okay. Cool," Jimmy said, his eyes darting from me to Lucy and back again.

"Something else?"

"Uh, yeah —" he said. "Miss Three Rivers?"

"Jimmy," she said with disappointment in her voice. "If we're ever to be friends and lovers, you're just gonna have to call me Lucy. Or Snuggle Muffin."

"Yeah, okay, uh — listen," Jimmy stammered, "Miss Carmela and Miss Sylvia, they really like you. I just want to make sure you treatin' 'em right, okay? I mean 'cause sometimes I walk past they house and all I can hear is your music —"

"EDM and techno. You like EDM and techno?"

"I'm just saying I know they can't half hear," Jimmy said, "but you might want to turn the music down a bit. And they got used to me cooking for 'em once or twice a week. If you could do that, I'm sure they'd appreciate it. Maybe trim they toenails once a month or so —"

"Their — toenails?"

"And paint 'em," Jimmy said. "They like that Sally Hansen *Sonic Boom* color in the summer. Number 226. You can get it at Walgreens or CVS."

"Anything else?"

"Them ladies will take good care of you, even if you don't care about 'em," Jimmy said. "I'm kinda hopin' you learn to care about them." Then he looked at me and said, "Anything I can do, Mr. Snow, you let me know, okay?"

"Thanks, Jimmy," I said. "Now go kick Brutus's ass."

Jimmy nodded to me. Then he nodded to Lucy and said, "Miss Three Rivers."

"Snuggle Muffin," Lucy said.

After Jimmy closed my front door behind him, Lucy looked at me and said, "Is Gomer for real?"

"He's as real as they come, Lucy," I said. "Be nice to him or you and me are gonna have problems. In fact, just stop all this hard-case bullshit, awright? It's exhausting."

Lucy put her ear back against the square black safe door. Slowly, she put her hand on the combination dial and began turning it one click at a time. Four numbers later, she gently took the handle, pushed it down and cautiously pulled the door open a half-inch or so.

"Sometimes, dudes booby-trap these things," she said, opening the door completely. She turned to me and said, "Ta-daa!"

Wearing rubber kitchen gloves, I removed

211

a .38 caliber Smith and Wesson revolver from the safe. It was secured in a plastic bag with three spent shells. There was about five grand in cash, all tens and twenties, and files stuffed with neo-Nazi flyers, propaganda, agendas, and phone numbers. There were four DVDs with the initials "BO" and dates over a two-year period. There was a thick file which held some very damning information on some very interesting people, including Barney Olsen, Esq. And there were three burner phones, one in a plastic bag with dried blood on it, and a digital recorder.

Finally, there were photos.

Young girls in various stages of undress and looking drugged to their eyeballs. Young girls gagged and chained over the bar in the secret room at Barney Olsen's house. Each photo had numbers written on back. Three of the numbers corresponded with the names in the files. The fourth set of numbers proved to be a coded mystery.

"What's all this shit?" Lucy said craning her neck to catch a glimpse of the photos. "What are those pictures of?"

"Nothing you should know about. Ever," I said, quickly stuffing the photos back into a file folder. "You were saying something earlier about a pterodactyl and a warp engine?"

"Yeah," Lucy said peering deeper into the safe. "Holy shit! How much money is that?"

"Don't touch anything!" I said, swatting her hand away from a stack of cash. "Warp engine, Lucy. Focus!"

"Okay, so all communications these days is high frequency digital, right?"

"If you say so."

"Awright, so imagine having your own private cell phone network run on old analog equipment at a low frequency. So low people think it's just background noise. Nobody cares about monitoring that end of the spectrum anymore. Whoever spoofed your phone is using re-tasked UHF antennas and twenty-year-old satellite TV dishes. And that junk is *everywhere*!"

"Can you locate the source?"

"I'm Lucy Three Rivers," she said. "The Original Digital-Diva! The Queen of Code! But you have to do something for me first, slick."

I felt my eyebrows furrow. "And that would be?"

25

If shopping malls are dying out, you could've fooled me.

I found myself at Twelve Oaks Mall in Farmington Hills, thirty miles northwest of Mexicantown. I was there on a Saturday afternoon with a smartass nineteen-year-old hacker, two elderly stoners — Carmela and Sylvia — and about five thousand zombie-walkers with shopping bags, texting on cell phones or gulping down Starbuck's coffee concoctions.

I figured Carmela and Sylvia would be infinitely more help to Lucy in choosing women's clothing than I could ever be. Plus, the trip might serve as a bond between the girls. So far, things were good between the ladies; just as Carmela and Sylvia had adopted Jimmy as their beloved son, so they had instantly taken to Lucy as a beloved daughter.

Lucy, on the other hand, didn't initially

appear comfortable with such attention and affection. The sign of someone who'd been scratching and scrapping on their own for too long.

I'd gone shopping once with Tatina at Paleet, a large and confusing mall in Oslo. I would have gone mad if not for two things: 1) I liked watching Tatina try things on, and 2) I knew I was going to be treated to a plate of Pinnekjøtt — salted, dried, and smoked lamb ribs — for having held her purse, carried her shopping bags and complimented how nice her butt looked in this dress or that pair of jeans.

I'd even complimented how nice her butt was when she tried on shoes.

I was getting nothing out of this journey to Twelve Oaks, save for the bill.

While the girls whirligigged through the Contemporary Women's section of Macy's, I sat on the solitary bench provided for bored husbands and confused boyfriends and had a pleasant phone chat with FBI Special Agent Megan O'Donnell.

"You pull shit like this again, August, and swear to God, I will shove a stick of dynamite up your ass and light a very short fuse."

"Well, that doesn't sound at all pleasant."

O'Donnell drew in a long, deep breath. "You're clear on this Taffy's escapade.

Barely. There was enough there — including the girl — to nail these bastards on statutory rape, drug trafficking, money laundering and an assortment of firearms violations. The guy you or Tomás put down was wanted on felony murder of a teenage girl in Indiana, so I don't think anybody's gonna come after you with a vengeance on that one. You're just lucky the local cops saw the mess, vomited and gladly handed it over to me and the State cops. I have the feeling those BMC assholes will want to go directly to a deal, so you won't even be implicated in your O.K. Corral-style gunfight. I cleaned up your mess, August, including your trashed rental car. Oh, and don't *ever* have your lawyer — what's his name?"

"David G. Baker."

"Don't *ever* have that annoying fuck-bag David Goddamn Baker call my office again!"

I'd have to remember to send G a case of good Pinot Noir for being an *effective* fuck-bag.

O'Donnell continued telling me what a pain in the ass I was. Meanwhile a sticky-faced kid crunching a luminescent orange sucker was staring at me.

I smiled at him.

He flipped me the finger.

His mom grabbed him by the collar, apologized profusely, then hustled him off.

O'Donnell finally took a ragged breath.

"Yeah, so anyway," I began, "I have this safe from the biker bar at home and there's stuff you need to see."

"Gee, I'd just *love* to see even *more* evidence I can't use, August, because you fucking stole it from a crime scene," O'Donnell said. "And by the way, I've got forensics people going over that lawyer's house — what's his name? The guy on the buses."

"Barney Olsen."

"I'll tell you this much," O'Donnell said. "Three bullet holes, no slugs. Bleach-degraded blood splatter. And neighbors who heard and saw nothing. Whoever cleaned that up was quick and professional. Bikers aren't exactly known for cleaning up their messes."

"Set a meeting of your white whale cabal tonight," I said. "LaBelle's. Eleven o'clock."

We disconnected.

"Is this all right?" Lucy said holding a bright yellow lacy-frilly-top-thing three inches from my face. "Carmela and Sylvia like it. I mean — it *is* okay, right?"

She held out the price tag for me to see.

"It's fine," I said.

"Yeah, we're cool, ladies!" Lucy yelled back to Carmela and Sylvia. They grinned and gave the thumbs-up sign. She started to walk back to the girls before stopping and turning to me.

"I, uh — I don't know how long I'll be around," she said. "I — don't stay nowhere for very long. You think Carmela and Sylvia will hold these for me if I go away for a while?"

"Every now and then, home is where you happen to land, kid. It just happens."

Lucy looked at me for a moment before saying, "So, I mean, is that a yes, they'll hold on to this shit for me? Or what?"

"Yes," I said. "They'll hold on to your shit."

"Cool!"

I bought Carmela and Sylvia silver charm bracelets before we left the mall. Amazing how the old girls had gotten under my considerably thick skin and settled on my heart.

"Oh, you didn't have to do this, Mr. Snow," Carmela said, grinning as she stared at her silver crucifix charm. "You're young. Pinch your pennies. That's why Sylvia and I can eat anywhere we want and watch the Netflix in our retirement. Because we pinched pennies at your age."

We got burgers at the Basement Burger Bar in downtown Farmington and finished with ice cream at Silver Dairy on Grand River Avenue, where I got a call from Tatina.

"Oh, my *God!*" she began. "You're *trending!*"

"I'm what?"

"Trending! On Twitter!" she said. "*And* YouTube! Oh, my God! Over two hundred thousand views on YouTube! You and Tomás and another man being arrested at that Mexican restaurant! Some sort of immigration protest!"

In the background one of Tatina's friends shouted something.

"Three hundred fifty *thousand* views!" Tatina said. "What is going *on* over there? Are they deporting *all* the Mexicans? If they are, come here, August! I mean we don't have to — you know — shack up. Is that how you say it? 'Shack up'?"

We talked for another five minutes.

Gooey stuff.

Stuff that might tarnish my former-marine, tough-guy image if it ever got out.

After we disconnected, I found the video on YouTube, much to my embarrassment. Me, Tomás and Trent T.R. Ogilvy being pushed into the back of an ICE SUV while twenty or thirty people surrounded the vehicle while chanting "I am a *Dreamer!*" and "Stop deportations *now!*"

I assumed the person who took the video was a young black man by his phrasing and the tenor of his voice. With me square in the final frame, he ended his narration by saying, "Ain't this some fucked-up shit? Brotha can't even get a taco in this town without gettin' jammed up!"

Later that evening I stood over Lucy's shoulder looking at one of her two laptop screens. She was wearing her new yellow lacey-top-thing and new jeans by some high-end French designer. Lines of numbers and clumps of symbols fluttered across both laptop screens. Lucy stared at the cascade of code, occasionally muttering "Yep," or "Saw that one coming" or "Bullshit."

"You're sure about the origin of the signal," I said.

"Were you like this with Skittles?" she said without taking her eyes from her laptop screens. "I mean, did you bug him while he was working? *Yes,* I'm sure of where the signal's coming from! Now go be annoying somewhere else."

"Thanks," I said before leaving her room at Carmela and Sylvia's house.

Twenty minutes later, I was at LaBelle's

Soul Hole Donut & Pastry Shop.

"You got some goodies to share, baby?" Lady B said as I gave her a kiss on her cheek.

"Sure do," I said. "Everybody here?"

"Everybody except Elena and Father Grabowski." Lady B walked me to the back of the shop. "He had some sort of Catholic thing. Y'all just love yo little rules, regulations, rituals and secrets, don't you?"

"And incense," I said. "Don't forget incense."

"Elena thought it best just to hang close with that big-ass brute she married to."

"That 'big-ass brute' just happens to be my godfather."

"Like I said," Lady B said with a smile. "Big-ass brute."

Most of the kitchen, including the floor and the round table where O'Donnell and undercover DEA/ICE captain Foley sat, was draped in plastic sheeting.

"Gonna paint the walls," Lady B said.

"This better be worth it," O'Donnell said as I sat at the table.

Foley glanced at his watch. Then looking up, he smiled at Lady B. "You got any of those strawberry-filled Long Johns, Lady B? I feel like a couple of those."

"Coffee, too, baby?" Lady B said, grinning.

"Cup of joe be nice," Foley glanced again at his watch.

"Got some place to be?" I said.

"Yeah," he said. "Home. In bed. You'll be glad to know Mexicantown's catching a break tonight. The team's in West Bloomfield, rounding up some off-the-radar Muslims and Chaldeans."

" 'First, they came for the Socialists, and I did not speak out — because I was not a Socialist.' "

"What's that supposed to fucking mean?" he said.

I took a seat at the small round table and handed O'Donnell one of the files that had come from the safe. Three very explosive pages.

O'Donnell opened the file. After a moment the color drained from her face. She whispered, "Jesus," before cutting her eyes to Foley, then me.

"Now you understand why it's better for me to have the safe than you," I said. I turned to Foley. "You keepin' an eye on Henshaw?"

Before Foley could answer, Lady B returned with a plate of Long Johns and a carafe of coffee. Sitting the donuts at the center of the table, Lady B carefully poured Foley a cup of coffee. He grabbed one of the strawberry Long Johns and took a big, satisfying bite.

"You're the best, Lady B," he said, his mouth full of the Long John.

"Oh, I know, baby," she said.

Then she pulled a 9mm semi-automatic gun with suppressor from her apron and fired into the back of Foley's head. His face slammed down into the plate of donuts. She fired a second bullet into the back of his head.

"Fuck!" O'Donnell shouted. She was on her feet, weapon drawn, aimed at Lady B.

I did the same, not sure if I was tasting Foley's blood or strawberry filling.

"Goddammit!" I shouted, aiming my Glock at Lady B. "What the fuck!"

Lady B quickly laid her silenced 9mm on the table and raised her hands.

"Y'all got about sixty seconds," she said.

"You just killed a federal fucking agent!" O'Donnell shouted.

"Fifty-five seconds," Lady B said.

"What the hell are you talking about?" I said.

"Foley was running the trafficking operation out of ICE. Not Henshaw," Lady B said.

"I *know* that!" I said. "It's in the file I just

223

handed to O'Donnell! Goddammit, Lady B!"

Lady B turned to O'Donnell. "Pay outs. Raids. Doctored detention logs. What y'all *don't* know is what brings us to the next thirty seconds of y'alls life. He was about a day and a dollar ahead of y'all: Three of his biker buddies is about to bust up in here and kill us all. Way I see it, y'all can read me my rights just before we all get dead — or we can take care of *real* business."

"Where?" I said.

Her hands still above her head, Lady B signaled that two men were about to breach the back door while one was preparing to come in through the front.

"We're not done here," O'Donnell said to Lady B.

"Oh, baby, I didn't expect we was," Lady B said.

I gave her a hard look and said, "When this is done, you and me are gonna have a serious chat about why you spoofed my phone."

Lady B, in possession of her suppressed 9mm again, moved quickly through the kitchen doors toward the front of the bakery.

"Go with her!" O'Donnell said.

"Baby-girl," Lady B said, "I been coverin' my own ass for thirty-five years." Then she said to me, "You stay right here, Young Snow. She gon' need a second hot barrel when they come through."

O'Donnell and I stood on opposite sides of the steel reinforced back door watching as thermite sizzled and burned through the lock.

. . . Three . . . Two . . .

26

. . . One . . .

The back door burst open. Two men in BMC biker gear rushed in with silenced revolvers.

"FBI!" O'Donnell said.

Neither man much cared which letters of the alphabet O'Donnell spouted.

They turned and leveled off to fire. O'Donnell and I put two slugs in each man. They dropped. One dead. The other soon to follow.

Lady B limped into the kitchen.

She'd taken a slug in her left leg.

"He's on the run," she said. "I caught him in the shoulder and thigh."

"Which way?" I said.

"Train station, across the park. I'll see if I can get this asshole to talk," she said. *"Go!"*

I ran into the thick heat and midnight darkness blanketing the space between the back of the donut shop and the looming carcass of the Michigan Central Train Depot. The land stretching out in front of the station was less of a park and more of an open sore. Any one of the moving shadows I saw could have been a homeless man looking for a spot to sleep or homeless woman looking for a private area to piss.

I made my way through Detroit's version of a Hieronymus Bosch painting, past faces pleading their cases from hell.

I spotted a shadow limping quickly away from the park and toward the train station.

A car squealed from beneath the Vernor Street underpass to the west side of the station.

Headlights flashed twice.

On the edge of the park, fifty yards from the car, I took a stance and fired three shots at the limping man's ride. I ran, closing the gap. The passenger fired off several rounds at me. We traded fire. A homeless man took a slug in the chest. One of my rounds shattered a rear passenger window. The car squealed away, leaving the limping man to fend for himself.

He ran for the cover of the train station.

I pursued him into the looming hundred-year-old train station.

Echo of labored breathing.

"You're losing a lot of blood," I called out

as my eyes followed the lead of my gun sight and his trail of blood. "The harder you make this, the more blood you lose. Talk to me and I'll get you help. Or you die the hard way. Your choice."

"Not much of a choice," the man said, his voice bouncing off the high, arching walls of the station.

"Only one you're gonna get." I moved through the flickers of shadow and light. "Your ride burned rubber outta here. Be smart and talk to me."

"So, what do you wanna talk about, asshole? The Tigers? The Constitution?"

"No, let's talk about something you actually know something about," I said. "Like who runs the trafficking ring. Or who killed Barney Olsen."

"Olsen's dead?"

I moved slowly up a wide staircase through an obstacle course of steel and concrete rubble, broken glass and junction boxes stripped of wiring. In a time before my birth, the train station had been a jewel in Detroit's crown with its Greek-inspired high-arched ceilings, frescos and gleaming chandeliers. Now, after decades of pillaging by copper strippers and antiques thieves, all that remained were the whispers of ghosts listening for the call of their train.

"Yeah," I said. "Olsen's been wiped off the planet. His place cleaned out. Guess that means the BMCs have their asses hanging out now. So tell me something."

A shadow appeared at the top of the staircase.

A shadow holding a five-foot length of pipe.

"Ever imagine how you'd go out?" the man said.

"Yeah," I said. "Never thought it'd be at a goddamn train station."

I snugged my Glock away and said, "So we doin' this old school?"

"Why not, homeboy?" the man laughed. "I got nothin' to lose."

"Yes," I said, picking up a four-foot length of pipe lying on the staircase. "You do."

I wasn't in an ideal position; fighting up an incline is infinitely harder than fighting down, especially if it's with bo-staff style. Everything Sun Tzu warned against doing in his military strategy manifesto, *The Art of War*, I was about to do. Always give a dying man a chance.

Of course, I never claimed to be the smartest guy in the room . . .

The man brought his pipe down with considerable killing force. I blocked it, pushed hard and gained a quick two steps up. He was bleeding from his left hip and I swept my length of pipe into his wound. He howled and limped back five or six steps, allowing me to finally reach the second level.

My advantage didn't last long.

He brought his pipe down. It glanced off mine, but not before catching the edge of my right shoulder. I could feel the sting of warm blood.

I backed him up another five feet, the sound of the colliding metal pipes echoing in the dim light and deep shadows of the station.

He brought his pipe into my right arm, then to the left side of my rib cage. I stumbled back. He advanced and brought his pipe down with crushing strength toward my head. At the last second, I blocked his strike.

His breathing was labored. Blood streamed out of his wounds.

I didn't want him dead.

I wanted questions answered.

I swept my length of steel pipe into his wounded hip, then up with a jab to his wounded shoulder.

He yelped, stumbled backwards and fell.

I quickly brought the tip of my steel pipe to his shoulder wound and pushed.

He screamed and released his pipe, letting

it roll away.

"I will shove this pipe all the way through and twist if you don't give me names," I said.

"They'll kill me!"

"You're already dead, asshole," I said.

Keeping pressure on the man's shoulder wound with the pipe, I knelt down, made the Sign of the Cross over his face and said, "Bless me, Father, for I have sinned. It has been blah-blah-blah since my last confession. Now you say something . . . and make sure it's something me and God wanna hear before the devil snatches your ass."

For a man who was losing blood faster than the Lions lose offensive yardage, he was quite talkative. Just before he lost consciousness I got a call from O'Donnell; in the background I could hear the squawk of sirens.

"You got a back way out?" O'Donnell said.

"I can find one," I said. "Why?"

"Because I don't want to have to explain you to my boss," she said.

"Tell the EMTs you saw a guy run into the train station," I said. "Maybe second level."

She disconnected.

Before leaving I touched the unconscious man's carotid artery: His pulse was weak, but he was still topside.

Then I found a rear exit out of the train station and ran into the thick midnight darkness.

"Notice the coffee and spice notes with dark chocolate and ginger on the palate," I said, carefully dispensing two fingers of very rare and expensive Glenglassaugh 30-year-old malt whisky into a Waterford Crystal tumbler — one of a set of four such tumblers my mother had given my father on his fortieth birthday.

O'Donnell sat at my kitchen island, hunched over the tumbler. Once I'd finished pouring, she took the tumbler to her lips, snapped her head back and swallowed the entire two fingers.

"Wow," I said. "Must be pledge night at Alpha Kappa Snow."

"I've been suspended."

I poured her more scotch.

"I read Director Phillips into the operation. Put him on the phone with his boss. After getting his ass chewed out by his boss, he chewed me out. Said I'd endangered an off-book operation. Said I was 'uncharacteristically irresponsible.' " This had to be killing her. O'Donnell loved her job. Loved law enforcement. And Phillips was someone she respected, even admired.

"What about Lady B?" I said.

O'Donnell gave a bitter laugh. "What about her? I handcuffed her to a support beam before I went out looking for you. By the time the cops, EMS and my office arrive, she's in her kitchen with four others making donuts and baking goddamn cookies. Place was clean as a whistle."

"If it weren't for her we probably wouldn't be drinking scotch," I said.

"She shot a man in the head, August," O'Donnell said. "She *executed* him. This isn't Dodge City and we're not the fucking Dalton Gang."

"Dodge City got nothing on The D," I said. "And the Daltons wouldn't have lasted two minutes past the stroke of noon on Mack Avenue and Helen."

Forty minutes later, O'Donnell was completely in the bag.

Refusing to let her get behind the wheel, I helped her to the staircase landing, assuring her my intentions were honorable. A key clanked around in my front door. O'Donnell reached for a gun that I'd deprived her of after her third whisky. Luckily, I was strapped and drew on the opening front door.

"I'm not interrupting you getting your

pecker wet, am I?"

Lucy.

After I put O'Donnell to bed, I came downstairs. Lucy was seated at my kitchen island with one of her laptops open.

"What are you doing up so late?"

"She your girlfriend?

"No."

"Thank the Sun God," Lucy said. "Too many black, red and brown brothas under the spell of white-girl witchcraft."

I held my phone up and showed Lucy a picture of Tatina.

"This is my girlfriend," I said. "And I don't cheat. Now why are you here?"

"Wow," Lucy said, looking at the photo of Tatina. "Nice. She live here?"

"Oslo. Now —"

"Wait a minute," Lucy said. "Oslo, *Norway*? You couldn't find a black girl in *Detroit*?"

"Lucy, swear to God —"

She turned her laptop screen to me.

I felt my mouth go dry and my blood begin to boil as I looked at the screen.

"Is that what I think it is?"

"Yep," Lucy said. "It ain't no milk and cookies keepin' me up, tough guy. By the way — you got any milk and cookies?"

27

It was a sweltering Thursday afternoon and I'd spent the last thirty-five minutes on I-75 North trying to avoid hitting orange-vested road crews that all looked like ZZ Top, elderly drivers going five miles under the minimum speed limit and SUVs with drivers apparently using underdeveloped telekinesis skills to make lane changes.

Summer freeway traffic in Detroit is enough to turn the Pope into a road-rage maniac.

"Wow," the young guy in the parking lot said. He was wearing expensive nut-squeezing jeans, a Tommy Bahama Hawaiian-style shirt, navy-blue Tony Lama cowboy boots and had a leather messenger bag slung over his shoulder. "Nice bike."

"Thanks," I said, not in the mood for small talk. I put the kickstand of my newly acquired Harley down, turned the engine off and dismounted.

"Me? I got a Kawasaki Ninja," the guy said trailing me to the door of SoundNation Recording Studio. "S'like having a rocket strapped to your balls."

"I'll remember that if I ever want a kid's toy strapped to my sack."

He laughed, came to my side and put his hand out. "Brad Lanzetti. Viral marketing manager, Shout-Out Communications."

I stopped and turned to him. "Listen. Brad. How 'bout you be somewhere else for about fifteen, twenty minutes."

"Hey, look, pal," he said. "I don't know what your problem is, but —"

I pulled my Glock and ratcheted a bullet into the chamber.

"Yeah, sure, cool," Brad said, high-tailing it away from the studio.

Inside, I approached Dahlia Delaney, aka White Girl, and said, "Duke in?"

"Mr. Snow! How nice to see you!"

"Duke," I repeated. "Is he here?"

"Uh — yes — but you know the routine, Mr. Snow —"

"Think I'll keep my gun this time," I said, holding up my Glock for her to see.

I walked past her and started down the ugly Jackson Pollock-style hallway.

"Stop right fucking there," she said. She

was holding her Smith and Wesson 686 Plus on me.

I walked back to her and quickly twisted it out of her small hand.

I turned and began walking down the hallway again.

"You're too nice to pull the trigger," I said.

"I'm not."

Behind me, White Girl pick up her desk phone. Her voice trembling, she said, "August Snow is here. Lock him down."

I got past three of the studios, no problem.

The Compton twins, like a meat-starved NFL defensive line, were waiting for me by the fourth and largest studio. Black America's answer to Elvis Presley — Blelvis — was in the studio wearing headphones and gyrating in front of a microphone.

I slowly laid my gun and White Girl's gun on the hallway carpet and said, "Let me pass and nobody gets hurt."

Funny thing about being well over six feet and having more muscles than humanly necessary: The mass and weight of such muscles tends to slow a person down, accentuating awkwardness in the effort to move quickly. Theoretically, being smaller and lighter would be an advantage in a confrontation with such human hulks. Of course, I only had to be wrong once with these mammoth killers; getting hit by either of them would be owning a face-full of M198 Howitzer cannon fire.

The twins charged me like two blood-thirsty tackles off the line of scrimmage.

One twin went high, the other low, both with their arms outstretched.

I kicked one in his head, sending him crashing into a wall. That gave me a split second to duck the other twin. On his way flying past me I was able to land two quick punches to his solar plexus. I knew that wouldn't be the end of it.

Unfortunately, I didn't expect they'd be quite so fast on their feet.

Both men, hunched and grunting like angry buffalo, sized me up for a second before making another run at me. This time I wasn't so lucky: One of the twins grabbed me around the waist and lifted me off my feet. I managed to keep both arms free. Just as I started feeling my ribs crack, the other twin came up behind his brother and landed two solid punches to my face. I felt warm blood spill from my nose and pool in my mouth. Another hit to the face or another three seconds in the vice-grip of the first twin's arms and I'd be slop-in-the-trough.

I could feel my ribs getting ready to snap from the twin holding me in a bear hug. I brought the palms of my hands hard and fast against his ears.

He howled, dropped me and stumbled backwards, holding his bleeding ears.

Knee to his ribs.

Kick to the sweet-spot just above his left knee.

He dropped like a three-hundred-pound bag of wet sand.

But not before his brother reached one of the guns I'd laid on the floor.

He leveled off.

I shouldered my way through the door of the fourth recording studio.

A bullet popped into the doorjamb.

"Stop! *Now,* goddammit!"

Duke.

He stood in the doorway of his office, fists planted in his hips and staring up at the Compton Twin holding the gun. The twin hung his head like a shamed child, then handed the gun quietly to Duke. With surprising affection, Duke said, "Look after your brother." Then he scowled at me. "Next time, make a mothafuckin' appointment."

I brushed myself off, wiped most of the blood from my face, then pointed to Blelvis and said, "Love your work, man."

"Thank you," he said with a half-smile,

half-snarl. "Thank you very much."

Today Duke was wearing lime-green plaid golf shorts with matching ankle socks, white buck golf shoes, a marine-blue polo shirt and matching Kangol bucket hat.

"I shoulda let Fin pop you," Duke said as we entered his office.

"You sonuvabitch," I said. "You sold them your old pipeline and you didn't tell me."

"What are you talking about?"

"The routes you used to traffic guns, drugs and women," I said. "You sold your proprietary smuggling routes while you were in prison. That's how you can afford this place. I've seen the banking records. The deep records. The Bank of Montreal. Bank of Canada. The Central Bank of Bahamas. Five years ago, you couldn't afford a pack of cigarettes at the prison commissary. Suddenly, you're shopping for Royal Oak real estate and recording equipment."

"You always prided yourself on being smart," Duke said, pouring himself a whiskey. "Why should I make your job easier? You a detective — so detect, mothafucka. And stop bleeding on my goddamn carpet!"

"I should have shot you when I had the fucking chance six years ago," I said.

Duke laughed, poured me a whiskey and said, "And yo daddy shoulda shot me fifteen, twenty years before that. Honor and integrity's gonna be the death of y'all Snow men. Here." Duke had reached into a desk drawer and pulled out a box of Kleenex. He slid the box to me. While I wiped blood from my face, he took a call.

"Ain't about a thang, White Girl," Duke said. "You done good. *Real* good, baby girl. We cool. You did everything right and then some. For real." He hung up and said to me, "See what you done did, mothafucka? You upset White Girl."

"She pulled on me," I said, dropping my used and bloodied Kleenex on his desk and grabbing the tumbler of whiskey. I knocked the drink back and tossed the glass on the sofa behind me. "Now let's stop fucking around, okay? Tell me who you sold your pipeline to or, swear to God, I'll bring this whole thing crashing down around that watermelon-sized head of yours."

"Ain't no reason to get all nasty 'n shit," Duke said. He took an appreciative sip of his whiskey and admired its amber color. "Truth is, I have no clue who bought my routes. Couldn't care less neither. Deal was done by intermediaries. Folks with lots of dirty cash and nowhere to wash it."

"You doin' laundry now?"

"This place is legit," Duke said. "One

241

hundred. Ain't washin' nothing 'scept my own funky drawers. Like I told you before, boy; the path I was on didn't serve me no more — and sellin' my routes was the cost of this new, healthier path."

"Give me a name, Duke."

"Or goddamn what?"

I smiled and slowly walked around to where Duke sat. In rapid succession, I grabbed a fistful of his polo shirt and punched him three times in the face.

"I'm not afraid of you," I said as Duke's bloodied head lolled on his neck. "Never have been. You wanna play the devil with me? Get to know the demons I've already wrestled with."

28

Two people were waiting for me in the lobby of SoundNation: Tomás and Lucy.

Tomás casually held a long-barrel S&W Model 629 at his side. Lucy, a dwarf next to him, held her six-inch Marttiini hunting knife, her arms folded across her chest.

"You came to see Duke without backup?" Tomás said.

"What's she doing here?" I said pointing to Lucy.

"Kid's hard to shake," Tomás said.

"I can handle myself," Lucy said defiantly.

"I'm reminded," I began, "of what someone once said about bringing a knife to a gunfight."

Lucy smiled innocently.

Then, in a tempered steel flash, she threw the knife. Behind me, White Girl — standing by her desk chair and crying — was pointing her 686 Plus at us in a trembling hand. Lucy's knife planted itself deep into the headrest of White Girl's chair. Enough of a signal for White Girl to drop the gun. She collapsed to the floor sobbing.

"You were saying?" Lucy said, walking past me to retrieve her knife.

Once Lucy had retrieved her knife I walked to White Girl and crouched near her.

"You're no good at playing tough guy," I said. "And Duke's gonna get you killed insisting you pretend to be one. Either get good with a gun — or get a new job."

Before leaving SoundNation, I gave Tomás a download on what transpired between Duke and me. His jaw flexed, veins enlarged and pulsed on his neck as I spoke. I told him I needed to fly solo on my next stop tonight and why, but after that I'd keep him well aware of my movements.

"And since I'm not ready to have another death of a kid haunting me the rest of my life," I said to Lucy, "you stay put by your computers or I'll drop-kick you back to Vegas. And you can explain to Skittles why you're back to jacking one-armed bandits and spoofing room keys instead of doing real shit."

Lucy was silent for a moment. Then she said, "Speaking of jacking, looks like somebody jacked your face up. What's up with that?"

I took Tomás and Lucy for a big plate of chorizo, shrimp, steak and chicken tacos at Taqueria El Rey as my act of contrition.

Later Thursday evening, while Lucy took a deep dive into the Sargasso Sea of the dark net, I took a chance and drove to a barber shop on West Grand River Avenue and 7 Mile Road, a stretch where black iron gates offer cold security comfort to liquor stores, fried fish restaurants and hair salons.

Smitty's Cuts & Curls has been in business for over thirty years. My father occasionally got a trim at Smitty's. He got a trim for the same reasons I, as a young patrolman and later a detective, occasionally got a trim at Smitty's: Dependable, boots-on-the-ground intelligence. From three barber chairs and, during the summer months, two lawn chairs out front, information was traded, bought, bartered, gathered and fresh-squeezed by Lucius "Smitty" Smith and his itinerate operatives.

If Smitty's Cuts & Curls had depended solely on haircuts and women's weaves, it would have folded twenty years ago. Instead, on a northwest Detroit street always teetering on the edge of bloody explosion or financial implosion, Smitty's thrived, protected by cops and thugs alike. Smitty mostly put in with doing the right thing even if he would swear on a stack of Gideon bibles he didn't care who gave or got the bullet.

One of Smitty's best operatives was a young guy named Sylvian Russo, aka "Sly," aka "Bags," aka "Sweets."

I knew him as "Sweets" and that's the name I shouted as I approached the lanky black man who was in the middle of a craps game with four other guys.

"Aw, shit, goddammit —" Sweets said just before cutting and sprinting west on 7 Mile toward the Southfield Freeway.

I quickly caught up to him, dragging him by the collar of his knock-off Prada shirt to an alley behind Aunt Loo Loo's Fried Fish Emporium three storefronts down from Smitty's.

"Jesus," I said, releasing his collar.

"Really, niggah?" Sweets said. "You gon make a brotha run in *this* heat? I mean do I *look* like I'm from damned Kenya to you?"

"You used to make me work for this," I said, trying to catch my breath in the thick humidity.

"Yeah, well." Sweets laughed. "You look like you's gettin' old, ma brotha. Thought I'd cut you some slack."

We clasped hands and gave each other "bro" hugs.

Sweets said, "Damn, boy. I done heard you was back in The D. Had some banking trouble a while ago. FBI and shit."

"You still got it, Sweets," I said. "And that's why I'm here."

I extracted a thick fold of hundred-dollar bills from my pocket, peeled off one and handed the crisp bill to Sweets.

"It's two these days, ma man," Sweets said. "Inflation and all."

I stripped off another bill. The cost of opening a dialog. He shoved the bills into his shirt pocket.

Smitty, as Sweet's contract employer, would get a healthy cut of the payment.

"Somebody bought Duke Ducane's guns and girls trafficking pipeline while he was doin' a nickel in Jacktown. I need to know who. And I need to know how ICE is involved with that purchase."

Sweets cocked his head and narrowed his eyes at me. He said, "Wha'chu up in this shit for, Snow? You ain't no cop no mo'. Word on the street is you some kinda neighborhood sugah-daddy. Like Spider-Man only without no superpowers or no cool mothafuckin' outfit."

"Money *is* a superpower, as anybody in the US Congress will tell you," I said.

"Seriously, though," Sweets said. "If'n I

had yo cash money, I wouldn't be carin' 'bout no everyday, down-here-below niggah shit. And I sure as hell wouldn't be chattin' up no hood rats in a dark alley. Me myself? I'd be in Belize or Columbia, some pretty brown thang on my lap bouncin' on my joint while I sucked down a piña colada and watched the sun rise."

"Ain't built like that."

"Yeah," Sweets sighed. "I know. You always was Captain Mothafuckin' America." Then he held out the palm of his hand. "Five," he said.

I peeled off seven C-notes, stuck them in the palm of his hand and said, "Two for you."

"Much appreciated, ma man," Sweets said, making the bills disappear. He took a sharp breath, looked around for a cautious second. Then, in a lowered voice he said, "Some brotha by the name of Tootie employed by Buddy Lane — you remember Buddy?"

I did. Chesterton "Buddy" Lane owned a small, seedy strip club in northwest Detroit — The Nappy Patch. The club was once a cash-stash for Duke Ducane, a place where he could hold money for short periods of time before moving it for a quick wash through ATMs he owned. After I put Duke in an eight-by-eight, Buddy Lane assumed he was heir apparent to Duke's vacated throne. Unfortunately, Buddy couldn't even claim the throne's foot stool. He ended up losing millions and was left with only his seedy strip club and a poor pimp's percentage of the prostitution run out of the club.

"Real ashy-lookin' niggah from Ypsilanti," Sweets said. "So, this Tootie, he goes out to see Duke in the joint, make the play, see what I'm sayin'? Tootie got no damn idea what he was talking to Duke about. He was coached to use coded words and phrases. And Duke knew the code."

"And Tootie takes Duke's coded responses back to Buddy?" I said. "Who'd Buddy pass Duke's code on to?"

"Don't know," Sweets said. "Rumor has it some small, high-tone S&M shop in Birmingham. Could be a way station for trafficked girls. Don't have no intel on that."

"You think Duke knows where this way station is and who runs it?"

"Word is maybe an old girlfriend," Sweets said. "But Duke ain't gonna talk. Whoever paid Duke didn't pay him to talk outside of his deal and he knows this. He talks, and whoever's running this new game comes down on him like a hammer in the Hand of God. This got to do with them two Mexican girls, right? One off the bridge, the other, Zug Island?"

I felt a lump grow in my throat.

"That's all I got, brotha-man," Sweets said. "We link intel and parley sometimes with Lady B, but we ain't got no comm-share with the south side Mexicans. I mean, we did twenty-five years ago when Maria Sandoval ran a listening post out of her dress shop on Vernor and Stair Street. You remember Maria?"

I did: My mother shopped at Maria's, dragging me along. I'd never forget the indignity of being a seven-year-old boy sur-rounded by women's clothing and custom-ers pinching his cheeks.

I had no idea until this moment that Ma-ria's was an intelligence hub for Mexican-town.

I peeled off another C-note and folded it into Sweets's shirt pocket.

"Please tell me you're getting out of this business soon, Sweets," I said. In the Ma-rines, I'd known intelligence professionals who had ghosted back alleys, drank cheap whiskey with killers and made dubious deals with any partially informed devil. There was nothing glamorous about what they did. Usually their lifespans were abbreviated and their bodies went unclaimed.

"Six more months and I'm out," Sweets said, grinning broadly. "Got me a small house on five acres in Comox, northeast coast of Vancouver Island. No TV, no radio, no nothin'. Just a fishin' pole, boat and some Marvin Gaye vinyl. When Jesus come back to put a hot, nasty sandal up *every*-body's ass, I wanna be somewhere He ain't never heard of."

I wished him Godspeed. "Should I — you know — hit you in the jaw or something? I forgot how this works."

"Naw, man, we coo," Sweets laughed. "That's white movie cop bullshit. I'mo get me some fish. You want some fish? Aunt Loo Loo for *sure* put her foot up in a basket of perch."

29

The following Monday, the noon temperature reached ninety. It was the second week
without rain and Detroit recorded its third
heat-related death; an elderly man alone in
a home without a fan or air-conditioning.
His water had been turned off by the city
for non-payment a week earlier.

I very much doubted prayer or the lighting of a Vigil candle would be of much use
to the man now.

Still, I found myself at St. Al's.

Father Grabowski was sitting on a beat-up
puke-yellow sofa in his office at St. Al's,
furiously scribbling on a yellow legal pad,
when I knocked on the open door and
walked in.

"Makin' a list and checkin' it twice,
padre?" I said.

As per usual, Father Grabowski stood and
gave me a hug.

"Just making a wish list for our seniors,"

he said. "You know. Silly stuff like food, clothing, shelter, donations to pay outrageous water bills and back property taxes that amount to pillaging the village."

"Have you talked to Lady B about the meeting you missed?" I said. "Frankly, I'm thinking you need to be as far from Lady B as humanly possible. At least for a while."

"Did you hear what I just said? About my *list*? The *seniors*?"

I pulled out my wallet, retrieved my lone charge card and handed it to him. "Just get it back to me by tomorrow. I need to get another rental car."

"You're serious?" Grabowski said staring at the card as if I'd just handed him a key to the Narnia armoire. "I mean, we're talking maybe a couple grand, August."

"Your limit is ten grand, father," I said. "We'll do cash after that. Now, about Lady B —"

"Yeah, it *has* been hotter than the bowels of hell," he said, pressing a stubby forefinger to his lips. "How's Tomás and Elena doing? Tell me about that girl of yours again. Tanya?"

"Tatina."

We play-talked about a number of inconsequential things as we made our way downstairs. The cool, dark thirty-pew overflow altar was a maddening echo chamber of concrete and marble. The only way any conversation could be understood was by whispering within an inch or two of a person's ear.

"I fear they may have bugged the place," Father Grabowski whispered, his breath smelling like bacon and cigarettes.

"Who?" I said. "ICE? Here?"

"Probably," Grabowski said. "There's a van out front on the boulevard. Hasn't moved in four days. I've seen a couple guys get in and out of the van. I think my sanctuary network's blown."

"I'll take care of the van," I whispered. "Forget what I said about Lady B. Get her in here to sweep for bugs. And call the diocese lawyer."

"Holy cow! Lady B can sweep for bugs? Just who the hell *is* she, August?"

"She's an enigma wrapped in a mystery rolled into a croissant."

"What are you gonna do, son?"

Back in Father Grabowski's office I used his desk phone.

"Nine-one-one. What's the nature of your emergency?"

"Madre Maria!" I said in an exaggerated female Mexican accent. "Oh, my God! That's not *right*! It's just not *right*!"

"Ma'am, calm down and tell me the nature of your emergency."

"I'm work to clean the St. Aloysius Catolic Church," I said. "I look out on the Washington Boulevard and me, I see a van. And I see men. They go in and go out of the van. And — oh, my God! — they *doing* things with each other in the van! In front of a House of God!"

Father Grabowski pressed a decorative sofa pillow to his face to stifle his laughter.

"The men in this van. You believe they are engaging in sex, ma'am?"

"That's what I say! Si! Yes! I don't care what the people they do for sex. But then they — they come out and make pee-pee on the street! I think one of the mans he got a gun!"

"I'm sending a patrol out, ma'am," the 911 operator said. "Stay inside. Stay safe."

"God bless you, Miss Nine-One-One lady! Gracias! Tank you!"

Forty seconds later, two DPD cruisers — lights flashing — rolled to a halt near the van. Father Grabowski and I stood on the grassy Washington Boulevard median in front of St. Al's and watched as three men emerged from the van, their hands raised. One of the men slowly reached into a shirt pocket and produced ID.

The DPD patrol sergeant reviewing the man's ID said, "Y'all ain't supposed to be perched this close to a church, hospital or school, are you?"

"We're within legal limits," the apparent van leader said. "I think maybe your people should back off."

"Back off?" the patrol sergeant laughed as he handed the leader's ID back. He turned to his partner, "Hey, Charley! ICE-man thinks we should 'back off'!"

"That shit's funny," his partner replied without seeming amused.

"I'm a federal goddamn agent!" the van leader snarled.

"And I'm a God-fearing son of east side Detroit who don't really give a rat's skanky ass what your tin star says," the patrol sergeant said. "Move your van or we can elevate this to your brass and mine, where-upon *my* brass will see what a good job I'm doing and *your* brass will see what a shitty job *you're* doing. Spyin' on a House of God? This ain't Moscow, mothafucka."

The two men traded Dodge City gun-slinger stares for a long time before the DPD sergeant's partner brought his shoulder-mounted walkie to his mouth. "Dispatch? Yeah, listen, we're gonna need a tow vehicle at —" The three ICE agents got in their van and the engine turned over. "Cancel that request, dispatch."

I told Father Grabowski this wasn't the end of things. It might take the ICE surveillance team time to regroup. But they'd be back. In the meantime, Lady B was to sweep the church for bugs.

After St. Al's, I needed to clear my head and try to put a few of pieces of the puzzle together.

Twenty minutes later I was slow-dancing in the second-floor boxing ring with Brutus Jefferies at his swanky downtown health club.

"The kid? Jimmy Radmon?" Brutus said after giving me two lightning fast jabs to my nose. "Whip smart. Soaks up karate like a sponge. Loves the philosophy. He'll be a red belt faster than anybody I've ever taught."

"Including me?"

"Including you."

I gave Brutus a right cross followed by an upper cut that glanced off the right side of his jaw.

"Pretty good," Brutus said. "You still droppin' your shoulder, though."

"How do I remember not to do that?"

"Just remember this —"

Brutus connected with a left cross to my

jaw, then a right cross, then sledgehammered my midsection twice. All of the air in me spewed out and, like a deflated balloon, I withered and fell to the mat.

"Yeah," I wheezed. "I think I'll remember now."

"Good," Brutus said, offering a hand to lift me up. "It took me a while, but I figured out how I know the kid."

"You know Jimmy?"

"Back when I was on the job," Brutus said as we bumped gloves and prepared for another round. " 'Bout a year before I got shot. Six-year-old kid, eating out of the garbage bins behind the Motor City Casino. Picked him up, took him back to his house — real shithole somewhere around Gratiot and Rosemary. Mom stank of weed. Don't know which dude in the house was his daddy. Long story short, I got him out and into foster care. Then the system did what they do best: lost him completely. Never did find out where he got to. Tell you this much, though; I made his case worker's life a living hell for about a year before the captain backed me off."

"Jesus," I said.

"What I tell you 'bout usin' the Lord's name in vain, August?"

For my transgression, Brutus popped me

in the face, backed me against the ropes, jack-hammered my stomach three times before finishing me with a tight-quarters right cross.

"You know, one of these days I'm gonna lay you out, old man," I said, spitting my mouth guard out and yanking my hands out of my gloves.

"Like I ain't heard that foolishness before," Brutus laughed. "You know, yo daddy actually *did* lay me out once. Worst beating I ever took."

"What was his secret?"

"Patience, persistence and sheer force of will," Brutus said. "See the same thing in you, young blood. Only somethin' different with you."

"Like what?"

"There were lines yo daddy wouldn't cross." Brutus tossed me a bottle of water. "That's why he never got promoted. Why he was never able to collar Duke Ducane. You? I got a feeling them lines is off on some far, faint horizon. And that do concern me a touch."

"Concerns me a touch, too, old man," I said after a swig of water. "But mostly, I sleep like a baby."

30

"She's *back*!" Tomás shouted. "My woman is *back*!"

Later that afternoon, Tomás and I drank cold Negra Modelo in front of his TV. We had been watching the Tigers get their asses handed to them by the Yankees even though we had acquired some new kid from Puerto Rico with a pitching arm capable of turning air into plasma.

During a local news break there was a live report from City Hall.

Elena stood at a microphone in front of a rare daytime Detroit City Council meeting making an impassioned speech about why Detroit should declare itself a "Sanctuary City." Behind her were about forty mostly Mexican-Americans waving little American flags and holding signs that read "I'm a Dreamer," "Sanctuary NOW!" and "Hands off Mexicantown!"

"We are business owners and day laborers, mothers, fathers and students," Elena said. "And we are doctors, lawyers, teachers, engineers, astronomers and astronauts. We pay our taxes and pledge allegiance. Now we want — we *demand*! — America pledge its allegiance to *us*. Mr. Mayor, City Council, will you pledge your allegiance to us? Will you declare — *right here, right now*! — Detroit as a Sanctuary City?"

Unfortunately, the mayor, as the reporter later informed us, was unable to attend the council meeting; he was on a five-day trip to Shanghai soliciting Chinese companies to do business in Detroit. Next stop on his knee-pad tour? Bangalore, India.

"Why's Irish importing brown when he won't commit to the browns he's already got?" Tomás wondered aloud.

The deputy mayor, a scholarly black woman in her fifties named Dr. Francine "Frankie May" Keyes, acknowledged that Elena's plea was important. She assured the crowd that the mayor — a "good Christian man" — would gladly give Elena an audience upon his return.

Tomás snorted. "Swear to God; the death of Christianity is coming at the hands of white Christian men."

After the news, Tomás and I lost interest in watching the Tigers lose. We took fresh beers into the sweltering eighty-seven-degree heat, where he watered Elena's bountiful vegetable garden.

"I'm heading over to The Nappy Patch tonight," I said.

"Fucking hell, Octavio," Tomás said, making sure the tomatillos got a good soaking. "Isn't that Buddy Lane's joint?"

"Yep."

"And your reason? I mean other than the opportunity to watch the living dead dancing, and the possibility of catching an airborne STD?"

"I think he knows a major roundabout for trafficking women," I said. "He's the intermediary who got the message to Duke that somebody wanted to buy his trafficking routes and safe houses. I think he may know where one of the major safe-house hubs is."

"You still doing this for Izzy?"

"No," I said. The humidity made my shirt stick to me like gauze to blood. "Izzy's gone. Can't do anything about that. But there's plenty of young women in Mexicantown running the risk of getting swept up, undocumented *and* citizens. And this place is my home."

Tomás smiled at me. "That's the first time since you been back I've heard you call this place home. How'd that feel, *cabrón*?"

"Strange," I said after a swig of beer.

I watched Tomás water Elena's garden for another ten minutes.

Then I told him I'd pick him up at nine.

Needless to say, Buddy Lane was none too pleased to see me.

When Tomás and I arrived at his grotesque lower east side strip club, no one looked like they were having much fun: The women dancing looked exhausted and the men looked bored. An elderly black man sat at the bar nursing a beer and reading a Walter Mosely paperback.

I told Tomás to grab a table and watch for trouble.

"Yeah, sure," Tomás said, nodding to the elderly black man reading at the bar. "He looks pretty sketchy. I'll keep a bead on him."

In the bar's back office, the mid-sixties Buddy Lane was dressed to impress. He wore black slacks with a satin stripe down the side seam, a white tuxedo jacket with black silk pocket square, a crisply starched white shirt and black satin bow tie. I'm sure in Buddy's mind The Nappy Patch was his Rick's Café in *Casablanca*.

Standing to my right was Buddy's muscle.

"You come into my business thinkin' you

some bad-ass private dick mothafucka?" Buddy yelled. His breath smelled like too many cigarettes and strong breath mints shoved in the crack of an ass. "You ain't *nothing,* Snow! You ain't even po-po no mo! You need to be gettin' yo half-ofay ass up outta here right damn now!"

"Suppose I decide to stay," I said. "Maybe enjoy one of your signature champagne cocktails and buffalo wings. You still be passing off rat hind legs as buffalo wings, are you?"

"Mothafucka —" Buddy made a move for his weapon of choice, a snub-nose .38 tucked beneath the left arm of his white tuxedo jacket.

As a former Marine and ex-cop, I was trained to effectively multitask even if there was a single mission with a single expected outcome. Because honestly: When has Plan A ever actually worked?

Even God is a Plan B kind of Guy.

Old Testament.

New Testament.

I punched Buddy Lane in the throat while simultaneously bringing my Glock out and holding it four inches away from his muscle's nose.

Buddy dropped to the floor in front of his desk, clutching his throat.

I deprived him of his .38, then to his muscle I said, "Don't I know you from some place? I'm usually pretty good with faces, but my gun's kinda blocking yours so I can't tell."

"Year and a half ago," the muscle said. "Bank lobby downtown. Security. You and my boss got into a mixed martial arts showdown. You was ready to come at me. That's when I quit."

"Right!" I said. I briefly looked around. "This the best you could do?"

"Everybody talkin' 'bout Detroit bein' a come-back miracle," the muscle said. "Got new construction everywhere and how many black folk you see on them construction jobs?" He sighed heavily. "Guess I'm quit on this job now."

Buddy was gasping for air and struggling to his feet.

I brought the back of a left fist to his head and he went down and out.

"What's your name?" I said.

"Kinsey Latrice."

"Mind if I call you Special K?"

"Like the cereal?"

"Sorry," I said. "Sounded more bad ass in my head. How 'bout just K?"

"You the one with the gun," K said. "Call me whatever you want."

"You're in good shape, K," I said. "How much you bench?"

"Two-eighty," he said. "Three. Dead lift 'bout four."

"Steroids?"

"Heck, no," K said. "Juicing's for punks. I used to bench guys for juicing."

Turns out K was once a strength coach for a small black college football team out of Georgia. College went bust and so did his job. Came back to Detroit to live with his seventy-two-year-old mother.

"If I lower my gun are we gonna have a problem, K?" I said.

"Naw," he said. "Sick of this place anyway. Women ain't supposed to be showin' themselves like this and brothas ain't supposed to be actin' a fool up in these places."

I stowed my Glock away. Then I borrowed a pen and paper from unconscious Buddy Lane's messy desk. After writing, I handed the paper to K. He looked at it and his eyes widened.

"You know him?" he said. "Brutus Jefferies? Fo real?"

"Old family friend," I said. "He's looking for a strength trainer."

I looked down at Buddy Lane. He was moaning, struggling to rejoin the conscious world.

K looked down at his former boss, too. "I don't have to use no gun or nothin' to pay you back for this job thing, do I?"

"No," I said. "In fact —" I took a couple bills from my wallet and shoved them into his massive hand. "Get yourself cleaned up. Haircut. New sweat suit and cross-trainer kicks — nothing ghetto fabulous. And bring donuts. Assorted. No nuts. He won't eat 'em. But he loves the smell of donuts. I'll give him a head's up and, if you play your cards right, you'll be taking your mom out for a nice dinner after your interview."

"Why you doin' this, man? You don't know me from Adam."

" 'And if you give yourself to the hungry, and satisfy the desire of the afflicted, then your light will rise in darkness, and your gloom will become like midday.' "

"Isaiah 58:10," K said.

He gave me his Nappy Patch business card.

"I ain't never handed a-one of these stupid cards out," K said. "Guess Buddy thought they made us look professional. Number at the bottom's my cell. You need anything that don't involve a ruckus, gimme a call."

"Stay strong, K," I said.

"Only way I know," he said before forever departing The Nappy Patch.

After a couple minutes of rifling through Buddy Lane's cramped office, I knelt, tied his hands behind his back with his alligator skin belt and slapped him awake.

"Time to wakey-wakey," I said. I had my Glock out and gave him a close look at it. "I need information, Buddy. And you're going to give it to me."

He spat in my face.

"You a two-bit Uncle Tom niggah just like yo dead old man," he said.

I wiped the spittle from my face.

Then I brought the butt of my Glock's grip down on the bridge of Buddy's nose. A crunch and sudden river of blood streaming down his cheeks. Buddy went under for a minute.

One of the strippers sashayed into the room. She froze and stared down at Buddy and me.

"Well, I been wantin' to do *that* for the past four months," she said.

"Would you mind getting a shot of tequila and a glass of water, ma'am?" I said.

"Who the fuck you be?" the stripper said.

"I'm Mr. Lane's leasing agent," I said. "Alexander Dumas. Mr. Lane is three months behind on his Cadillac Escalade payments."

"He ain't got no damn Escalade."

"Not anymore he doesn't."

The stripper got a shot of tequila and a glass of water. Before she left, she said, "When dumbass Buddy wake the fuck up, tell him Monesha done throwed up on stage and I ain't cleaning that shit up." Then she left, closing the door behind her.

I slapped Buddy awake. "You're going to tell me where the hub for the trafficked girls is and who runs it."

"Or fuckin' what, ya dumbass spic-niggah?"

I grabbed the shot of tequila and poured it on the broken and bleeding nose. He grimaced from the sting of alcohol.

"That's it?" he laughed. "That's all you got, niggah?"

"Funny you should ask," I said.

From his desk I grabbed a cigarette lighter shaped like a hand grenade, shoved his jacket kerchief in his mouth and lit the tequila on fire.

After a few seconds, I doused his burning nose, cheeks and shirt collar with the glass of water. Considering his muffled screams I think he got the message that I wasn't fucking around.

"I could do this all night," I said. "But I'm guessing you don't want me to do this all night. A name, Buddy. A location. Or next, it's a weenie roast. Oh, and Monesha done throwed up on stage."

A couple minutes later, I emerged from Buddy's office and headed for the door of the strip club.

Tomás joined me.

"Get what you came for?"

"I did."

"And Buddy?"

"He's fine," I said. "A little hot under the collar, though."

31

"Here," Lucy said. "Taste this."

The next day I found Lucy Three Rivers in Carmela and Sylvia's kitchen. She held out a tablespoon of her chili for me.

"No," I said.

"Why not?"

"Because I can smell it."

"You can really be a real dick sometimes."

"I know. You wanted to see me? Where are the girls?"

"Riding the QLine," Lucy said, tossing the spoon and chili it held into the sink. "They thought it'd be nice before stopping at the DIA's café for lunch. They asked me if I wanted to go but I said I'd rather shove red-hot knitting needles in my eyes. Okay, I didn't say that, but riding the QLine all day? Then eating an overpriced sandwich surrounded by paintings of a vengeful white man's God? No, thanks."

"Still," I said, "you wanted to make the

girls dinner. That's progress. I mean, it smells like a cow fart apocalypse in here, but you're coming along."

"A little encouragement might be nice," she said. "I don't need two of you man-babies biting my head off."

"Two?"

"Jimmy," Lucy said. "I think his girlfriend dumped him. Why are guys such twisted emotional wreckage?"

Lucy opened her laptop on the small kitchen table. "So anyway, I found the place your friend Buddy Lane told you about. 8384 Toblin Circle, Birmingham, Michigan."

She brought up a street-level picture of the house, an expansive two-story Tudor in a five-house cul-de-sac. Courtesy of Google Earth, we could see the street and most of the house. A local upscale real estate firm provided us with three-year-old 360-degree views of the exterior and video of the interior of the massive house, plus drone video of the house and neighborhood.

"Sold five years ago to a Lincoln and Marybeth Hamilton from Springfield, Ohio, then again two years later to a William Mae-bourne of Colorado Springs. He leases it out to a Genoa Enno, LLC, as a rental for Genoa big wigs from Frankfurt, Paris and

Amsterdam."

"Who's Maebourne?"

"Far as I can make out, he's an accountant," Lucy said. "Does mostly Air Force family taxes and financial planning. Owns a couple rental properties. This is the biggest one. He seems pretty active with his other properties, but not so much with this one."

"It's possible he doesn't know he owns it," I said. "What kind of business is Genoa?"

"A made-up one," Lucy said. "Website says they supply high-tech autonomous navigation systems for cars, trucks, cargo freighters. Their financials *look* real, but feel front loaded. Even the warts and blemishes on their quarterly reports look manufactured. For shits and giggles, I did a scan of the faces of the guys on their Frankfurt executive page and ran the photos through my own facial recognition software, which is *really* awesome. Guess what?" Lucy hit two keys and up popped the smiling, silver-haired CEO of Genoa Enno, LLC, Hans Ruger Gremel. She backed out from the close-up of Gremel. His photo shared a page with seven other portraits of smiling, silver-haired white men. Some were dressed like airline pilots. Still others were dressed like chefs, fishermen and doctors. "Mr. Gremel is a no-name model from a stock photo company out of Paramus, New Jersey. They went bust six years ago. Then I had an idea."

"Am I gonna like this?"

"Probably not," Lucy said, grinning. "Okay, so I hacked a NOAA satellite —"

"Jesus, Lucy!"

"— 'cause those puppies got everything — high-resolution cameras, infrared, ultra-violet spectrum, real-time layered scanning. They scan over a million square miles of the earth's surface every freakin' day, dude! So anyway, I hacked the one that covers the Great Lakes — BR-128NTG, or 'Benji,' — and had it do a focused infrared, thermal and layered scan of the cul-de-sac in general and 8384 Toblin Circle specifically . . ."

She pointed to a photo of Toblin Circle and the five houses in the cul-de-sac. Four of the houses had spots of light, streaks and flares of white, red and yellow. Thermal and infrared imaging. The fifth house — 8384 — was a nearly complete black rectangle.

"Holy shit," I heard myself say.

"I'm guessing as close as you can get to military-grade radio wave insulation and infrared shielding." Lucy looked up at me. "It's a Faraday cage."

"NOAA can't trace this back to you?" I said.

Lucy laughed. "You mean *us,* buffalo soldier. And heck no! The propeller-heads at NOAA'll probably think they got a tenth of a second of space noise or interference from the bazillion satellites junking it up out there."

Even though I was a bit shaky with Lucy hijacking a multi-million-dollar US government weather satellite, I was also proud of her.

As a reward, I took her to the Honeycomb Market. We bought ingredients to make proper chili: fresh jalapenos, red and black beans, pinto beans, ground chorizo beef, uncured bacon, Mexican-spiced flank steak, tomatoes, Honeycomb's own blend of chili powder spices, brown sugar and a six of Negra Modelo beer.

"You put *beer* in chili?" Lucy said, watching me pour two bottles into the simmering pot.

"You got a better idea?" I said.

About forty minutes into cooking chili with Lucy, I got a heavy-breathing call from an "UNKNOWN" number.

"You're blind and in the badlands, partner," the caller said in a hushed, conspiratorial voice. "And you need help. *My* help. I got info you need."

"Why so generous, friend?"

"Because I'm a nice guy, motherfucker," he said. "Now, you want what I got or not?"

"And let me guess," I said. "You can't give me this information over the phone?"

"Go ahead. Be a smartass," the caller said. "More girls are gonna wash up on the river front wearing Barbie clothes. You want to shut this shit down or not?"

"I do."

"Then I need ten g's," the caller said. "You got that kinda bread, right?"

I told him I did. He gave me an address and meet time.

Then he disconnected.

Lucy held out a steaming spoonful of chili to me.

"Good," I said after a taste. "Add a bit more smoked paprika."

I called Tomás.

"You're shitting me," Tomás said. "Ford Field? You know what security's like at Ford Field? Even when the Lions aren't playing?"

"I do."

"And you're still doing this?"

"I am. Whoever it is, they're a serious player and I don't think they ride Harleys, drink cheap beer, or braid their ear hair. They've probably cleared a path for me past Ford Field security. They're killing me to send a message to anybody else screwing with whatever operation this is."

"And what about me?" Tomás said.

"I doubt there's a bounty on you, Tomás."

"Well, that's bullshit," Tomás said. "What am I? A fucking vegan taco?"

Ford Field pushes nearly two-million square feet of red brick, glass and steel at 2000 Brush Street. When the Detroit Lions aren't bashing helmets and bruising bones with opposing NFL football teams on the field, you'll likely see Beyoncé, bull riders or monster trucks. I love Ford Field for the exact opposite reason I also love Lambeau Field in Green Bay: At Ford Field, you're warm and cozy with a cold beer under the skylights, safe from the ravages of a Michigan winter. At Lambeau Field in Green Bay, you're outside freezing your ass off while watching the Packers hammer it out like gridiron gods in a blizzard. Just like when I was a kid playing football in a foot of snow.

But regardless of the stadium or team allegiance, this is an age of foreign terrorists with pressure cooker bombs and home-grown terrorists with AR-15 assault rifles with bump stocks.

Security at Ford Field was a reflection of the times.

In a waste can outside of Gate A was a

Detroit Lions security pass on a lanyard belonging to a Sephus Goins. I cringed to think what may have happened to Mr. Goins. I flashed the pass in front of the reader. The light turned green and the door clicked open. Tomás quickly followed me in. I told him if anybody was going to put me in the crosshairs it would either be on a diagonal from Section H or from the west facing end zone, Sections M or 01. My bet was on a diagonal from somewhere in Section H since the yardage and elevation from end zone to end zone would require fairly expensive sniper skills.

Section H was where a discount killer would perch: Shorter range, clearer and faster shot, less ground to cover for an escape.

Before Tomás left for Section H, he whispered, "How come you don't got fifty-yard line season tickets?"

"I need to see two consecutive Black-And-Blue championships under their belt," I said. "Then I'll think about it."

"Wow," Tomás said with a grin. "Real hardass."

Then he disappeared into the labyrinth that was Ford Field.

Tomás understood there was nothing I could do for him if he got caught. Likewise, if I got nailed I didn't want a hint of my stink on him.

Even with the security pass, navigating to Section 137L demanded more stealth than had been required of me in a long time. There are very few shadowed corners in Ford Field.

Although none of Ford Field's security team carried lethal weapons, they were nonetheless lethally trained and smartly deployed. In a post 9/11 world, they couldn't afford to be anything less.

After five minutes I made it to Section 137L and looked around.

Four men in the opposite end zone were huddled around a large patch of Astro Turf that had been ripped up. Two of the men took turns stepping into the bald spot and bouncing on it. They didn't notice me. If they had, I doubted very much they would have cared. They had more important business. Like fixing a bald spot in the end zone of a $500 million football stadium.

I figured if I was going to get shot, I might as well get comfortable. I took a seat and imagined myself suited up in a snappy Lions "Honolulu Blue" uniform, taking the hand-off at the twenty-five-yard line, cutting right through the hole, juking left and finding daylight — the thirty . . . thirty-five and first . . . forty . . .

"Hey —"

My football fantasy was interrupted by the echo of a security guard at the fifty-yard line, fifteen rows up in the shadows of the upper level. He was approaching what appeared to be a maintenance man.

"Where's Mica?" the security guard said. "I thought he —"

"Yeah," the maintenance man laughed. "Day off. Guess I'm the lucky sonuvabitch, eh?"

"Yeah," the security guard laughed. "Hey, listen. Mica ever fix that scanner on the promenade?"

"Yeah," the maintenance man said. "Yeah, he got it."

"Wasn't no scanner needed fixing," the security guard said before speaking into his headset. "Bronze One, this is —"

That's as far as the security guard got before the maintenance man shot him twice.

With my Glock out, I leaped down the staircase, two, three steps at a time.

Another shot.

This time from Tomás.

He'd caught the shooter in the hip. The shooter had no choice but to jump onto the field. Tomás squeezed off two more rounds.

Misses.

More Astro Turf would have to be replaced.

Tomás spotted me on the field.

"Go!" he shouted, kneeling by the wounded security guard. "Get that fucker!"

The shooter was at least thirty-yards away. Even with a bullet in his hip, he was widening the gap. The four men that had been huddled over the bald spot either hit the deck or ran.

I knew I couldn't catch the shooter.

But a 9mm bullet traveling at over 800 mph could.

I took a stance, anticipated timing, calculated deceleration, angle of descent . . .

. . . then fired three times.

He dropped.

"Oh, my God!" Tomás bellowed from the stands. "Ladies and gentlemen, he is *down* at the ten-yard line! And what a hit from the kid out of Wayne State University!"

By the time I got to the shooter he was trying to crawl his way to freedom. He'd caught one of my bullets in his lower back.

"You — fucker," he growled. "I can't — feel my legs!"

"And I can't feel pity," I said. "Who sent you?"

He lost consciousness just as a swarm of Ford Field security descended onto the field, yelling for me and Tomás to drop our weapons.

32

"Isn't this the part where you yell at me, then I have a witty retort, then you yell at me some more?" I said. Shaking a fist in the air, I did an intentionally bad impression of Detective Captain Leo Cowling. "Snow, you cretinous *Philistine*! You scurrilous *vagabond*!"

Cowling just sat behind his desk staring dispassionately at me, tapping his fingertips methodically. I was in one of his visitor chairs, free of handcuffs or leg shackles. In fact, I was enjoying a nice cup of iced chai tea from one of the 14th Precinct's new upscale vending machines.

Finally, he smiled at me and said, "Ya know, I finally figured you out, Snow."

"Oh, yeah?" I said, taking a sip.

"Yeah," Cowling said. "See, you this baboon-sized asshole 'cause you actually a manic depressive. You need a continuous adrenaline rush to feel both alive and

283

worthy of folks' affection. Without that turbo-charged, psycho-chemical rush, you'd crash and burn. You'd realize how little you're worth to yourself or anybody else."

"Wow," I said. "That's actually pretty good."

"I ain't as dumb as you look, mothafucka," Cowling said. Then after a moment of silence he said, "Ford Field? Fo' real?"

"Where is my associate?"

"Coolin' out in an eight-by-ten downstairs," Cowling said. "Thinkin' about naming a couple holding cells after you and Pancho. The Imbecile Suites."

"Out of curiosity," I said, "why haven't I been burned upon the faggot yet?"

"We don't use the word 'faggot' 'round here no more," Cowling said. I decided not to regale him with my knowledge of 16th-century British execution techniques. "Besides, you'd love that martyr shit, wouldn't you? Far as I can tell, Mayor Pro Tem got a call, then he called a couple district representatives, who blindsided the commissioner, who has an emergency conference call with Ford Field management, who end up talking to my commander, who tells me to buy you a fucking cup of coffee while everybody's community relations departments run around sniffin' each other's asses.

I get to babysit you until somebody makes a decision."

"Shit truly does run downhill to where, I imagine, your mouth is right now?"

"Fuck you."

"I've got a few friends at the FBI," I said. "Maybe —"

"Word is, your *only* FBI contact — that little blonde heifer — done been kicked to the curb," Cowling said. "I know what plausible deniability smells like, Tex-Mex. Somebody somewhere with a black-on-black pay grade got *every* body spooked on this latest Snow shitstorm."

Cowling's administrative assistant poked her head in his office and said, "Sir? I have Commissioner Renard on line one for you."

"And the Snow Shitshow begins," Cowling sighed. He picked up his desk phone, hit "1" and said, "Yessir. Good afternoon."

Cowling listened for a moment, only contributing the occasional "yessir" or "I understand, sir," finally closing out the one-sided conversation by saying, "Thank you for your call, Commissioner."

Cowling slowly, gently laid the receiver back in its cradle.

Then he reached into a desk drawer, pulled out a roll of TUMS antacid tablets and popped two in his mouth.

After crunching and swallowing, Cowling looked at me and said, "You're free to go."

"And my friend?"

"Signing for his belongings at the booking desk."

"Wow."

"Yeah," Cowling said, making no effort to hide his disgust. "Wow."

"Well," I said standing. "Thanks for the chai. You wouldn't know the brand —"

"Get the fuck outta my office."

I was half way out of his office when I stopped, turned, and said, "Hey, listen; do I get my parking validated here or —"

"Motha—" Cowling shouted. Suddenly jumping out of his chair, he grabbed his gun out of its shoulder rig and slammed it on his desk. "— *fucka!*"

I took the hint and left.

Tomás was standing at the booking desk, slipping his belt — a thick, hand-tooled leather affair with images of the Stations of the Cross — through his pants belt loops.

"Jesus," the booking sergeant said, holding up Tomás's HK Mark 23 Caliber .45. "That's a beautiful piece."

"Ain't it, though?" Tomás extracted his wallet from the oversized plastic bag and slipped it into his back pocket.

"First pistol ever made specifically for US

Special Operations Command," the booking sergeant said as he turned the weapon lovingly over in his hands.

"Field tested, battle proven," Tomás said, grabbing his cell phone from the bag.

"How much this beauty run you?" the booking sergeant asked.

Tomás told him what he paid for the weapon.

"Get the fuck outta here!" the sergeant said. "Seriously? Who's your guy?"

Tomás told him who his guy was and that if the sergeant decided to buy from his guy he should use Tomás's name to get a better deal. Then he took his gun and slipped it under his shirt and into the small of his back.

I got my stuff.

The booking sergeant had nothing to say about any of my belongings.

As soon as we got outside of the 14th, my phone rang.

"What's this all about, August?" O'Donnell said.

"What's what all about?"

"Did you send me a text telling me to meet you at the Painted Lady?"

"I didn't leave you any text. I don't text. I call. Or play Candy Crush."

"Well, I'm here," she said. "What the hell's —"

"Are you strapped?"

"Yeah," she said.

"Twenty minutes," I said. "And stay sharp."

Once Tomás drove me back to Mexicantown in his recently acquired classic Ford truck, I told him I had to split in another direction.

He asked what was going on and I told him frankly I didn't know.

"Watch your ass, compadre," Tomás said.

"I will," I said. "Stay locked and loaded, mi amigo."

Nothing like riding a Harley on a hot day past the million orange safety cones and white-boy road crews working in futile, multi-million-dollar efforts to fix winter-ravaged roads before the coming winter wreaked havoc on them again.

Weaving in and out of traffic that was slowed or stalled by road construction, I made it from Mexicantown to Hamtramck, aka Poletown, in less than twenty minutes.

The Painted Lady Lounge, off of Joseph Campau Avenue on Jacob Street in Hamtramck, has been around since — well — no one quite knows. The ancient Victorian house, dressed in peeling pink and turquoise, unapologetically makes Detroit's "Top 10 Best Dive Bars" list every year. It's refreshingly antithetical to craft beers, tapas, edamame salads and sushi. In its time, The Painted Lady has poured hundreds of thousands of whiskey, vodka, schnapps and bourbon shots and snapped the caps off of millions of bottles of Pabst Blue Ribbon, Schlitz and Stroh's. The place has served without reservation or hesitation Detroit's collision of cultures: Polish and Italian immigrants and blacks in search of respite, a cold beer and a working jukebox. These days, you might see a Sikh US postal worker eating a sandwich at the bar or young Muslims on the sneak sharing a beer and basket of fries with Chaldean friends. And always an abundance of college kids.

"What the hell's going on?" I said, standing over the booth where the recently relieved-of-duty FBI agent Megan O'Donnell sat.

Sitting across from her was the ICE agent I'd come to know as Henshaw.

"August," O'Donnell began, "this is —"

"I know who the fuck he is," I said before grabbing a fist full of his shirt collar and dragging him out of the booth.

"Hold on, partner!" Henshaw said. "I come in peace!"

I drew back a heat-seeking fist and was about to let fly when something cold and blunt pressed into my cheek: the hickory of a Louisville Slugger baseball bat.

"Shit like this don't start until around seven thirty or eight," the short redheaded bartender said as she pressed the bat into my cheek. "You're about three hours early, sport."

"Sorry, Duchess," O'Donnell said to the bartender.

"No problem," the bartender named Duchess said. Slowly, she retracted the baseball bat from my cheek. "How 'bout something cold to cool you out, big guy?"

I let go of Henshaw and said, "You got martinis here?"

"We got gin in a glass and vodka in a glass," she said, grinning. " 'Bout the only choice you got is ice or no ice. Don't much feel like looking for a jar of olives — and I wouldn't count on finding one anyway."

"Vodka," I said. "Ice."

"Cool," Duchess said. "Now sit down and make nice."

I sat next to O'Donnell.

"I thought you were in Quantico visiting Frank," I said to O'Donnell, locking my eyes on Henshaw.

"Yeah," she said. "Three days. Long

enough to get my tank topped off." O'Donnell caught me staring at her. "What?" she said. "Guys can say shit like that but I can't?"

"So, who called us here?" I said.

"I did," Henshaw said. "Through my ops director."

33

His real name is Ryan Lassiter.

He works for the DEA and for the past two years he's been deep cover as "Harlon Henshaw" with Immigration & Customs Enforcement. According to O'Donnell, Lassiter was the one who alerted his DEA bosses to the possibility of rogue ICE units involved in kidnapping and trafficking, operating originally out of California, New Mexico and Arizona.

No one believed Lassiter until a coyote was caught with eight drugged and nearly suffocated young women stowed in a hot, false-box cargo van outside of El Paso. The man claimed to have *inmunidad* — immunity. He said men with the DEA and ICE told him he could avoid arrest and prosecution if he helped them execute "black-box deportations" of the illegals.

"Where's this guy now?" I said.

"In the ground," Lassiter said. "Shanked

thirty times at Lewis in Buckeye, Arizona. And *nobody* gets shanked thirty times at Lewis. At least not without the kind of precise planning and tactical execution that your average max rat is nowhere near capable of."

"A hit?"

"Pretty sure it wasn't a dispute over a piece of pie," Lassiter said. "Caught him in one of three CCTV blind spots. A lifer took the fall. Aryan Nation asshole affiliated with the Bruderschaft Motorcycle Club. Three months later the lifer's old lady — some chain-smoking mattress pad — buys a new condo and a tricked-out Ford F-150. Cash. I know you won't believe me, man, but I'm truly sorry for everything I've put you and everybody else through. I haven't enjoyed a goddamn bit of it. But I'm doin' what I gotta do 'cause this shit's got to end."

"Did you know Foley was dirty?"

"As a pig," Lassiter said. "He's the reason I got dropped in. Shadow the shadow. But he was only one dirty piece to this filthy puzzle and I wasn't about to sacrifice two years just to snag his sorry ass. He's gone dark. Nothing. Just — poof."

O'Donnell and I exchanged quick glances.

"Lassiter's on the level, August," O'Donnell said. She held up her phone and showed me Lassiter's DEA ID and agent profile. "I had an agent that owes me one vet him on the sly. He's neck-deep in this and he's given the DEA and FBI some good, actionable intel."

"We've documented a couple routes," Lassiter said. "We know some of the women are sold back to coyotes, or forced into high-end prostitution at loosely affiliated sex clubs working out of high-end resorts in Riviera Maya, Puerto Vallarta and Los Cabos. Corporate clientele level. Anywhere from three to five mil in estimated quarterly revenue. As you might guess, the Mexican authorities aren't exactly jumpin' at the chance to help us."

"Cut one tentacle off, there's seven more," I said. "And knowing where some of these women end up is not finding the head of the beast and chopping it the hell off."

I sat back for a moment and sipped my vodka.

Between the three of us, we had everything and we had nothing.

"I wouldn't blame you if you pulled the chute on this one, Snow," Lassiter said. "You're a private citizen and you got no skin in the game."

"No skin in the game?" I said. "Pretty fucking ironic thing to say, don't you think?"

"I didn't mean —"

"No, I'm sure you didn't," I said. "But truth is, some folks are born with skin in a fucking game." I took a breath. Standing, I said, "I live in Mexicantown, Lassiter. ICE agents spend half their time pounding down good Mexican food then, instead of paying the fucking bill, they arrest and deport the cook because he sold a joint to a cousin eight years ago. And that same joint that got the brown guy booted from the country is what white guys are lining up for at their pot dispensaries if they're not starting their own grow houses. So 'no skin in the game'? Fuck you."

"August," O'Donnell said. "Come on. Sit down. Let's —"

"Let's what, O'Donnell?" I said. "Hold hands and sing that old time Ghulla-Geechee Kumbaya? Why is it when white folk suddenly take a tumble into the shit they want to work with the black or brown guy who wakes up every day drowning in it? No, O'Donnell. Not this time. You do what you gotta do. I'll do the same."

"August —"

I threw a couple bills on the table and walked out.

When I got home, it was early Tuesday

evening. The temperature hadn't abated from its noon high of eighty-six, but now the air had the consistency of tepid soup.

Seated on my porch steps was Jimmy Radmon wearing Carhartt work shorts, a plum-purple Club Brutus T-shirt, and looking worked to sweaty exhaustion. He was drinking a luminescent green bottle of Mountain Dew.

"You okay?" I said, wheeling the Harley into my driveway.

"Yeah," Jimmy said standing. "Sorry. I probably shouldn't —"

"Go inside," I said. "I have the feeling we've both had pretty crappy days."

I left the Harley in my shed next to the stripped-down Olds 442 (the boys had sanded it smooth and begun patching) then went into the house through the back door.

Jimmy was seated at my kitchen island, guzzling his Mountain Dew. He had a ten-thousand-mile stare in his eyes. That stare that removes you from yourself.

Jimmy gave his head a slight shake, then said, "I'm sorry, Mr. Snow. I don't mean to —"

"To what? Bring goddamn Mountain Dew into my house?" I grabbed a fistful of ice out of the freezer and dropped it into a tall glass. "Yeah, well, don't ever do it again.

And that goes for Cheetos, too." I poured myself a generous glass of water, took an appreciative gulp, then set out a bowl of my homemade salsa and taco chips. "What's up, kid? I hear you're flying solo to the prom."

"Uh — what?"

"The girl you were seeing," I said. "What's her nickname? Mothra? She broke up with you."

"*I* broke up with *her,*" Jimmy said. Then he said, "You ever be around somebody that you like but you don't like some of the stuff they do? And it kind of — adds up?"

"Yeah," I said. "My accountant and my lawyer."

Jimmy smiled. Then he said with deadly seriousness, "You know I don't like being around no dope, right, Mr. Snow?"

"I do."

"I mean except for Carmela and Sylvia," Jimmy said. "But even with they brownies I feel a little — you know — twitchy. I seen what that nonsense do to people. Messes with they mind. This girl I was seeing — she liked to smoke dope before we watched a movie — you know. It — changed her. Not in a bad way. Just not in a *real* way. See what I'm sayin', Mr. Snow?"

"I see what you're saying."

"I ain't judgin' nobody," Jimmy said. "Everybody got the right to do what they got to do. But me myself? I — seen too much of what that stuff do to people. And it just — reminds me of what I don't wanna think about. Don't wanna be around."

"Does it bother you when I drink?"

Jimmy laughed. "Aw, shoot no, Mr. Snow. You got a more clear head on a couple beers than most people what never touch the stuff. And with what you been through, you done earned the right to do you, dawg. It's just —"

"You can't force yourself to overlook something that goes against your principles, Jimmy. And you can't change your experiences to fit someone else's life. You may like her. And she may like you. That doesn't mean you're meant for each other. You're one of the kindest, smartest, most talented people I've ever had the privilege to know. I'm kinda glad I didn't kill you when we first met."

Jimmy laughed. "Me, too."

"You'll find somebody, kid," I said. "She's out there, bumpin' around in the dark just like most of us. And when you finally bump into each other, well — instead of the formless void, there shall be light."

"Like Miss Tatina?"

"Like Miss Tatina," I said.

This was the first time in years I thought about my dad and me, sitting on the steps at the back of the house, under an early summer night sky, his hand on my shoulder, having "the talk" after Clare Rutilani broke my middle-school heart. It felt good to know I had at least a modicum of hard-won wisdom I could pass on to a young man who I suspected had seen more shit in his first ten years of life than I'd seen in my first twenty.

34

From the outside you'd think Mr. and Mrs. Peter and Patsy Americana lived at 8384 Toblin Circle Drive, Birmingham, Michigan. Some nice silver-haired retired couple with closets full of bright cardigans and spiffy golf slacks.

Lucy had given me a good satellite's overview of the house. Of course, here on earth, my curse is noticing the little off-kilter details in otherwise idyllic settings. Like the discreetly placed state-of-the-art security cameras.

Security cameras in the wealthy northwest suburb of Birmingham were nothing unusual; residents jealously guarded their amassed fortunes and affluent lifestyles. But six front-facing cameras had to be a paranoid record. I could only imagine how many cameras monitored the sides of the house and the four-car garage in back.

With the gleefully self-righteous disposition of a Seventh Day Adventist, I flashed my pearly-whites at the double door peep-hole camera and gave the doorbell button a good push, apparently activating the bells at Oxford's Church of St. Mary the Virgin.

After a moment the door cracked open, revealing a third of a pretty woman's face including one emerald-green eye.

"Yes?"

"Hi! My name's August Snow."

"Are you selling something, Mr. August Snow?" the woman said, scanning me from head to toe. I doubted very much she was admiring my Adonis-like body. "I'm afraid we don't do solicitors."

"No," I said. "I'm not selling anything. But I bet *you* are." The woman narrowed her single green-eyed gaze at me. "And from the sound of things, you just cocked the hammer on a short barrel .32. Maybe a .38? Tell Miss Reinbach — The Major — it's important we talk."

Reluctantly, the woman opened the door.

Her other eye was also emerald green, making the set supernaturally beautiful.

She was dressed for sex and murder; a short black leather skirt, form-fitting black lace bodice, seamed black stockings and black stiletto heels. Secured around her length of smooth white neck was a black lace choker bearing a silver skull.

"You have lovely eyes," she said, easing the hammer down on her Smith and Wesson .38. "Like — chocolate milk."

"Thanks," I said. "And may I say your eyes —"

She slapped me hard across the face.

As I recovered she said, "That nine-milly you're carrying? Keep it stowed, lover, or someone might get hurt. We clear?"

"As a Pictured Rocks stream."

"So, what brings you here, Mister Snow?"

"What brings me here is a long story. Suffice it to say people are trying to kill me probably because of this house — and I want to know why."

"And you know Miss Reinbach — how?"

"That's between me and Miss Reinbach."

"You sure you want to play it like that?"

"No other play," I said. "Now you can go get her, or I can take that peashooter from you and find her myself. What's it gonna be, Green Eyes?"

Green Eyes stared at me for a few long seconds, then said, "I'll see if she's available."

"By the way," I said, rubbing the cheek she'd slapped, "I'm not paying for that."

She smiled at me. "Not now you aren't."

The foyer was pleasantly decorated with a

ceramic tile floor, cream-colored walls hung with expensive abstract art and several vases overflowing with colorful flowers. To my left was a brightly lit study with leather club chairs, antique side tables, tall bookcases and a large fieldstone fireplace. To my right was an open concept dining room that I imagined shared space with an equally large kitchen.

Nothing that said tie-me-up-tie-me-down.

Save for maybe the mortgage.

The wide staircase at the back of the foyer was railed with nice wood, the steps covered with an oriental-style runner. Above the staircase was a discreet bronze plaque bearing the engraved words, *Lasciate ogne speranza, voi ch'entrate.*

Abandon all hope, ye who enter here.

"Mr. Snow!"

An athletically built strawberry-blonde woman in her mid-fifties wearing a form-fitting couture dress and expensive shoes walked briskly toward me, her well-manicured hand extended. I took her hand and we shook. It was a strong handshake.

" 'And I thought the major was a lady suffragette.' "

"McCartney?" Smiling, she narrowed her eyes at me. "Aren't you're a little too young to appreciate Sir Paul?"

"My mom was a McCartney fan. Wings. Not Beatles. A sucker for the Paul and Linda love story."

"Come!" she said brightly. "Let's talk!"

I followed The Major upstairs and down a long hallway, past eight black doors to a set of black double doors at the east end of the house.

A striking young black woman emerged from one of the eight rooms we'd passed.

"Ms. Reinbach?" the young woman said.

The Major turned and grinned affably at the young woman.

"MarKesha, darling!" The Major said. "You're here early."

"My noon chem lab was canceled," the young woman said. She held up a white leather bodice and matching mask. "Sorry to interrupt, but is this the set you ordered for me?"

"Yes," The Major said. "Why? Is something wrong?"

"The cat-o'-nine-tails is black. It's supposed to match."

The Major sighed heavily. "This is the third time. Don't worry. I'll take care of it, dear."

"Thank you."

MarKesha disappeared back into her room.

Next to the double doors leading to The Major's office was a keypad. She pressed five numbers, the doors unlocked and I followed her in.

The Major's office was less whips-and-chains and more Nantucket retreat; the built-in bookshelves were crowded with volumes old and new and the expanse of her large desk appeared to be antique cherry. There were two well-worn leather wingback chairs positioned in front of the desk and a white leather chaise near a tall window. Perhaps the only window with normal curtains that let the early Tuesday afternoon sun in. The hardwood floors were adorned with casually strewn Persian rugs.

She gestured to one of the wingback chairs and I sat.

"Drink, Mr. Snow?" The Major said.

"If it's on the house."

She laughed. "I'm not *that* avaricious. Just because we are trained in the art, science and psychology of S&M doesn't mean we lack in good manners and civility. Whiskey's fine?"

She poured two neat tumblers of whiskey and handed one to me.

"So," she said, taking a seat behind her desk. "No one calls me 'The Major' save for old acquaintances and a few special clients.

I think I'd remember you as a client; you have a certain — carriage — about you. So, an acquaintance? Perhaps a charity function?"

"Duke Ducane."

The color drained from her tanned and freckled face. She stared wide-eyed at me for a disbelieving moment.

"You — work — for Duke?"

"No," I said. "But I'm the ex-cop who put him away for a nickel in Jackson. I got to know a lot about Duke. Like how he trusted a woman named Florence Elizabeth Reinman enough to let her run prostitution for him. She disappeared with two million of his bucks six months before I collared him. Probably the only time in his life he's ever displayed a heart that could be broken. Another reason why I've had this nagging feeling that I didn't quite collar him so much as he gave up. With you, it went beyond business-arrangement trust. It was love."

"What do you want?"

"This is a hub for kidnapped women trafficked for high-end sex clubs. I want to know who you work for and where the next stop in the pipeline is for these women."

The room flooded with silence. She took an unsteady sip of her whiskey and, trying to be as subtle as possible, pressed a button under the desk top. Then she said, "I honestly have no idea what you're —"

"I don't have time for this," I said. "I'm guessing you're scared of both your new employers *and* your old employer — Duke Ducane. Duke has no idea you're here. No idea you're doing business in his backyard. And no idea you seeded this business with his money. You need a minute to decide who you're most afraid of?"

"You fucker."

"That I am," I said snapping back the rest of my whiskey and pushing the empty tumbler across the desk to her. "Here's the deal: I walk out of here with a name, maybe you get to keep your little shop of orgasmic horrors. Otherwise, Duke finds you and dumps pieces of you in each of the Great Lakes. 'Heaven has no rage like love to hatred turned / Nor hell a fury like a pimp scorned.' "

The double doors behind me opened and Green Eyes stormed in, holding the black-hole business end of revolver on me.

"First you slap me," I said to Green Eyes. "Now you're gonna *shoot* me? Are we married and nobody told me?" To The Major, I said, "Well, I had to try, right? I can see I've worn out my welcome, so — no harm, no foul?"

I offered my hand to The Major. She stood and signaled for Green Eyes to lower her weapon. Then, reluctantly, she put her hand out to shake mine. In the space of a second, I had her wrist and pulled her halfway across the desk. I had my Glock out and pointed at her forehead.

"I shoot your employer, you're out of a job," I said to Green Eyes.

I didn't like the way she smiled.

"Go ahead. Shoot her," Green Eyes finally said. " 'Bout damned time I got a promotion."

I had the sinking feeling I was pointing my gun at the wrong person.

"Anna?" The Major said.

"Oh, for God's sakes!" Anna erupted. "You really think I *like* working for you? You and your — your pathetically outdated '90s fashions and superior attitude! Jesus! Eight years of you cherry-picking my ideas to improve the business. It was *my* idea to bring in this new organization! *My* time! *My* negotiations!"

"You — you're like a daughter to me —"

"And you're like a stupid cow to me!"

"You *bitch*!"

"Put a bullet in her, Snow," Anna said.

"My gift to you. Then I put a bullet in you. Or try to get the drop on me and I kill you. Then I shoot her with your gun. Makes no difference. Sure, it's a little messy, but the new organization? They'll have this cleaned up in an hour."

"I take it this new organization doesn't much like fuck-ups or hostile takeovers?"

"Let's just say at this early stage of operations they prefer changes with cleaner sight lines."

The young black girl named MarKesha appeared in the doorway wearing her new white leather bustier. She saw us, our guns, and screamed.

A tenth of a second distraction was all I needed.

I swept my Glock from The Major's forehead to Anna Green Eyes, fired twice.

She fell. I released The Major and kicked Green Eyes's gun away.

The Major quickly reached into a desk drawer and had a 9mm half way out when I brought my Glock back to her.

"Seems Anna has more value," I said. "You, on the other hand?"

With my gun I gestured for The Major to take a seat in the middle of her sofa. She did, keeping her hands flat on top of her thighs.

I knelt by the wounded Anna and said, "Unless you've got a doctor client that can get here in fifteen minutes, you're gonna bleed out. Tell me what I want to know and I'm sure The Major will get you help."

"Fuck her!" The Major spat.

"No, fuck *you,* ya skeezy dinosaur!" Anna replied.

"Okay, maybe I was wrong," I said to Green Eyes. "Either way, you're done. I'll help you as much as I can. But you're cashed out, so tell me what I want to know —"

"You tell him, we all die!" The Major shouted.

Contrary to popular belief, most people who've never been shot before and suddenly find themselves with a hot bullet burrowing through their flesh will likely give up any information required to staunch the pain: bank PINs, where grandma's jewels are hidden, battalion coordinates. With a through-and-through bullet wound gushing blood on her right side, Anna Green Eyes told me what I wanted to hear.

I performed quick triage on her, enough so she wouldn't bleed out. Then I said to The Major, "Show me where you keep the women."

"Go to hell, you bastard."

I smiled, pulled out my phone and punched a number.

"White Girl?" I said. "Listen, it's — yeah, I know I'm an asshole — listen, is Duke in?"

"Okay!" The Major said. "Jesus! Just don't — *please*!"

I disconnected. "How 'bout that tour."

35

"I have two master's degrees," The Major said with a renewed sense of superiority. She led me down a wide first floor staircase to the "dungeon" where the majority of her business was conducted. "A degree in psychology from Northern Michigan and a degree in pharmacology from Miami University. Does this surprise you, Mr. Snow?"

"No," I said, keeping my gun trained on her back. "A lot of shitty people have degrees."

The eight second-floor private rooms near her office were reserved for the crème de la crème of The Major's S&M clientele. Black Card members with money to piss away on even stranger, more specialized sexual proclivities.

Downstairs was another matter.

Below the first-floor leather pub chairs, bottles of eighteen-year-old single malt whiskey, Waterford crystal, side tables bearing copies of *The National Review* and *The American Spectator* was "the Dungeon."

"Some people don't physically react the way others do," The Major said, intent on educating me in the art and science of sadomasochism. "They have deeply recessed psychological and physical pleasure and pain receptors. As a result, they have higher pain and pleasure thresholds. Their sexual needs are mostly normal, but they simply can't achieve an endorphin release unless these higher pain and pleasure thresholds are met. It's about the very human need to feel a transcendental physical release. We're professionals, Mr. Snow. We provide a needed service. We know what each client needs to achieve an acceptable level of euphoria."

"Wow," I said as we reached the Dungeon "That's *very* interesting. You know what else is interesting? The physics of bees in flight — but you don't hear me fucking yammering on about it. Now move."

Oddly enough, I was beginning to gain an appreciation that such a place could successfully exist in socially and politically conservative Michigan.

God Bless America.

The Dungeon, all black tile and flickering LED torch lamps, was expansive and subdivided into suites. As we passed one of the suites, a door opened and a tall woman with spiked white hair emerged, leaving the door slightly open.

"Lilith," The Major said. "Everything good?"

"He's 'kiting' now," Lilith said. "I'm gonna warm his bottle."

The Major felt obligated to briefly explain to me what 'kiting' meant: The human body and mind as a "kite" lifted high on sustained endorphin release through the stimulus of pain.

I told her I didn't give a shit.

Before Lilith closed the door, I glanced in the room: tied to a large horizontally suspended metal tube circle, dressed in a diaper and displaying a number of welts on his chest was the guy I got my evening sports report from on one of the local TV stations.

The Major finally came to a black metal door with a keypad.

She pressed five numbers. There was the heavy chunking sound of a lock disengaging.

She opened the door and we entered.

There were no vases full of flowers here. No framed artwork or leather pub chairs. It was a forty-by-forty concrete room with one sink, a toilet with no walls and twenty filthy cots. Hanging off the railings of two cots were handcuffs. It smelled of sweat, damp concrete and unflushed urine. There were empty two-liter bottles of soda pop and fast food wrappers strewn on the floor, along with a large waste can overflowing with empty water bottles, and paper towels and soiled panties. A spot on the concrete floor looked like someone had tried to scrub blood away.

"Jesus," I said, looking around at the hovel.

"I was going to — there were plans — to make this more — accommodating," The Major said.

"Yeah. Sure."

"We're giving them a *life*!" The Major suddenly bellowed. "These women! What the hell else would they have? Hiding from immigration? Always on the run! At least now they'll make more money in a *day* than most people see in a goddamn *month*! A fucking *year*!"

"You made choices for them nobody has the right to make."

I gestured with my Glock for her to move toward the toilet. I grabbed a set of handcuffs from one of the cots.

"You're a stupid fuck!" she yelled as I

315

handcuffed her to the toilet plumbing. "You don't know the shitstorm you're starting! They'll come for you! They'll cut your balls off and feed 'em to ya! You hear me?"

Leaving the room, I pushed the heavily insulated door closed.

Then using the butt of my gun, I hammered the keypad into a useless collection of broken LED lights, disconnected wires and smashed circuit boards.

Several women in various stages of S&M dress emerged from their suites.

"The fuck's going on?" one of the women asked as I passed.

"Toilet's backed up," I said making my way back down the dark hallway, past the screams, howls, moans and whip lashes.

Back upstairs, there was a blood trail through the foyer to the back of the house. I looked out at the four-car garage. One of the garage doors was up, the garage itself empty.

I was just about to walk out of the kitchen when I noticed something small and shiny on the floor.

A green contact lens.

Walking out to my recently acquired Harley bike, I called Tomás and filled him in on what had transpired.

"Holy shit," Tomás said. "And you went

without me?"

"I didn't think your heart could take it, mi amigo."

I gave him a download on the information I'd just acquired and how we had to act fast.

"I'm in," Tomás said without hesitation. "But seems like we're gonna need more than us for this one. Makes me wish Frank was here."

"Me, too."

"What about the FBI lady?"

"How 'bout we discuss this in front of your gun locker?"

"Now you're talkin', *cabrón.*"

36

"So, let me see if I've got this right," Tomás said. "Some new organization's running rogue ICE units and neo-Nazi biker gangs to grab up girls and move 'em *out* of the city while they move new girls *in*?"

"Yep."

"And the girls they're moving *out* pay for the new girls coming *in*?"

"Uh huh."

"Why?"

"That part I haven't quite worked out," I said. "One or the other makes some sort of perverse sense. But opposite and simultaneous paths along a single pipeline? The rogue ICE units look like they're only responsible for moving women out. Maybe double-dipping selling some of the women as drug mules. But who's moving new women *in* — and why?"

"I think the 'why' is pretty obvious," Tomás said. "Prostitution. But this? This is a big undertaking just to run a few new whores through strip clubs, casinos and hotels."

"Let's agree to call them sex-workers. Being forced into selling sex — or choosing to sell sex — doesn't make these women 'whores.' It makes them victims, survivors or entrepreneurs."

"You gotta stop watching public TV," Tomás said. "How'd Barney Olsen fit in?"

"This organization probably ran ICE and biker payments through Olsen," I said. "But let's say he starts skimming payments and women to feed his own habits. With the heat two dead women brought, this new organization probably had no choice but to disappear Olsen. There's something very — antiseptic — about whoever these people are."

"Guess we'll know more about these fuckers tonight."

"Guess so."

We sat in old webbed aluminum lawn chairs in front of his open gun locker. Elena was back to breathing fire, leading a DACA sit-in at City Hall. The folks at City Hall were damned if they knew what to do about the sit-in.

Then again, they were damned if they knew what to do about *any* thing on any given day.

"I've never asked you this before," I said while admiring Tomás's newly acquired Winchester SX4 rifle. "But exactly why do you have so damned many guns?"

"I ever tell you my pops got robbed at gunpoint?" Tomás said.

"No."

"Oh, yeah," Tomás said. "My mama, too. Me and my sister was with 'em both times. All we had was migrant cash. We didn't know nothin' about banks. What migrant does? A week's worth of back-breaking work —" he snapped his fingers "— gone. Both times. The looks on their faces — like they'd failed each other. Failed us. Robbers even made us take our shoes off — the 'wetback wallet.' Nothin' like lookin' into your parents' eyes and they look back at you like they failed you. Looking down the barrel of a gun is when you realize what real power looks like. When you realize how valuable life is. And how quick and cheap it can be." Tomás took a long pause. Then he said, "Your mom ever tell you stories about the four sun gods?"

"No."

"Creepy old Aztec stories about how the universe was created and destroyed four times by four suns. Four times people have inhabited the earth. And four times, wiped out by the fifth sun. All because the gods grew jealous of each other. Started pissin' on each others' golden boots. The fifth sun rides in, wipes out the old gods and everything they created and ushers in a new age. I look around, Octavio, this 'new age' ain't that cool. The gods are at it again and we're smack dab in the middle of their pissing match. You know I ain't much for ghost stories or religion. But if the new 'gods' are thinking about catching me unaware and in the middle, I'm unloading every weapon I got. Every bullet. Every clip."

Tomás and I talked about tonight's mission and the conflagration we were soon to set off. I hadn't managed to get much out of Anna Green Eyes, but what I did get from her while she bled on the floor of the Major's study was vital: a freighter — the *Federal Shoreland* — docking tonight, the Nielsen Emery Terminal at the Port of Detroit. An iron ore freighter taking on fuel and crew supplies.

And eight women.

Seven or eight well-armed men guarding the ship and human cargo.

That's what Anna Green Eyes said I could expect.

"You won't even get past the fucking

gate," she'd said to me. "These guys chew Boy Scouts like you up for breakfast!"

"Well, they'd better come hungry."

If Anna Green Eyes said seven or eight well-armed men, then Tomás and I had to be strapped for fifteen or more.

"You figure they're BMC biker crews?" Tomás said.

"Yep. But they're still just the wranglers. The hired help."

"Still," Tomás said. "Ain't nothin' sweeter than kickin' Nazi ass."

Once we selected primary weapons and ammo, we loaded secondary artillery into the covered bed of his everyday Ford-150. Then we went to my house.

I pulled up Google Earth and we took a detailed look at the Nielsen Emery Terminal, a sprawling shipyard with two freighter loading docks, two berths for repair, stationary cranes and rail loading gantries. There were stacks of freight containers and five long, low corrugated metal buildings where various and sundry goods and equipment were stored. A sixteen-foot-tall fence topped with razor wire ran the serpentine one-mile length of the terminal. There were two entries with roll-away gates large enough for trucks, and a gate security booth manned 24/7.

"It's possible they've added security or moved things around," I said, staring at the laptop screen. "No telling how old these photos are. But I'm guessing nothing's changed much. They rarely do at freight yards. Only hang-up we could face —"

"You mean besides getting shot?"

"Yeah," I said. "Besides getting shot. This is a Foreign Trade Zone shipyard. And that means some areas are outside of US Customs jurisdiction."

"Which means they're out of US cop jurisdiction," Tomás said. We were quiet for a moment. Then Tomás said, "We really are flying by our ass-hairs on this one." He squinted at the overhead photo of the docks and said, "Well, we can't go in here on account of there's water. We got no boat and I ain't fuckin' swimmin'. So, it's looking like the southeastern security gate. How many cameras you figure?"

"Ten, maybe fifteen," I said, "manned by a couple of regular Joes just trying to make this month's mortgage payment. Our guys are probably huddled around Dock 1 and any freight containers on the dock ready for loading."

"That's where the women are?"

"That's where the women are."

We gave each other a fleeting look, leaving

volumes unspoken: Volumes that men and women for millennia had written in blood. The stratagems and campaigns, insurgencies and wars, lost soldiers' names and riderless horses, all covered over by indifferent epochs of sand.

There are things you come back from. And things from which you never return.

"Time?" Tomás finally said.

"Be here at nine," I said.

"You wanna have dinner with Elena and me?"

"No," I said. "You guys go ahead."

"What are you gonna do?"

I was going to do exactly what Tomás planned to do: Immerse myself in the sight and sound, smell and feel of someone I hoped would remember me should I this very night pass from existence. Someone who would accept me into the DNA of their memory and add me as another thread in the diaphanous fabric of their soul.

No, not Tatina.

She already knew my soul in both what was said and unsaid, felt and anticipated.

Why give her a reason to worry six thousand miles away.

No, Tatina would know how much she had meant to me. She would receive a cashier's check in a bouquet of roses, an Octavio Paz poem — "Touch" — and a note that simply read, "I'm sorry." Money doesn't make loss or mourning any easier. But it still provides a bit of cushion at the end of the fall.

The ladies of Café Consuela's agreed to stay open late for me.

I offered a cash incentive.

"You think we wouldn't do this for you without your money?" Martiza said before ordering me to sit in the restaurant's lone booth.

"Never insult me with your money again, Octavio."

Sitting across from me in the small restaurant's solitary booth were Jimmy Radmon and Lucy Three Rivers.

"So, what's the occasion, Sherlock?" Lucy said.

"No reason," I said. "Just thought it was as good a time as any for the three of us to sit down and have a meal together. And no, this isn't me matchmaking. Whatever happens between you two is your business."

Jimmy and Lucy gave each other a nervous look before bringing their eyes back to me.

"Can I have a margarita?" Lucy said. "I mean, I know I'm only nineteen and . . ."

"I'm not a proponent for underage drinking," I said. "But in this case, yeah, sure. Regular or strawberry?"

"They make *strawberry* margaritas?" Lucy said, her eyes lighting up.

I looked up at Martiza and, in Spanish, I said, "A strawberry margarita. Light on the tequila."

She smiled and nodded.

"Just a Coke for me, ma'am," Jimmy said.

We didn't order. We simply ate whatever the ladies of Café Consuela's made for us: Chicken Posole soup with homegrown poblano peppers and fresh radishes; queso empanadas; the house grilled shrimp and blackened salmon Quesadas; chicken and grilled vegetable tacos with homemade chipotle sauce; fresh guacamole and chips.

I supplied the salsa.

"You're learning," Martiza said after tasting half a teaspoon. "*Si*— you're learning."

This I took as high praise indeed.

After dinner, I took Jimmy aside and said, "You still got that envelope I gave you last year?"

"Yessir," Jimmy said.

"Good."

"I ain't never opened it," Jimmy said. "You told me not to unless you — I know what it is, Mr. Snow. And you already done did enough for me. I don't never want to open that envelope."

"Frankly, I'm hoping you never have to,

Jimmy," I said. "But like I said then, I'll say now; you've put your stamp on Markham Street. And when I'm not around, it's yours. I don't trust anyone more than you and Carlos to take care of it."

"I don't know what you into, Mr. Snow," Jimmy said, "but if you need backup —"

"You've been backing me since we met," I said. "Your only job now is to be the best version of yourself."

With Jimmy settled at his new house, I got Lucy back to Carmela and Sylvia's.

On the front porch I gave her the same kind of envelope I'd given Jimmy. She stared at it for a few seconds. "What's this?"

"Something for your future," I said. "Don't open it now, okay? Just — you know — put it somewhere safe —"

"Is this, like, your last will and testament?" she said. " 'Cause that's kinda creepy and I don't want to be responsible for, you know, making burial arrangements or having you cremated. How'm I supposed to do that shit and I can't even make decent chili?"

"No," I said. "It's not my last will and testament. It's something for you. But don't open it for a while. Promise me."

She stared at the envelope for a moment more.

Then she hugged me. Long and tight.

When she released me, I could see her eyes were wet.

"You're a moron," she said, quickly wiping her eyes. Then she turned and walked into Carmela and Sylvia's house.

37

By nine-thirty of a steamy Friday evening, the sun was fully submerged beneath the leaden horizon. It was still a stagnant, suffocating eighty-two degrees with a sauna-like drizzle threatening to become a full-on sweltering rain. Perfect weather to sleuth around the dismal confines of a shipyard along the Detroit River.

I was dressed in heavy tactical black and sporting twenty pounds of weaponry and ammo. Tomás, dressed the same, was carrying even more weaponry and ammo. The rest of our gear was under a tarp in the bed of his truck. Hopefully we wouldn't need any of it.

We'd parked on West Fort Street near an old two-story dock warehouse that had fallen into disuse. Using the low, slump-shouldered buildings and jagged shadows as cover, we made our way on foot south to the Nielsen Emery Terminal. In this part of town, the only company we expected was the occasional homeless vet and rats the size of Buicks.

Halfway to the terminal, Tomás decided he wanted his new Winchester SX4 rifle with him. He'd left the rifle in the bed of his truck.

"Be a shame for her to miss the sights, being new in town," he said.

I didn't mind the delay. It gave me more time to scope activities at the terminal and possibly find an answer to the question "What the hell am I doing?"

When Tomás returned he had a surprise for me.

Lucy Three Rivers.

"She was hiding under the tarp in my truck bed," Tomás said.

"Goddammit, Lucy!" I said. "What the hell are you doing here?"

"After you left Carmela and Sylvia's I wondered what you were up to," she said. "So, I opened the envelope. I know I wasn't supposed to — but you hand me an envelope, I'm gonna open it. You really got that much money to be handing out? I mean, thanks, but I don't want you to die so I can get some stupid money. Plus, you never asked me if I *un*spoofed your phone. I heard what you and Tomás were talking about.

The dock. The women. The shitty bastards holding those women. I want to help."

She was dressed in a black T-shirt bearing the words "Fade to . . ." rendered in white, black jeans and black Converse All-Star high-tops. Strapped to her right hip was her 10mm handgun. Strapped to her left thigh was her Marttiini Lapp hunting knife. Under her eyes were thick dashes of black paint.

"Swear to God, Lucy —"

"Let me do this," she pleaded. "You've helped me more than anybody ever has. Besides Skittles. And my mom."

I drew in a slow, deep breath of the thick, hot air in an effort to bring my blood pressure down from the stratosphere.

"People are probably going to get killed tonight, Lucy," I said. "I don't want one of those people to be a kid who hasn't seen her twenty-first birthday yet."

"I lived most of my life freezing my ass off on a rez outside the Sault," Lucy said. "I've seen old women die of exposure and babies die of malnutrition. And I've seen elders cry over the bodies of young bucks who drank themselves to death or blew their brains out because they felt even the fucking gods forgot their names. So, don't you ever talk to me like I'm a baby with a talcum powdered ass, dude. You can call this whole thing off on account of me — and eight women get shipped off to God only knows where to do God only knows what. Or I'm with the hunting party. Your choice, Sherlock."

I gave Tomás a hard look.

"Don't look at me," Tomás said. "I kinda like the kid."

Still seething, I held a rigid forefinger an inch away from Lucy's face and said, "You do *what* I say *when* I say it. You put me or Tomás or any of those women in danger, I'll shoot you myself. You are non-lethal backup only. Do you understand me?"

She looked at me for a moment before saying, "Can I give an Indian war whoop?"

"Goddammit, Lucy!"

"I'm kidding!" she said. "Yeah, I understand. Now let's go be heroes."

I turned and walked away.

Behind me I heard Tomás chuckle and tell her, "You're a piece of work, kid."

Tomás has always had a good singing voice. A nice baritone that brings old Mexican folk tunes to soulful life. Late in the evening at backyard barbeques, after my father and Tomás had drunk their fill of beer and tequila, Tomás — feeling both ebullient and maudlin — would sing Mexican folk songs. My father would accompany him on his Fender acoustic. My mother and Elena — though certainly displeased by the amount of booze the two men had consumed — would nevertheless swoon at the music.

Tomás even sang at his daughter's *quinceañera* and her wedding. Both times had him sweating bullets. He'd never sung sober before.

Tonight, Tomás was singing "You Belong to My Heart."

He was also doing a wobbly drunk walk and dragging a rotting plank of wood across the chain links of the port security fence.

I hid in the shadows in front of the wide truck gate entrance near the guard shack, ready to cover Tomás. Lucy was crouched low ten feet behind me and quiet as a mouse.

"Hey," a young, lanky, zit-faced guard said, approaching Tomás from the guard shack. "What the hell you doing, man?"

"My — my Maria — she's gone," Tomás whined as he banged on the fence with the wood plank. "She's just — fucking *gone*! Puta!"

"Hey, listen," the guard said. "You need to get gone. I mean *now*. This is private —"

"I can't live without her! I don't *want* to

live without my Maria!"

Tomás — more of an old-school method actor than I would ever have imagined — slammed his body against the chain link fence and, weighed down with faux grief, began sliding down the fence, weeping. The guard fumbled out his Taser and came within inches of the fence and Tomás.

"Listen, bro," the guard said, "I don't wanna have to use this, but —"

Before the guard could finish his sentence, Tomás had the black barrel of his HK Mark 23 auto .45 through the fence and inches away from the guard's chin.

"How much do you make an hour, amigo?" Tomás said, shedding his sloppy drunk theatrics. "See, I'm thinking it ain't nearly enough to take a bullet for. Am I right?"

"Yessir."

I came out of the shadows and stood behind Tomás's right shoulder.

"What's your name?" I said to the guard.

"Lloyd," the guard said, quivering. "Lloyd Hormsby. Sir."

"Good strong name," I lied. "Listen, Lloyd Hormsby, you got a chance to be a hero tonight. But first you're going to walk down to the gate and open it for us, right, Lloyd?"

"Wrong."

I felt a cold metal gun barrel press into the base of my skull and a gruff voice behind me said, "Tell your buddy to lay his piece nice and easy on the ground or he's gonna have your brains all over the back of his shirt."

Slowly, Tomás laid his .45 on the damp ground.

"Here's what's gonna happen next, assholes —" the voice behind me said.

The gun barrel eased away from the back of my head. Then out of the corner of my eye I saw the gun appear over my right shoulder, dangling upside down by a forefinger hooked in the trigger guard. I grabbed the gun and spun around.

Behind me was a tall, beer-bellied older guard showing me the palms of his hands. Riding him, piggyback, was Lucy Three Rivers, the tip of her six-inch hunting knife held in the guard's left nostril, a thin crimson line of blood slowly following the blade's shimmering edge.

Tomás quickly picked up his gun. "Open the gate, Lloyd Hormsby. Now."

Hormsby stood as if trying to pull himself out of a waking nightmare.

"Goddammit, ya dumb country fuck!" the older beer-bellied guard growled at his young partner. "Do what he told you to do!"

Tomás turned to the beer-bellied guard and said, "You got a ninety-pound girl riding your back and holding a knife up your nose. I don't think I'd be calling Lloyd Hormsby a 'dumb country fuck.' "

"Lloyd," I said calmly. "It's time to go."

Blinking himself back to life, Lloyd Hormsby nodded that he understood and began taking measured steps toward the gate-mounted controls forty feet away.

38

Zip-tied, gagged and seated on the floor of the grimy guard shack were the Magnificent Mr. Lloyd Hormsby and his unpleasant beer-bellied boss. I crouched by Hormsby and said, "It may not feel like it now, Lloyd, but you're doing a good thing. A brave thing."

Lloyd grunted and nodded. I'm sure he felt a bit less than brave hog-tied and gagged with one of his own dingy tube socks.

I looked at Lloyd's partner and said, "You? You're gonna die a lonely alcoholic binge-watching *Gilmore Girls* on Netflix."

"Uk ooo!" Lloyd's boss grunted. Which, in the language of the recently zip-tied and gagged, translated to "fuck you."

"You set?" I asked Tomás.

Tomás had been studying the six CCTV monitors. "I got seven guys. Three by a south stack of cargo boxes, two by the freighter smoking, one walking our way —

ninety seconds — and one taking a piss in the river by a loading gantry. I'm sure there's more, Octavio, but this equipment was considered crappy a decade ago."

"Sound like good odds to you, compadre?" I said, smiling up at Tomás.

"Even Steven," Tomás said, returning my smile.

I turned to Lucy. She was kneeling by the two subdued guards, casually twirling her hunting knife. I said, "You stay here."

"You kidding me?" she groused. "I gotta babysit these two shit stains?"

"You," I said with a bit more emphasis, "stay here."

"Thirty seconds." Tomás crouched by the CCTV control panel and racked one in his new rifle.

"Fine," Lucy grumbled.

The beer-bellied guard suddenly tried to call out, banging a shoulder heavily into the wall of the guard shack. Lucy quickly pulled her 10mm from its hip holster and brought the butt of the gun hard across his face, knocking him unconscious.

Too late.

The man approaching the guard shack got the message.

"Rover One! Rover One!" the man said into his walkie. "We got uninvited!"

Kicking the door of the guard shack open, the man saw Lucy and the two guards huddled on the floor. He brought a black muzzled TEC-9 machine pistol to the three of them. Simultaneously, Tomás and I stood: I put two rounds in him — one center mass, one in his head. Tomás sent him flying out door with a blast from his new rifle.

In the lethal space of a tenth of a second, the party had started.

"Rover Three," a frantic voice crackled over the dead man's walkie. "What the fuck's going on? Rover Three? God*dammit!*"

Tomás and I exchanged a glance, then we both looked at Lucy.

We had to move out. Away from Lucy. Away from the two guards.

"Lucy!" I yelled. "Stay low!"

"Yeah! Right! *Go!*"

We did.

Tomás and I ran toward the *Federal Shoreland* freighter, keeping at least thirty feet between us.

The freighter's engines were slowly spinning up.

The kidnapped women must have already been loaded on board.

Two muzzle flashes.

Bullets shredding the blacktop between

Tomás and me. Tomás drops and rolls behind a discarded cargo container. I run for the cover of dumpsters near the warehouses.

Bullets hammer into the metal dumpsters.

With every second, the engines of the freighter spin faster. It's only moments away from embarking. I glance up at the dock's control tower and decide it's time to give the dock master a wake-up call: I fire the remaining clip in my Glock 17 at the control tower. Maybe — just maybe — two of the seventeen bullets will hit the tower's window, diverting the dock master's attention away from moving the freighter safely out of port.

I switch out clips and take a quick look around the corner of the dumpsters.

On foot, a BMC biker with a TEC-9 is twenty feet away from being on top of me.

He fires, the bullets thudding into the dumpster, narrowly missing me.

I push the dumpster.

Hard.

It rolls toward the man, distracting him. I spin out from behind the moving dumpster and fired three shots.

He drops.

No time to bust an arm patting myself on the back. More shots ring out, finding the concrete to my left. On my feet, I grab the dead biker's TEC-9 as I pass his body.

Any man or woman who served in combat can tell you about the cold-sweat terror of a night firefight: the pyrotechnics of tracer bullets searching for warm flesh; the sound of bullets thumping into the earth inches away from you. Is that sweat or a buddy's blood spraying? Is that breathing mine or the enemy's?

The anomalous weightlessness and unbearable gravity of seconds slowly stretching into an eternal black hole.

I heard the thunder of Tomás's rifle twice to my eleven-o'clock position, maybe forty yards away. It was time we got back together.

Suddenly . . .

. . . silence.

The second worst thing about a night firefight is abrupt silence.

Is this that solitary moment before a bullet hits the heart?

"Whoever the fuck you are," a voice echoes through the cascading darkness and grey mist, "you need to stop fuckin' around right now. Lay your weapons down, come out and we won't kill you."

"You promise not to kill us?" I yell back, checking the clip of the TEC-9 and trying to calculate the location and range of the man's voice. "Because I've been lied to before. Winifred Brousse. Seventh grade. She said she liked me, but she didn't *like* like me. She *like* liked my best friend Tony Alvara."

"Okay, smartass," the voice booms. "Have it your fucking way."

Two bursts from an automatic rifle.

While I was echo-locating whoever had been talking, they were echo-locating me.

And they were pretty good at it — the shots came within six feet of me.

"Enough of this shit," I grumble to myself. I spin out from behind a stack of concrete pipes, elevate the barrel thirty degrees and unload the TEC-9.

A shooter perched on a gangplank thirty-feet up and some thirty feet away took most of the bullets. His body tumbles through the air before slamming hard to the ground and shattering at least 183 of its 206 bones.

I roll back to cover.

"You still among the living?" I call out in Spanish.

"If you call this 'living,' " Tomás replies in Spanish. "You?"

"Havin' the time of my life."

"All right!" a voice calls through the darkness. "Enough of this shit, goddammit! Say something, bitch!"

My heart stops.

There is a moment of cruel silence. Then, "I'm sorry, August!"

Lucy.

"They — they shot those two guards," Lucy said. I could hear her choking back tears. "They just — they killed Lloyd Hormsby! Like he was *nothing*!"

"Seriously, dudes," the man laughs. "Where'd you get this one? Some fucking carnival face-painting booth? Jesus! How desperate *are* you guys?"

"Fuck you, dick-breath!" Lucy yelled.

The sound of a slap.

"Stop wasting my fucking time and come out!" the man shouts. "Or tiny tot gets a bullet between her tits!"

Seconds after Tomás and I lay down our weapons, we're surrounded by nine battle-hardened BMC bikers with a variety of automatic and semi-automatic weapons. The biker who had talked us out — a tall, pocked-face maniac with a black moustache attempting to cover a harelip — had a fistful of the back of Lucy's shirt collar in his left hand and an M&P 380 auto in his right. Lucy's wrists were cuffed behind her back.

"Okay, so let's talk about who sent you," the man said while holding Lucy. "You associated with anybody — the Osoverde brothers? Pavel Ochinko? Maybe that fat fuck Xiang Lao?"

"We just came to get the women," I said. "No association. No plans other than cut 'em loose from your stink."

"Oh, my God," the man said. "Really? I mean, like, white knight shit?"

"Your Birmingham safe house is blown," I said. "Your ICE associates are under FBI surveillance and they can't wait to toss you losers into super-max. The girls, the drug mules, the coyotes — it's all about to fall. It's time for you to bug out. So why not just let the girl go? Keep us, but let her walk."

"As the saying goes, homeboy," the biker said, pulling Lucy up to her tiptoes by her shirt collar, "that ship has sailed. And from the sound of things, you have no idea — not a fucking *clue*! — who you're dealing with. And that's sad. It's so sad I find myself wanting to tell you who you're fucking with — but, I mean, if I told you I'd have to kill you. Which is looking like an inevitability anyway." He pressed his face into the back of Lucy's neck and took in a deep breath of her. Then, performing for his band of biker cutthroats, he said, "What do you think, brothers: Toss her onto a moving freighter — hoping to miss the propellers — and collect another ten grand? Sell her for parts?

Or maybe *all* aboard the train?"

Ten of the men chanted "Train! Train! Train!"

Two made a "Woo-woooo!" sound and laughed.

One made a choking sound.

The biker making the choking sound suddenly stumbled toward the man holding Lucy while clutching his throat.

He crumpled to the ground, blood gushing from his neck.

A dull pop twenty meters away.

Another man's head blossoms red, spraying Lucy and her captor with blood and brains. Lucy's captor throws her to the ground and begins firing his gun into the assassin's cover of darkness. Lucy rolls and quickly brings her legs through the loop formed by her handcuffed wrists so that her hands are in front. Her captor suddenly levels his weapon at her. Lucy deflects the gun with her hands and plants a knee in the biker's nuts. Twice. Then, swinging onto his back as if mounting a horse, she brings the chain links of her handcuffs around his neck and pulls him into her. Choking, he desperately tries to bring his gun over his shoulder to fire at Lucy's head. He only manages to shoot off his right ear. He drops to the ground, unconscious.

"Don't kill him!" I yell to Lucy. "We need him!"

I could only hope she heard me.

Tomás and I grab up the weapons of the dead and begin firing: Tomás takes out three of the bikers in short order. I manage to drop four. And our avenging guardian angel puts assassin's bullets into the heads of two more bikers. The last man dropped his weapon and fell to his knees, lacing his fingers behind his heads. A position I'm sure he was familiar with.

Echoing footsteps on a freight container.

Tomás and I brought our weapons up.

"I don't ask for much," suspended FBI Special Agent Megan O'Donnell said. "Just the occasional Save-the-Date for when the goddamn festivities begin."

"Well, aren't you a sight for sore eyes," I said, admiring O'Donnell's tactical look, smartly accessorized with a Barrett M98B sniper rifle. "How'd you —"

"The kid called me," O'Donnell said. Then, gesturing with her head, O'Donnell continued, "Uh — looks like Lucy's got some 'splainin' to do —"

I turned: Lucy had backed her mustached captor against a cargo box, her six-inch hunting knife embedded to the hilt through the bottom of his chin.

"Okie-dokey, honey," I said, grabbing her hand and pulling the six-inch blade out of the man's chin and mouth. "That's enough of that."

"You fucking piece of *shit!*" Lucy screamed at the biker as he choked on his own blood. Lucy, crying and inconsolable, kicked at him. "I'll *kill* you! I'll *kill* you, you skunk-fucking bastard!"

A cell phone in the man's pocket began ringing.

I hand Lucy off to Tomás and say to the man as he spits blood, "You mind?" Then I pull a flip phone from the man's jeans and answer.

"May I presume the merchandise is on its way?" a man's cultured voice says.

"Yeah," I tersely grunt.

"Good," the man said. "Miss Olivier will have your shipping fee the day after tomorrow, seven thirty at The Whitney. And please do clean yourself up this time."

"Sure."

The man disconnected. I pocketed the bleeding man's phone, then turned to a still furious Lucy and say, "It's over."

"Yeah," Tomás said, pointing to the freighter. "It's sure lookin' that way."

The *Federal Shoreland* freighter was slowly churning away from the dock.

39

The freighter hadn't moved far from its dock and it wasn't moving fast — but it was under way.

"I'll mobilize the Coast Guard," O'Donnell said.

Frankly, I wasn't listening to O'Donnell. Instead I found myself pointing to a tall mobile gantry, its cargo loading arm still slung over the deck of the moving freighter.

"You know how to work one of those things?" I said to Tomás.

"Yeah," Tomás said brightly. "Back in '93 I did a short stint as —" Then he gave me a look. "Oh, you are just *bullshitting* me, right?"

"Bring 'em home, marine," O'Donnell said with a definitive nod to me.

By the time we reached the gantry, the *Federal Shoreland* was slowly beginning to churn away from the dock, powering up to make its entry into the channel leading to the Detroit River's freighter lane. Tomás would have to extend the upper loading arm another eight to ten feet if I were to have a good shot at landing on the deck.

He fired up the gantry and I began climbing the scaffolding of the loading arm.

From that height I could see numbers beneath the ship's name. Numbers that corresponded with the numbers written on the back of the photos of women I'd pulled from the biker club's Spring Lake bar headquarters safe; ship registration numbers.

At the very top of the scaffolding I climbed out onto the loading arm and gave brief thought to my namesake, poet Octavio Paz . . .

"One of the most notable traits of the Mexican's character is his willingness to contemplate horror: he is familiar, even complacent in his dealings with it."

. . . and then I jumped.

Somehow, I managed only to break my left pinky finger before rolling and coming to my feet on the freighter's deck.

Sprinting to the wheelhouse, I pushed myself through the door and leveled my Glock at the two men standing at the glowing control panel.

"Who the bloody hell are you?" the grey-bearded man I assumed to be the captain said as he glared at me. Instinctively, his younger first mate raised his hands, appearing ready and able to piss himself.

"I'm the guy telling you to turn this boat around. You've got eight women stowed away, probably held hostage in the supply hold of this ship."

"There aren't any women on my ship," the grey-bearded captain snarled. "Now explain yourself, son. Who the hell —"

"I'm the guy with the gun telling you to turn this goddamn tub around. *Now!*"

"You pointing a gun at me won't make turning a hundred tons of steel around any faster or easier." We stared hard at each other for a moment. Then he glanced at his first mate and said, "Go down to the supply hold. Radio back."

"Aye, sir," his first mate said before walking a cautiously wide berth around me and out of the wheelhouse.

"Stop the goddamn engines," I said.

"If I stop the engines, then she drifts," the captain said. "And if she drifts, then it's likely we run aground in a channel wall. And if that happens, nobody's going anywhere. Best to navigate into the channel where I'm better able to maneuver. What would they be doing here, these women?"

"I don't know if you're playing dumb or if you're being straight with me," I said. "But let's assume for a second you're being straight: These women have been kidnapped and are being trafficked. This ship is one link in a pipeline from Canada through Michigan then south, east and west. And my guess is, you and other freighters have been transporting women like this into prostitution, domestic slavery and maybe even black-market organ sales for the past year."

"Dear God."

"Yeah," I said, still holding my gun steady on him. "Dear God."

As we waited for the First Mate to return, we simply stared at each other with me holding him steady in my gunsight.

"Am I your first?" I finally said to the white-bearded captain, who appeared unimpressed by my presence.

"My first what?"

"Pirate."

The wheelhouse door opened behind me.

"Okay," his first mate said. "We're all just gonna breathe easy, okay?"

His forearm was locked tightly around the neck of a frightened-looking young brown woman. Pressed against her temple was the short barrel of a revolver.

"What the hell are you doing, McKenzie?" the captain blurted.

"You," the first mate named McKenzie said to me. "Put your gun down. Easy, okay?"

"McKenzie, I'm your *captain*!"

"Sir! Just — just shut the fuck up, okay? Please? I don't want to hurt anybody. Swear to God I don't."

"Seriously?" I said. "You don't want to hurt anybody? 'Cause it looks to me like that's exactly what you're prepared to do. The way I see it, you've got three very bad choices."

"Come on," McKenzie pleaded. "Put your gun on the floor. Please."

"Crappy choice one," I said. "You kill me and toss me overboard. Then you kill your captain and somehow make it look like an accident. After that you deliver the girls, collect your pay and disappear. And there's nothing more pathetic than an amateur trying to disappear."

"Jesus Christ! Will you just put the gun down!"

"Then there's shitty choice two," I said, slowly bending to appear as if I was complying with his request to place my gun on the wheelhouse floor. "You see the profound error of your ways and pray for the mercy of the court at your sentencing. And for a crime like this, I don't think mercy is in the stars."

He laughed, confident he was only hours away from a life-changing paycheck.

"Then there's three, which isn't really a choice," I said, still holding onto my gun and crouched near the floor. "It's more of a lousy permanent condition."

"Condition?" McKenzie said, not knowing whether to point his gun at his captain or me. "What are you talking about?"

"Three is somebody on this boat pulls the duty of washing your brains off the wall behind you."

He issued a quick, nervous laugh. After a second or two of seeing the deadly intent in my eyes, he brought the barrel of his revolver to me . . .

. . . but not fast enough.

Even at an awkward, crouched angle, I fired.

The bullet grazed the top of the young woman's left ear before entering McKenzie's mouth at a thirty-degree angle, exploding the back of his head and painting the wall behind him with blood, teeth, bone and brain.

His remains collapsed to the floor.

The young woman, screaming, ran to me

and I held her. In Spanish I told her it was over, that she was safe, and that we'd get her home.

Behind me, the captain radioed the shipyard.

"This is the freighter *Federal Shoreland*," he said. "We are returning to port."

"Say again, *Federal Shoreland*?" a voice crackled back. "Is there a problem?"

"Yeah," the captain said, staring at his dead first mate. "Pretty big one."

Four DPD cruisers had arrived on the scene, their lights flashing.

O'Donnell called the FBI knowing that the first thing they would do upon their arrival would be to put her in cuffs.

Of the eight women in the freighter's supply hold, five were undocumented Mexicans and one was Honduran. They had all made secret homes and quiet lives of servitude in Detroit and Ann Arbor. The last two were a black girl and a white girl, neither past the age of fifteen, holding hands and looking as if they'd just barely survived the world-ending fires of the apocalypse.

Three of O'Donnell's FBI colleagues surrounded her; one agent had his handcuffs out and ready. After a minute or two, the agents started to walk away. One of the agents stopped, turned back to O'Donnell and tossed his handcuffs to her.

"When you see the boss," the agent said, "put 'em on, okay? Makes everybody's life easier."

The agent saluted O'Donnell, then walked away.

"Goddammit, August," O'Donnell said with an exasperated sigh. "Why do you do shit like this?"

"You're gonna have to shoot me to stop me, Megan," I said. "You gonna shoot me?"

"The temptation is always there, August." Then, continuing to stare at me through narrowed eyes she said, "Ah, hell. Goddamn bullet would probably ricochet off you and catch me in the forehead."

"Thanks," I said.

I hustled the undocumented Mexican and Honduran women to Tomás.

"Get them to Father Grabowski," I said. "He'll know what to do."

Tomás started to move the six women to his truck, but a uniformed Detroit cop intercepted him.

"Hey, whoa, hold on," the cop said, taking a stance in front of Tomás and the women. "Who are you? Where are you taking these women?"

O'Donnell stepped in between Tomás and

the uniform, flashed an FBI ID she had no right to flash and said, "This man is with me. These women are witnesses to a federal crime and vital to an ongoing FBI investigation. They are being taken into protective custody. Is there a problem, officer?"

The officer ran his eyes over Tomás, O'Donnell and the six women before jerking a thumb over his shoulder and walking away.

I called Father Grabowski, waking him out of a dead sleep, and gave him a heads-up. With his network, in less than four hours he'd probably have the six women praising Baby Jesus over a good breakfast in Windsor, Ontario.

"I'm going to hell for this," O'Donnell said, standing next to me and watching the swarm of Detroit police and now State police and FBI agents; forensics people in white moon suits photographing bodies and weapons, yellow cones marking shell casings, the dockmaster being scrutinized. And the last of the living BMC bikers being marched to squad cars. "I am definitely going to hell for this."

"Where's Lucy?" I said.

"Four blocks away in my car," O'Donnell said. "I left her a flask of Irish whiskey."

"She's not legal."

"Then I am definitely taking the express handbasket to hell."

"Pretty girls don't go to hell," I said. "They go to Tuscany. Besides. The way I see it, you get a spanking in Director Phillips's office. Then he pins a medal on you. You might even get your picture hung in the cafeteria — 'Employee of the Month'!" We watched the methodical documentation of the dock carnage for a minute or two. Then I said, "Those four shots you took tonight? Out*standing*! I owe you big time, Megan."

"Yeah, well, a woman really shouldn't just rely her looks," she sighed. "It helps to have a skill. And by the way — it was only two."

"Two?"

"I only took two shots tonight, August," O'Donnell said.

40

For as much as I believe in God, the possibility of miracles and the existence of angels (and the willingness to admit I am far from being one) I doubt very much any of God's legions of seraphim carry sniper rifles.

So, who made the other two sniper shots at the dock, catching a bad guy in the head and giving Tomás, Lucy and myself a new lease on life?

Drinking a beer on the stoop of my house two nights after the dock firefight (and after answering several hundred questions posed by Detroit PD, State cops, FBI, Homeland Security, ICE and DEA, with my trusted attack-dog attorney David G. Baker vigorously defending my dubious virtue) I had a feeling I couldn't shake. That uneasy feeling of having been watched over a period of time from a distance. Every movement documented and annotated, every breath logged and tagged, every uttered word entered into an invisible ledger.

I didn't like the feeling of someone doing to me what the Marines had taught me to do so well: put a human life in the crosshairs and wait patiently for the killing moment.

Between sips of my beer, my eyes kept landing on the house of a new neighbor. Trent T.R. Ogilvy.

Qui audet adipiscitur.

Who Dares, Wins.

Ogilvy was former SAS, which made him if not a brother-in-arms, at least a distant and highly respected cousin. And if anybody could shoot out the eye of a flying sparrow at two-hundred yards it was British SAS.

But all indications were Trent T.R. Ogilvy was who he said he was; a late-stage hippy with a ridiculous man-bun hairstyle doing socially conscientious works through an internationally recognized charitable organization. All while grossing out a few neighbors with his morning front porch yoga routine.

Whatever his background, Ogilvy had at no cost brought computers and Wi-Fi to people living in Detroit's information deserts.

Who says America doesn't need foreign aid?

Lucy had checked him out. As deeply as she burrowed into his digital footprint, he appeared only to be Trent T. R. Ogilvy, trust fund kid from an aristocratic English military family that possessed eight decades worth of commendations and decorations from the Queen herself. Ogilvy, it seems, had even served briefly with Prince Harry in Iraq.

Maybe I should just sit on my stoop, listen to the white-noise of traffic on I-75, drink cold Mexican beer and count my lucky stars.

Maybe I should just be grateful for two nights without ICE patrols creeping through the 'hood while they reassessed what kind of State-sponsored terror organization they wanted to be when they grew up.

And maybe I should just get back to flipping houses and daydreaming about Tatina naked in my bed. Or naked in her bed.

Maybe.

At seven thirty the next morning, the biker's phone rang and I answered it.

"What happened?" the man on the other end said.

"What do ya mean, 'what happened'?" I said trying to keep my replies terse.

"The shipment," the man said. "Our —

merchandise. It should have arrived at the next stop four hours ago."

"I put 'em on the boat," I said. "I don't drive the fuckin' thing."

"Miss Olivier is, of course, concerned —"

"Just have my fuckin' shipping fee ready tonight."

There was an exasperated sigh at the other end of the phone. "Again, it is highly suggested you not bring any firearms as Miss Olivier travels with her own well-trained and equipped security detail."

"Should I bring flowers or condoms?"

The man hung up.

I showered, dressed and decided to make my way to Trent Ogilvy's house for a pleasant softball interrogation. As grateful as I was for whoever took those other two sniper shots, I found myself in need of an actual name and a face toward which I could direct my gratitude. Mysteries, enigmas, puzzles and paradoxes were best left to God Almighty.

And NPR's Will Shortz.

I had just closed my front door behind me when I saw Lucy Three Rivers walking north toward Vernor Highway. She was nearly dwarfed by her oversized backpack.

"Going somewhere?" I said, catching up with her.

"Yeah, I uh — I gotta go, okay?" She nervously shifted her weight from foot to foot.

"You know you can stay," I said. "This is just as much your neighborhood as it is mine."

"Yeah, sure," she said, unable to look at me. "Whatever."

We stood quiet for a moment, letting the warm morning slowly wash over us.

"This isn't about what happened at the dock, is it?" I finally said.

"No," she said, finally looking at me. "No, that was — I've never been a part of something that — you know —"

"Meant something?"

"Yeah." She issued a brief smile. After a moment, she said, "Being happy. It feels like — uncomfortable. Like a lie. I don't trust it. I mean, one minute you're dancing with it — laughing and, you know, grabbin' each others' goodies — next thing, it's cutting your fuckin' throat."

"Happiness as a prelude to betrayal," I said. "I hear ya."

Awkward silence. Then she said, "It's not that I'm not grateful —"

"But you've got to go away," I said. "See if what you've felt here stays with you for a while. See if it's got a draw on you after a couple months, maybe a year."

"Yeah," she said, looking away from me. Her eyes began to fill. "Whatever."

"You need money?"

"No." She wiped her eyes on her shoulders. "I'm good. I, uh — I left that letter you gave me at Carmela and Sylvia's. I don't need to be carrying somebody's fuckin' last-will-and-testament around with me. I need money, Skittles'll work something out where I get paid."

I brought out my wallet, emptied it and shoved the bills into one of her oversized cargo shorts pockets.

"Any idea of which way you're heading?" I said.

"U.P.," she said. "Back to the Sault. Ain't said 'hey' to my mom's spirit in a while. Maybe see what's new in Mackinaw City — which I'm sure ain't jack squat."

Out of nowhere, she hugged me tightly, wept for about five seconds and almost as quickly pulled away.

"Hey! Where you goin'?"

It was Jimmy.

"I'll let you kids talk," I said.

Lucy attempted to smile at me.

I attempted to smile at her.

I walked away, turning back long enough to see Jimmy and Lucy shake hands. Then, standing on tiptoe, she gave Jimmy a kiss on his cheek.

Then she made her way to Vernor Highway, turned right and disappeared.

I arrived at Trent Ogilvy's house just in time to see my real estate agent's grandson, Claymont, hammering a for sale sign into the modest lawn.

"Hey, Clay," I said. "What's going on?"

"Hey, Mr. Snow," Clay said. "Seems Mr. Ogilvy moved out couple nights ago. Left instructions with Grandmomma Jesse to put the place up. Not much left inside. Said to donate any profit to charity. Gave her a couple grand in case there's a loss — which there ain't gonna be since white folk done rediscovered Southwest Detroit." Clay reached into a pants pocket and pulled out a folded envelope. He held it out to me and said, "Left this for you."

I took the envelope. Scrawled on it was a name that I no longer recognized: Lieutenant August O. Snow, FOB Lion, United States Marine Corp.

I opened it.

Inside was a small, worn piece of a map.

Korengal Valley, Afghanistan.

There were old stains on the map.

Blood from another time, another place.

41

14:58.

The call at Forward Operating Base "Lion" in the Panjshir Province, Afghanistan: Eight British SAS pinned down in the Korengal Valley by at least twenty Taliban.

I was, by helicopter gunship, six minutes out.

My spotter, Corporal Maximillian "Maxie" Avadenka, and I dropped in less than half a click north of the SAS team. Close enough to see the Taliban noose tightening on the Brits.

Three minutes. Seven Taliban killed from five hundred meters. A corridor for the SAS team to bug out. Four minutes more and Maxie and I took out another five enemy combatants.

Of the eight SAS, six made it out alive.

For Maxie and me, just another day in the sand.

Four days after the engagement, we get a bottle of good Irish whiskey. A note written on

SAS Forward Command letterhead: "There for us. There for you. Anywhere. Always. Semper fi, mates."

Before I left for The Whitney restaurant to meet the mysterious Miss Olivier, I checked the website for Ogilvy's charity group — Global Community Action Corp. It was the same website Lucy and I had checked several weeks earlier. Everything was the same save for one rather sizable difference: The photo of the Director of International Community Outreach — Trent T.R. Ogilvy — was not the man who had briefly been my Markham Street neighbor. Now, Trent T.R. Ogilvy was a well-dressed, thickly built black man in his fifties.

I was wearing a light grey checked linen Hackett London suit, white shirt, baby-blue socks and black suede Bruno Magli loafers for my dinner date with the mysterious Miss Olivier.

No tie. Ties are for suckers, especially during a steaming Michigan summer.

You can search the world and not find a restaurant equal or better than The Whitney. The Romanesque revival mansion was built of rose-colored jasper in 1894: fifty-two rooms, twenty fireplaces and a number of Tiffany stained-glass windows. It was the family home of lumber baron David Whitney, Jr. Today, the 22,000 square-foot mansion is known for its understated opulence and unmatched cuisine.

There were only three other vehicles in The Whitney's parking lot: a black Lincoln limo with blacked out windows and two serious-looking Chevy Suburban SUVs.

Inside, it was cool and sedate. There was innocuous live jazz music coming from the landing between the first and second floor.

I was greeted by three men: Two looked like they only ate glass and babies. The third was considerably shorter, thickly built and wearing black-rimmed round glasses.

"I'm afraid the restaurant is reserved for a private affair tonight, sir," the short, thick man said. I recognized his voice; the man who had called the biker at the freight dock and me this morning.

"Yeah, I know," I said. "Miss Olivier."

The man stared at me for a long time before saying, "And you would be?"

"The King of Spain on Tuesdays and Thursdays," I said. "Right now, I'm just a guy who'd like a few minutes with your boss. Do I give my drink order to you or what?"

Again, the short man stared at me for a moment, then gestured for the two gorillas flanking him to check me out.

One of the gorillas stepped forward with a wand and with an English accent said, "Open your coat, raise your arms and spread your legs, sir."

"Is this going to tickle?" I said. "I'm a little ticklish."

The other gorilla took out a semi-auto .45 from a shoulder rig and stood holding it with his hands casually folded.

The muscle running the wand over me nodded to the short man, indicating I was clean, and stepped back. His partner replaced his gun back in its shoulder rig.

The short man with glasses escorted me upstairs. On the landing was a jazz quartet — baby grand piano, double bass, simple drum kit and trumpet. The quartet was flanked by two more security guys.

"Hey, fellas," I said to the quartet. "Y'all awright?"

"Oh, yeah, brotha," the drummer said, shaking his head no. "Couldn't be better."

I was escorted to a private dining room with a fireplace.

Even though it was still a muggy eighty-three degrees outside, a small fire burned brightly in the fireplace, its yellow light playing off the room's single chandelier and stained-glass window portraying Saint

Cecilia, patron saint of music. Considering the restaurant's history, I half expected to see the ghost of David Whitney rise up from the floor, cocktail in hand, critically eying the woman seated at a small round table draped in white linens, sipping white wine and picking at a large salad.

The woman was nice looking, sophisticated, perhaps in her early fifties with short, severe jet-black hair and an expensive but conservative suit. She sat as if she were a mannequin posed to look bored.

Miss Olivier.

There were two other people in the room with her.

One was a nondescript man in a nondescript suit looking intentionally bored. I'm sure to Miss Olivier, he was invisible until needed.

I recognized the other person.

Anna Green Eyes.

"Well, you're looking better than the last time I saw you," I said to Anna Green Eyes.

"Jesus!" Anna Green Eyes said, taking out her gun and aiming it at me.

"Is that truly necessary?" the woman calling herself Miss Olivier said to Anna Green Eyes. She had an upper-crusty English accent and sounded eternally disappointed.

"He's a fucking *cop,*" Anna Green Eyes

said, not putting her gun away.

"*Ex*-cop," I said. "Now I'm just a gadfly man-about-town."

"He's the one who fucked up the safe house," Green Eyes said.

"*And* shot you. Remember that?" I said. "Wow. The times we've had."

"Ma'am —" she started.

Miss Olivier said to me, "I assume you've done all of this in an effort to replace Mr. Krenshaw? Perhaps become our vendor of choice in the region, mister — ?"

"Snow," I said. "August Snow. And if Mr. Krenshaw was the smelly neo-Nazi biker with the harelip and porn-stache, then yes. I hope you're not disappointed."

"He was quite good at his job," Miss Olivier said. "But he smelled, took drugs and used rather offensive language to describe certain people. I loathed dealing with him, but — well — business is, after all, business."

"Ma'am —" Anna Green Eyes began.

"Would you tell her to put her gun away?" I said, pointing to Anna. "Then have her get me a drink. Scotch."

The stoic Miss Olivier moved her unblinking hazel gaze from me to Anna.

Anna reluctantly holstered her gun and limped out of the room in a huff, presumably to fetch my drink.

"I'm more than willing to hear what you propose, Mr. Snow," she said. "Naturally, since we're still working out the kinks of a relatively new operation, we'd like to minimize any further damage. Am I clear, Mr. Snow?"

"Perfectly."

"And just to reemphasize, should we have any further meetings you are to attend them sans weapons."

"No problem," I said. Then nodding to the invisible man, I said, "I figure if I need a gun, I'll just take his."

Miss Olivier's bored bodyguard flashed his eyes at me.

Anna returned with my drink, setting it gently in front of me. We exchanged glances before she took several steps back and resumed her sentry post.

"I must admit, your actions, though destructive, revealed a weakness in the system we hadn't quite anticipated," Miss Olivier said, lifting her glass of wine to me. "And for that I commend you."

"And," I said, raising my glass of scotch to her, "I must say you are quite the psycho sack of shit. You're the monstrosity that cut a distribution deal with a few rogue ICE units, right? The sicko who bought up Duke

Ducane's trafficking routes?"

"I'm not sure I like your tone, Mr. Snow."

"And I'm on the fence over brussels sprouts," I said. "Who gives a shit on either count, right? I'm pretty sure you and your merry band of mercs had everything to do with the disappearance of Barney Olsen, Esquire. So, fuck you, Cruella."

"I take it you're not here to replace Mr. Krenshaw?" Slowly she sat back in her chair, her hands folded with poised precision in front of her.

"You take that correctly, Miss Queen of the Fucking Undead."

I reached into my suitcoat jacket. Anna and the invisible man took a quick step forward. I pulled out a piece of paper, unfolded it and sat it in front of Miss Olivier. It was the coroner's photo of Izzy.

Miss Olivier glanced at the photo. Then she took a sip of her wine.

"Suicide from the bridge," she said, bringing her soulless eyes back to me. "Needless to say, there have been — speed bumps — along the way. Mr. Olsen's — club — was one of those unfortunate speed bumps. We've since made adjustments. This sort of thing, I can assure you, won't happen again." With well-manicured fingertips, she slowly pushed Izzy's morgue photo further from her and closer to me. "Do you know what many of the great cities in the world have in common, Mr. Snow?" I didn't answer. She was going to tell me anyway. "The availability and variety of clean, organized and exclusively priced sex. Do you really, honestly believe millionaires — *billionaires* — go to Las Vegas, Monaco, Ibiza, Playa Mujeres for strategy breakout sessions followed by a bit of high-stakes poker? No. Certain — appetites — can only be satisfied by well-trained, well-paid, beautiful women and young men who exceed most any sexual fantasy."

"Detroit?" I said. "Really?"

It was the first time I saw Miss Olivier form the hint of a smile.

"My organization — like any business wishing to survive in today's global marketplace — actively searches for ways to expand our business model. Niche markets. Detroit's recent rebound has not gone unnoticed globally. It's less an anomaly and more a model for sustainable growth."

"But you're kidnapping and trafficking women out of the city."

"Yes," she said. "And the commodities we move out help to finance the higher-quality commodities we bring in: Very select, high-end commodities from Russia, Ukraine,

France, Ghana, South Africa, Montenegro and Spain. Commodities that will build, enhance and maintain this city as a truly world-class sex destination."

"Hey, listen, Frau Humpenstein, I don't give a shit about you or your organization," I said. "Any more rogue ICE units or neo-Nazi biker gangs come to my neighborhood, I'll kill 'em. I'll kill 'em all. I will stack their bodies on your doorstep just before I put a bullet in you."

"Perhaps I can arrange a safe-zone. Anything else, Mr. Snow?"

"Yeah. There's one more thing I want."

"That being?"

"His gun," I said pointing to the invisible man.

The room was frozen silent for a tenth of a second.

Enough time for me to grab Miss Olivier's dinner fork, spin out of my chair and plant the fork in the invisible man's right eye. I reached inside his suit coat, grabbed his gun and fired through his jacket at Anna, catching her in the stomach.

Her .38 was out, but before she could level the weapon at me I pushed the invisible man into her. He caught the bullet meant for me and the two crashed to the floor.

I stepped out of the dining room.

The bodyguards by the jazz quartet took stances on the staircase. Before they could fire, I unloaded three shots, killing one and sending the other tumbling down the staircase with a bullet in his right hip.

I walked back towards Miss Olivier, who sat in wide-eyed horror.

Standing over her I ejected a bullet from the gun's chamber and dropped it in her glass of wine. Then I ejected the clip into her salad.

"Her name was Isadora Rosalita del Torres. She was nineteen." I picked up the coroner's photo of Izzy, refolded it and put it back in my suit coat pocket. "You so much as have an unkind thought about me six-thousand miles away and I will step out of your dreams and kill you in your bed. You and anybody else who comes after you."

Noise from downstairs.

Five men wearing black balaclavas, helmets and military uniforms with semiautomatic rifles quickly ascended the stairs.

No time to move.

One of the men took a firing stance four-feet away from me.

He didn't shoot.

Four of the men hustled into the room. One dropped a black bag over Miss Olivier's head. Two scooped her up. The four moved her into the hallway and down the staircase.

The man stationed on me followed the other four men and Miss Olivier, leaving me alive and alone in the private dining room.

After forcing air back in my lungs, I leapt two, three steps at a time down the staircase.

"You guys awright?" I say double-timing past the musicians on the landing.

"Worst gig *EVER!*" the drummer said.

No bodyguards, dead or alive. No little man with round glasses.

I got to the door in time to see Miss Olivier hustled into the back of a black Chevy Tahoe, no plates.

One of the last men standing by a second black Chevy Tahoe started to get in, hesitated, then turned to me. He took off his helmet and balaclava. Smiled. Saluted. Then got in the SUV and closed the door.

Trent T.R. Ogilvy.

Three SUVs sped past me, bouncing onto Woodward Avenue and racing off into the night.

Looks like I'm stuck with the check.

42

"So, what's the deal?" I said, swallowing a large bite of my turkey Reuben. "You still FBI? Or you looking for exciting career opportunities at WalMart?"

O'Donnell issued a hint of a smile. "Still FBI. With caveats."

"Caveats," I said. "Is that like fish eggs?"

We were in a booth at Schmear's Deli in Campus Martius enjoying a noonday repast; me with a gigantic Reuben, mound of sweet potato fries with honey-horseradish dipping sauce, and Schmear's new Watermelon Lemongrass Iced Tea (passable); O'Donnell fiddled with her large Cobb salad, which was accompanied by a glass of water. If history is our teacher, O'Donnell would pick at the salad, then box up the remains for dinner tonight and lunch tomorrow.

"It went pretty much like you said it would." O'Donnell stabbed a piece of Romaine. "Director Phillips tore me a new one in his office for about fifteen minutes. Then he shook my hand, said 'Good work' and half-jokingly promised to boot me to the moon if I ever did anything like that again."

"You're lovable!" I said brightly. "I mean, come on. Look at that face! How can anybody get mad at the poster-girl for parochial schools? By the way. Was that sniper rifle yours or FBI property?"

"On loan," O'Donnell said coyly. "Another sin I'm doing penance for."

I told O'Donnell about my very interesting dinner engagement at The Whitney a couple days earlier.

"Essentially, you're asking me what I know about that, right?" she said.

"You're connected," I said. "Thought you might know a bit of something."

"And if I did, you somehow think you're entitled to know what I know because — why exactly?"

"We're ol' pals?"

O'Donnell uncharacteristically blurted out a laugh.

"You crack my snowflake ass up, August," she finally said.

Then she asked for a carry-out box for her salad.

Before leaving, O'Donnell said, "Some

answers you'll never have, August. Then again. There are times when the answers to life's most vexing mysteries lie at the center of a strawberry cream donut and a nice bourbon."

"She ain't never gonna trust me again, is she?"

It was a thick, eighty degree late June evening and I was sitting at the lone round table in the kitchen of the Soul Hole Donut Shop. I was eating a strawberry cream-filled donut and sipping Pappy Van Winkle's Family Reserve bourbon from a jelly jar that had Winnie the Pooh stenciled on it.

Lady B stood by a big Hobart double oven, drinking her bourbon. The whole place smelled like warm confectioners' sugar and flour.

"She'll come around," I said. "O'Donnell's biggest battles are with herself. She has a very strict personal code of conduct that sometimes doesn't jibe with the way things play out in the real world."

"I like that white girl," Lady B said. "But down here in the Big Black Below, you got to be quick and ready when whatever goes down. I had no choice but to put that man down, else y'all woulda been about a month in yo graves."

"I understand," I said. I looked around at the tight array of kitchen equipment — the butcher block tables, sinks, ovens, racks, mixing bowls and large trays. "Still don't know how you got rid of the body so fast."

"Y'all want me to tell you?"

"Would it ruin my appetite?"

"Probably."

"Then hell no."

We took sips of our bourbon, using the silence to run a thousand questions about each other through our brains.

Then I said, "How long have I known you, Lady B?"

"Since you was 'bout seven or eight," she said, grinning broadly. "Yo momma and daddy used to bring you here on Halloween 'cause they knew I had a warm cinnamon donut and fresh apple cider for you. You all dressed up like Mickey Mouse or some spaceman. Oh, you was the cutest thing!"

"According to a recent Gallup Poll, nine out of ten women — and two out of ten men — think I still am," I said. "That being said, I guess I really don't know much about you. I certainly didn't know you were capable of putting a bullet in the back of a man's head."

Lady B swirled the bourbon in her jelly jar glass. "Well," she began. "Like I said —

here in the Big Black Below . . ."

Then she said, "I been a lot of things in a lot of places for lots of reasons, young Snow. You know where I's born?"

"By the accent, I'd say somewhere in southeastern Georgia."

She smiled. "Seattle, Washington. Went to school in Georgia. You know where else I went to school?"

I said nothing. I simply waited for the answer.

"NYU," she finally said. "And TUM, Munich. Trinity in Dublin. Language arts. Linguistics and ethno-cryptology. Tell you the truth, son — I don't even remember what I used to sound like. Sure wasn't no down-home Georgia girl." She took a seat across from me at the table. "You wonderin' 'bout that English heifer, right? Miss Olivier? Margot Allister Wentworth. Ex-MI6 but not no spy or such. Financial assistant director, covert operations. Budgets, allocations, opposition economic analysis, false-front business constructs. A glorified accountant staring at spreadsheets all day. Finds out she's pullin' down 18 percent less than her male colleagues. And baby goes boom. You know how white folk get when they been shorted a dollar and cheated a dime. Next thing you know, she's way deep gone. Come out of the dark four years ago working for this trafficking cartel out of Hong Kong making ten, fifteen times what she was making shiftin' numbers around for the queen. This whole thing? The kidnappings? The women? The sex clubs? Wasn't nothin' but numbers to her. Logistics and analytics."

I stared at Lady B for a moment before I said, "How —"

"Got me a couple contacts at the British Consulate over there in Chicago," Lady B said with a wink. She poured herself another shot of bourbon. "Amazing what you can learn when you grease the palms of a consulate domestic, cook and janitor. Shoot son, we may not say much when we cleanin' yo house, but we sure as hell got our ears on."

"Miss Olivier," I said. "She the one that cultivated the relationships with ICE?"

"Probably not," Lady B said. "Don't know who ran her. Ain't got time or inclination to care. Hard enough keepin' an eye on this backwoods-ass city with all the newbies struttin' in the front door and the old steppers creepin' out the back."

I told her I admired her information network. I openly wondered if she ever thought about a merger with Smitty's Cuts & Curls. Seemed like a natural fit.

"Oh, baby, you know us colored folk," she said. "Gets us a little green half acre and ain't nobody else allowed to tip a toe on it. Rather salt that little bit of earth than let another sista plant a seed." She took an introspective moment staring down at her glass, then said, "We could have this whole damned city wired if we all just come together for a minute. But . . . well . . ."

We were quiet for a moment before I raised my glass to her and said, "Thanks for saving my life, Lady B."

She grinned. "Oh, honey, anytime, any day."

"You ever do anything like this for my father?"

Lady B suddenly roared with laughter. "Once," she said. "Had to parley some shit twix yo daddy and Duke Ducane. A loan Duke done give him. Wasn't nothing but a minute's holla."

"A — loan?" I said in disbelief. "My dad took a loan from Duke Ducane?"

Lady B sighed heavily, put a hand on mine and said, "Yo daddy took a loan from the devil so he could save his angel. You remember when yo daddy took yo momma down to the Cleveland Clinic for a couple weeks? They was doin' some sort of ovarian cancer clinical trials down there. Two weeks in a hotel on a cop's pay? Plus, don't no insurance pay for no clinical trials. Ducane heard about yo daddy's predicament. Loaned him the money. No interest. No special favors. That's what yo daddy demanded and Duke abided by it. Eventually yo daddy paid Duke every penny back, son. Wished he could've paid for more of your college, but — well — a deal's a deal."

I sat for a moment feeling the earth fall away from me.

Then I gave Lady B a kiss on her warm, plump cheek and left.

43

There is no path forward.

No dream to realize.

No hope that can be offered in good faith.

Father Grabowski, through his undocumented underground, managed to move Carlos, Catalina and their son Manny across the span of the US/Canada Bridge and into the temporary shelter of a small apartment in Windsor, Ontario. A safehouse the old priest had used for others who sought better than that from which they came only to find the flame in Lady Liberty's torch extinguished.

It felt like a strange death, sitting on my stoop, staring across the street at the empty house where Carlos, Catalina and Manny had, less than three days ago, lived.

No lights.

No sounds.

Only a cocoon of darkness insulating this house where Carlos once found refuge and hope in the arms of his wife. Where Catalina shone like a courageous and compassionate beacon. Where Manny, his eyes and smile brighter than all the stars in all of God's galaxies, waved to me as he ventured to school and before bounding up the steps home again.

I didn't even have a chance to say goodbye to Manny.

God . . .

. . . damn.

I could have easily, angrily and with all valid justification laid blame at the cloven feet of ICE and a wayward government for the loss of my friends, my neighbors.

I mostly laid blame at my own feet.

At least Carlos and his family made it to Canada: Three bodies — a Somali man, his wife and baby — were found dead today in North Dakota just shy of Emerson, Manitoba. Police suspect the family got lost on their sojourn north; chilled at night, heat exhaustion and no water during the day. Animals dragged most of the baby off into the wilderness.

Sitting on my stoop, nursing a beer, I felt as if I was looking across the street at an empty vessel that had once been filled to overflowing with the warmth of familiar voices. Now, those voice were gone. Vanished so quickly not even the chill of ghosts remained.

Carmela and Sylvia, each carrying a glass of wine, joined me on my stoop.

They joined me without greeting.

Without quiet words of consolation or sympathetic whispers.

Sylvia sat a step below me, an arm draped over my leg. Carmela sat a step above me, an arm around my shoulders. Together, we drank and stared at the empty house across the street where beloved friends once lived.

This was our *velorio* — our wake — where prayers settled on the tongue like ash.

For two weeks after Carlos and his family had been spirited across the Detroit River, I did light-sleep duty throughout the night and early morning ready to meet any and all fed-plated SUVs crawling down Markham. I wasn't sure what I would have done having spotted a patrol, but I kept my Glock loaded and a nice piece of hickory by the door.

I was simultaneously relieved and disappointed there were no patrols after two weeks. Exhausted, I found myself indulging in a well-earned afternoon nap on my sofa.

Before my sofa nap I got a Skype call on my phone from Lucy.

She was wearing an oversized hoodie, her neck wrapped with two scarfs.

"You look cold," I said.

"Oh, gee — ya think, Sherlock?" she said. "It's sixty-three degrees up here! And that's today's high!"

"People miss you," I said. "I miss you."

"And Jimmy?"

"And Jimmy, too."

"Sylvia and Carmela still got my shit?"

"I'm pretty sure the old girls do —"

"Good."

She disconnected.

My wonderfully levitating nap was interrupted when my doorbell rang.

For someone to ring my doorbell indicated I needn't interrupt my midafternoon slumber. It simply meant later I would find one of those annoying door hangers dangling from the storm door handle announcing a new lawn fertilizing service or the opportunity to get one of two dying daily newspapers at a fantastically discounted price. Maybe a copy of Watchtower announcing Jesus's great displeasure with how I was living my life (no news there).

I decided to let the two rings of the doorbell go unanswered.

Unfortunately, there was a third, fourth and fifth ring followed by some very insistent knocking.

Shirtless and wearing only a pair of fleece Wayne State Warrior basketball shorts, I schlepped to the living room window and discretely pulled the sheers back for a peek: Parked at the curb was a black Chrysler 300 with tinted windows and chrome wheels. A black man — maybe early thirties — wearing a white track suit, white Adidas court shoes and a white Kangol bucket hat had his ear pressed against the door.

I opened the door and said, "May I help you?"

"He here?"

" 'He' who?"

"Aw, come on, man." The man lifted a corner of his track suit jacket revealing the handle of a .38 short-barrel. "I ain't playin'."

"Ooo!" I said raising my eyes from the gun to the young man's bloodshot eyes. "Scary."

"Fo real, niggah," Track Suit said. "He here?"

"I haven't the foggiest as to whom you are referring, sir," I said. "However, I do know this: You've interrupted my nap and for that alone I am justified in my rights to tie your dick in the shape of a tiny giraffe and throw you into oncoming I-75 traffic."

Just as he was about to lift his jacket again,

Jimmy mounted the steps. Seeing the man in the white track suit, Jimmy froze.

"What are you doing here?" Jimmy finally said.

"Yo, hey," Track Suit said turning and sizing Jimmy up. "Damn! Look at you! Wearin' a tool belt'n shit — lookin' all gainfully employed."

"You know this guy?" I said to Jimmy.

"Yessir," Jimmy said quietly staring at the man. "He's my, uh — brother."

"Cutter," Track Suit said to me. "Tha's what people call me on account I cut deals when I need to and flesh when I have to." Then he turned to Jimmy and said, "You ain't got no hug for yo big bro?"

Jimmy took a step back and said, "What do you want?"

"Oh," the man calling himself Cutter said. "It's like that, huh?"

"How'd you find me? What do you want?"

"Momma been shot," Cutter said. "She at the doctor's office. Been axin' for yo ass."

"I — I don't —"

"Jimmy," I said. "Come up for a second."

After a moment's hesitation, Jimmy came up to the door. I said, "I'll drive. Give me a minute."

"Hey, man," Cutter said to me, "this be about family, so —"

"He *is* family," Jimmy said. "He goes or I don't."

For a large number of Detroit's indigent community — the homeless, beaten down and elderly — the "doctor's office" was Detroit Receiving Hospital. In a city constantly at war with its own soul, Detroit Receiving was as close to battlefield triage as you can get: doctors and nurses running twenty-four/seven on waning hope and bad coffee.

Jimmy's mom was in a crowded ward of the nearly dead.

Near the nurse's station was a Detroit cop leaning against a wall, flipping through a well-worn issue of Sports Illustrated. He saw the three of us — Jimmy, his thug brother and me — emerge from the elevator, instantly assessed our threat-level, then went back to his magazine.

After fifteen minutes, Mrs. Radmon's doctor appeared.

He was a broad-shouldered white man with a shock of salt-and-pepper hair, five o'clock shadow and ruddy complexion. The name on his white coat read "Dr. Tim Seibert."

"I know you," Dr. Seibert said without judgment to Cutter. "Who might you gentlemen be?"

Jimmy told the doctor who he was.

I introduced myself and said I was a friend of Jimmy's.

The doctor cut his eyes between Jimmy and Cutter. "Either of you mind my discussing your mother's condition in front of Mr. Snow?"

"Oh, hell yes," Cutter said.

"No," Jimmy said glaring at his brother. "What you say, you can say to Mr. Snow."

Cutter shrugged. "Ain't no thang."

"I'm going to interpret 'ain't no thang' as yes, I can discuss your mother's condition with Mr. Snow present," Dr. Seibert said. Then he said, "There's no way around it; she's going to need a lot of care. The bullet passed cleanly through with minimal damage, but it's what we found unrelated to the bullet wound that concerns us. She has what we suspect is alcoholic cardiomyopathy which is just another way of saying enlarged chambers of her heart that might eventually lead to heart failure. Complicating things even further is her history as an intravenous drug user —"

"She ain't used in five years, man," Cutter said.

"Five years. Fifty years. Doesn't matter," the doctor said. "It complicates her heart condition due to a number of collapsed veins from her intravenous drug use."

"Just do yo damn job, mothafucka," Cutter said taking a step into the doctor.

I started to intervene, but the doctor — apparently a veteran of too many years on the DR's front lines — calmly looked at Cutter and said, "And I will. But you steppin' in my square now and swear to whatever God eases and pleases you, you need to step off — you feel me?"

I was positively tickled pink by Dr. Seibert.

With Cutter shut down, the doctor said, "She's awake — groggy, but awake. Both of you individually can have two minutes. That's it. She needs rest. Am I understood?"

Jimmy said, "Yessir. Thank you."

Cutter said, "Cool."

Dr. Seibert left, presumably to check on his myriad other patients.

Jimmy went behind the curtain to see his mother. I stood guard outside the curtain.

I heard a woman's slurred voice say, "Jimmy? Baby, tha's you? I — you come for your momma, didn't you, baby."

After a silent moment, I heard Jimmy's low, rattled voice. "I'm here to tell you don't ever come looking for me again. Don't send my so-called brother lookin' for me. Maybe you gave birth to me — and I ain't even sure about that — but you ain't never been no momma."

"Oh, baby — why you — why you got to be —"

Cutter took a step forward and I stepped into him.

"Can you fire a gun that's been shoved up your chicken-and-biscuit black ass?" I said. "Frankly, I'd pay good money to see that."

Cutter dropped back.

"You're nothing to me," I heard Jimmy say. "Don't never come near me again."

Jimmy threw the curtain aside and stormed toward the elevator.

"Show up in my neck of the woods again and Jimmy won't have to lift a finger," I said to Cutter, "I'll do the killing. I will do it slow and I will do it in ways even the devil can't imagine. So . . . I mean . . . we cool?"

I didn't wait around for an answer.

In the car, Jimmy wept for a couple minutes then apologized.

"Nothing to apologize for," I said. "Been kind of rough lately. For both of us."

"Yeah," Jimmy said. "Rough. Lucy gone. Carlos . . ."

"I know exactly what you need."

"Ice cream?"

"Uh — no."

"The block party tomorrow?" Jimmy

guessed.

Forty minutes later, Jimmy and I were in our karate karategi — him with his blue belt, me with my fourth-degree black belt.

"Good to see you, Mr. Snow," Kinsey Latrice — K from the Nappy Patch strip club — said.

"Job's working out?" I said.

"Job's workin' out," K said grinning.

"I heard somebody 'bout to get they butt kicked," Brutus said, entering the upstairs dojo.

"Just stay out of the way, old man," I said to Brutus. Then I turned to Jimmy and said, "Don't hold back. Use what you know. Improvise. And —"

I didn't have to opportunity to finish my thought.

Jimmy came in quick, grabbed the lapels of my karategi, shoved a boney right hip into me and flipped me.

I landed on the mat.

Hard.

Boisterous laughter from a corner of the dojo.

"Oh, God!" Jimmy said. "Mr. Snow! God, I'm sorry! I am so —"

"What?" I forced a laugh. "Like you hurt me or something?"

He'd hurt me.

"Hey!" I shouted to Brutus and K. "Go ahead and laugh! Once I'm up, I'm in *every-body's* ass starting with you, old man. So y'all better start runnin'." I held my hand up to Jimmy and quietly grunted, "Help me up, kid."

ABOUT THE AUTHOR

Stephen Mack Jones is a published poet, an award-winning playwright, and a recipient of the prestigious Kresge Arts in Detroit Literary Fellowship. He was born in Lansing, Michigan, and currently lives in Farmington Hills, outside of Detroit. He worked in advertising and marketing communications for a number of years before turning to fiction. His critically acclaimed debut novel, *August Snow,* has been nominated for the Hammett and the Strand Awards.